ALL SHOT TO HELL
SIN DEMONS

MILA YOUNG

HARPER A. BROOKS

All Shot To Hell © Copyright 2021 Mila Young & Harper A. Brooks

Cover Design by Jervy Bonifacio | Phoenix Design Studio
Editing by Dara Horcasitas of Refined Voice Editing
Proofreading by Nic Page and Robyn Mather

Visit our books at
www.milayoungbooks.com
https://harperabrooks.com

All rights reserved under the International and Pan-American Copyright Conventions. No part of this book may be reproduced or transmitted in any form or by any means, electronic or mechanical, including photocopying, recording, or by any information storage and retrieval system, without permission in writing from the publisher/author.

This is a work of fiction. Names, places, characters and incidents are either the product of the author's imagination or are used fictitiously, and any resemblance to any actual persons, living or dead, organizations, events or locales is entirely coincidental.

Warning: the unauthorized reproduction or distribution of this copyrighted work is illegal. Criminal copyright infringement, including infringement without monetary gain, is investigated by the FBI and is punishable by up to 5 years in prison and a fine of $250,000.

DEDICATION

For the girl who sets too many goals
-Harper A. Brooks

For the girl who eats all the brownies
-Mila Young

CONTENTS

Sin Demons Series	vii
All Shot To Hell	ix
Chapter 1	1
Chapter 2	9
Chapter 3	17
Chapter 4	35
Chapter 5	49
Chapter 6	66
Chapter 7	80
Chapter 8	100
Chapter 9	124
Chapter 10	135
Chapter 11	148
Chapter 12	161
Chapter 13	193
Chapter 14	215
Chapter 15	228
Chapter 16	247
Chapter 17	260
Chapter 18	276
Chapter 19	295
Chapter 20	308
Chapter 21	332
About Mila Young	341
About Harper A. Brooks	343

SIN DEMONS SERIES

Playing With Hellfire

Hell In A Handbasket

All Shot To Hell

To Hell And Back

When Hell Freezes Over

ALL SHOT TO HELL

Playing devil's advocate with three demons? There's no way I am ever going to win.

Things were finally going right for us. We got the relics back. We defeated the dragon. I thought we'd won. But we've ended up losing so much more…

Cain's severely wounded, and I don't know how to save him. Losing him shouldn't bother me, but it does. A lot.

Elias and Dorian have a plan: seek out help from people who wield the darkest and cruelest of magic. We soon find that the only one with enough power to bring the Prince of Hell back from death is a master of death itself. But nothing can be done for free and the price has us traveling across the world and facing a slew of new dangers, ones none of us are prepared for.

Even with everything shot to hell, the demons

remain a constant temptation I don't need. Being with them only seems to fan the flames, but letting me go depends on finding all of Hell's relics.

And if I'm being honest, I'm not sure what I'll do once my soul is freed.

CHAPTER ONE
ARIA

"Be careful who you trust, the devil was once an angel." -Unknown

Seconds feel like hours. My chest is wound so tight, every breath in is needle sharp and painful, but I can't move. Can't even think straight as I stare at Cain's slumped body and his blood darkening the ground around him.

Before I can fully process what's happening, Dorian's arms wrap around me and he's lifting me off the ground. We're running through the shipment yard so fast, the frigid air bites at my face and ears. Fear crawls through my chest as the distance between us and Cain grows. There's no way we can just leave him.

"Elias has him," Dorian says as if reading my thoughts, and at that second, Elias appears around a metal container, racing after us with Cain in his arms.

When we make it to the Town Car, Dorian opens the back door and then the front. "You're going to have to sit on my lap for this drive, little girl."

I'm still having a hard time finding my voice, so I only nod. He slides into the front seat near the driver and pulls me in close. Right then, Elias appears and lays Cain onto the back seat, only to climb inside after him.

The door isn't even closed when Dorian barks at the driver. "Step on it, Holmes." And as if the older man's dealt with situations like this before, he punches the gas pedal, and we speed away.

Peeking over Dorian's shoulder and into the back seat, I gasp in horror. Cain's wounds look even worse this close. His skin is ghostly pale, almost translucent, from blood loss, and his eyes are closed. I stare at his chest for any hint of movement, any sign that he could be alive, but see none.

"Is-Is he breathing?" I ask, my voice coming out in a fearful squeak.

Dorian guides my face to look at him instead. "He's going to be okay."

But even I can hear the slight waver to his words. He isn't so sure either.

Elias and Dorian exchange weighted looks, and my stomach sinks. Losing Cain just isn't an option. It isn't.

With his hands firmly on my hips, Dorian twists

me to face forward again. "We are almost home," he says, as if all we need is to step one foot in the mansion and Cain will be right-as-rain again. As if it's that simple.

"It's coming... It's coming..." a soft voice sings.

I glance down at the box in my hands, almost forgetting I was even holding it still. It vibrates in my grasp, and the relics' eerie and muted song wafts through its seal and lock.

Since no one else has reacted to the sad drumbeat or creepy lyrics, it seems only I can hear the strange music, like before. I lean in closer.

"It's coming... Coming... Coming..."

Coming? What's coming? I don't understand.

As if understanding my thoughts, the relics continue their singing. *"Death... Death... Death..."*

Icy cold dread snakes up my spine.

Are they talking about Cain?

When the car pulls up to the front of the house, Dorian throws open our door, and we jump out. Elias is already picking up Cain from the back seat and cradling him in his arms. He is just as lifeless as before, and it kills me to look at him. It only makes the relics' song feel more real.

Dorian and Elias hurry into the house, leaving me behind. The demons are so occupied with their fallen friend that they disappear inside without so much as glancing my way again. I find myself standing in the gravel driveway, watching the Town Car pull away. Alone again with the relics in my hand.

Here it is. I've been given another opportunity to run for it. Make my escape. But again, I'm pausing.

What is wrong with me?

"Aria, dear, are you coming?" Dorian's gentle voice wafts from the front door.

"Yeah," I say as I turn and head inside. Dorian is already halfway up the stairs, waiting for me. When I hurry up to join him, he takes the box from my hands and bends his elbow my way in an offering. I slide my arm through, grateful for the extra support right now.

"He's in his room," he says, meaning Cain, and leads me toward his bedroom on the second floor. When we reach the door, Elias is standing there with worry wrinkling his brow. It's so unsettling, seeing concern on his ruggedly handsome face—the man never seems deeply fazed by anything. It only makes my gut twist even more.

"Are you sure she should be in here?" Elias asks Dorian, his voice soft.

"Why wouldn't she be allowed?"

I free myself from Dorian and head right for the four-poster bed where Cain lays deathly still. His clothes are drenched in blood, and I'm convinced he's dead. No other living person could survive those wounds.

The relics' ominous song plays again in my head. *"It's coming... Coming... Coming... Death... Death... Death..."*

Dropping to my knees by the bedside, I skim my

fingers over Cain's forehead and feel that his skin is icy cold, too. I can't stop staring at his closed eyes and his chest, which barely moves with his shallow breaths. The combination of grief, sorrow, and anxiety is painful. I don't want to lose him. I *can't* lose him. Just the thought of it leaves me shaky and sickly.

I lose myself for a moment in the feeling, unable to look away from his almost serene expression. If it wasn't for Dorian and Elias's frantic whispering behind me, I would've completely forgotten they were in the room with me.

"He wouldn't want her here, seeing him like this, and you know that." Elias's tone is sharp.

"Well, he's a little indisposed right now, and she's not doing any harm," Dorian replies. "She's worried about him."

"As she should be. Look at him."

"Shush, will you?"

"We need to figure out what we're doing next," Elias growls in aggravation.

"And we will," Dorian snaps back just as aggressively.

"We're running out of time."

"I *know* that."

I fist the bedspread in my hand as my annoyance rises. Hearing the two of them bicker like an old couple is the last thing I want to deal with right now.

"Will you two just shut up?" The words fly from my lips. Probably not the wisest thing to say to two powerful and reckless demons, but at the moment, I don't care. It needs to be said.

To my surprise, silence answers me, so I look over my shoulder at them. They're both watching me intently with sympathy in their eyes.

My chest pinches, and I sigh, my frustration fading into sadness. Frowning, I glance back at Cain. "He wouldn't want you fighting like this."

"She's right. This isn't productive," Dorian agrees.

"That's what I was saying," Elias grumbles, but that only wins him a hard elbow jab in the gut. He shoots Dorian a deadly glare.

"*We're* going to make some phone calls," Dorian goes on, "see what we can find that can help speed up his healing."

"More souls?" I ask.

"He's going to need a little more help than that," he replies. "We're going to have to call in some favors."

"What happens if we…" My sentence dies as my throat dries. I swallow a few times, hoping it'll help. "If we can't save him, will he go back to Hell?"

That's what he wants, isn't it?

Elias and Dorian exchange looks again, probably wondering how much they should reveal to me.

After some hesitation, Dorian steps forward. "That's not exactly how it works," he begins carefully. "We're damned souls, and damned souls out of Hell lose the perk of immorality."

I wait for him to continue, but when he doesn't, I ask, "What does that mean?"

"When we die, we cease to exist," Elias replies. "Our souls are eradicated."

Wait, *eradicated*? Like, gone forever? Poof?

Oh. My. God.

The true gravity of the situation sucker punches me. Hard.

I think I'm going to be sick. My stomach roils, and bile burns up my esophagus with impending vomit.

"But we're not going to let that happen," Dorian assures me. "Cain's taken a bullet for us multiple times. It's just time to return the favor."

Cautiously, they move to the door, but as Elias steps through, Dorian waits behind. "Aria? Are you coming?"

My fingers graze the back of Cain's hand. The thought of leaving him when he practically has one foot in the grave seems impossible.

"Can I stay?" I ask meekly. "Please?"

Elias's harsh "no" is cut off by a quick wave of Dorian's hand.

"Of course you can stay," he says despite Elias's wide eyes. "We'll be in my room down the hall. Holler if anything changes."

Dorian shoves Elias into the hall and closes the door behind them. With the soft *click* of the latch, the room sinks into an uncomfortable and deafening silence. It seems to suck all the air out of the room, leaving my lungs tight. Looking back down at Cain, my eyes begin to prickle with impending tears, but I fight them to keep them at bay.

I shouldn't be shedding a single tear for this man—this demon. I'm not supposed to be feeling anything for him at all besides pure hatred, and maybe some relief that there's one less demon controlling my life.

But no matter how many times I tell that to myself, the tears still gather at the thought of losing him, and I'm forced to blink rapidly like a psycho to stop them from spilling over.

Unsure even what to say, I wrap my hand around his and squeeze a little tighter. As my gaze drifts over him again, the sparkle of something shiny in his torn shirt pocket catches my eye. Reaching over, I gently pull out a slender gold chain and wing pendant, and my heartbeat falters.

It's the necklace he'd given me with his crest. The one I had ripped off my neck and thrown at him in a fit of disgust before our trip to Missouri.

I can't believe what I'm seeing. He's been carrying it around with him? But why?

Examining it more, I'm surprised to find that it's completely intact, its chain mended with no evidence of it ever being broken in the first place.

And that means, at some point, he'd had it fixed.

For me.

CHAPTER TWO

ARIA

My stomach clenches as I cradle the necklace in my palm. The gold glints against the sunlight drenching the room, but considering how badly things turned out recently, it ought to be pouring down outside, thunder shaking the ground. The sunny weather feels wrong when my insides are so shattered.

The fact we defeated Sir Surchion still feels surreal, especially when it came at such a grave cost.

I curl my fingers over the necklace, feeling the metal still cool against my touch. It's so small yet seems to weigh so much in my grasp.

I lift my gaze to Cain where he remains laying in bed, unmoving, still pale as death.

"Why did you have to go and get the necklace fixed?" I whisper to Cain, well aware he can't hear me. Maybe that's why I feel so comfortable to speak my mind, to not hold back.

"It would have been so much easier to deal with this… with you… you know… if I hated you. But you had to change that, didn't you?" My voice crackles, and I swallow the boulder in my throat, then glance back down to the pendant.

Deep inside, I know the necklace isn't the only reason I find myself sitting by this demon's bed, worried about him, holding back more tears that are threatening to fall and never stop. With it comes the heartbreaking pain of watching Cain slipping farther from me.

I refocus on the wing.

A single wing with tiny indentations to make it appear like feathers cover the surface.

A pendant that hangs from a thin golden chain.

The more I look at it, the more my eyes prick.

How can this stupid necklace affect me so much?

"I shouldn't have thrown this at you. I didn't mean what I said… But you knew, didn't you?" I look up at him through my lashes as a tear loosens and rolls down my cheek. Mentally, I slap myself for letting myself feel such things for demons. "You must have."

Silence hangs heavily in the room, thickening the air, and I draw in sharp, shallow breaths as I blink away the tears, refusing to let any more fall.

"I hated you… and I should still hate you." I catch the tear sliding over my jawline with my hand and wipe it over my pants. Without even a second thought, I collect the necklace and thread it around my neck, then clasp it closed.

The wing falls over my top, nestled in the middle of my chest. "Just so you know, Cain, this doesn't mean anything. Nothing. Don't get any ideas."

Part of me half expects him to pry open an eye and look at me after that comment, but he never moves an inch. Instinctually, I lower my gaze to his chest and watch how slow it rises and falls.

I sit on the side of the bed and reach over to push loose strands from his brow. My fingers slide into his luxurious hair, the sensation reminding me of the last time we kissed. The heat of his lips, the intensity of his hands pressing me close to him.

Heat flares deep within me at the memory. I bend forward so my face hovers inches from his, and the question wells in my mind about what I'm doing. Yet the memory of us together swirls on my thoughts with vengeance. Beneath the smell of coppery blood, I inhale his masculine scent, and he smells so good. I close my eyes, letting myself float on the memories, my pulse racing.

My lips brush his lightly, like somehow I hope that a single kiss might awaken him, to remind him he's not alone. Half expecting a reaction, I pull back when it doesn't come. I close my eyes, shaking under the reality of how badly injured he is. *Please get better.*

Pain flows over me with the fear that he won't come out of this, and it tears through me like a blade. I open my eyes and push more hair off his face, then I sit there for I don't know how long, watching over him, my eyes tearing, guilt chewing my insides that somehow I hadn't done more to protect him.

The scenario with the dragon replays in my mind on an endless loop. If only I had reached out and grabbed Cain's arm, dragged him closer to me.

I swallow the lump in my throat, needing to stop going down this guilt trip before it swallows me whole. The truth is, we were lucky to defeat the dragon and even luckier he hadn't taken us all out.

"I guess you've grown on me," I say.

I shake my head at how ripped apart I feel. How can I feel this way for a demon, anyway?

He owns my soul.

Bought me to cover a debt.

Controls my life.

And if he survives, he has every intention of returning to Hell… Maybe even forcing me to go with him.

I need to get my head screwed on straight.

Licking my dry lips, I climb to my feet. I shift my focus back to my necklace, running a thumb over the wing, then I glance over to Cain again, the man… the demon who has affected me so much. Just like Dorian and Elias. These three burst into my life, and I doubt anything will ever be the same again.

Maybe I'm looking at this all wrong, seeing my stay here as temporary, doing anything to leave… but what if that's been my mistake all along? What if I can gain more by staying here, finding out about my past, uncovering more about who exactly these demons are? And working out who I am.

I chew on my lower lip as a flare of decisiveness crosses my mind, so I straighten my posture and say with confidence, "I've made up my mind. I'm not going to run away anymore. I'll stick around with you three. At least for a while. Hell is still out of the question, but we'll cross that bridge when we get to it. So... I guess what I'm trying to say is... I'm calling this home for now." I'm babbling. I know it. But whatever. "That's even more reason for you to get better quicker."

Still, he doesn't move.

Even if I am speaking mostly to myself, there's a sense of strange relief to have made that decision. I've said it aloud, so that makes it real, right? And I have every intention of keeping my word.

Now Cain just needs to get better. Wake up.

He can't die... he just can't. The pain in my chest returns at the thought of losing him—really losing him. Forever.

"Cain... Please don't leave me, too."

Tears burn my eyes and I rub them away, hating how I can't stop thinking of the relics' words.

"Death... Death... Death... It's coming..."

DORIAN

*E*lias breaks our eye contact and turns his back to me, returning to staring out the window, letting the situation darken his mood further. Fire crackles in the fireplace, throwing shadows across my bedroom. Aria remains with Cain in his room, and there is no mistaking the agony on her face. Somehow, the sin demon of Pride himself has wormed his way into her heart enough that she worries for him.

Part of me had expected her to be slightly indifferent, but I'd been wrong. And I have been a fool to believe that what was going on between us was just lust. That notion sits heavily on my mind, and they are not thoughts I want to entertain at this point.

Our priority is saving Cain, because we sure as hell didn't get kicked out of the underworld to lose him to a damn dragon attack. We have so much more to achieve. We've finally found three of the harp's relics and now have Aria on hand to help us track the rest. So fuck, there is no way Cain is dying on us now.

Elias lets out a loud breath through his nose as he turns toward me. "Maybe we can find a way to contact Carbas?" he suggests, his voice tight like it pains him to say the name.

"That arrogant prick? Did you forget when he challenged you to a fight in front of Lucifer? If it wasn't for Cain intervening, you'd be dead by now." The asshole reported directly to Cain's father, not to mention was given thirty-six legions to command. That kind of power screws up demons' heads, and Carbas made sure everyone remembered his role.

Elias snarls under his breath. "I bet that asslicking dick still prances around Hell in his lion form like he's a god." Dark shadows gather under his eyes, which dance with anger. "But the bastard heals diseases."

"So does Lucifer, but we sure as fuck aren't going to ask for his help, either." Though I won't deny the notion had crossed my mind to speak to Maverick about this. Problem is, this was what they wanted from the beginning, wasn't it? Cain eliminated. I would just be handing them the opportunity to finish him off on a silver platter. Not a chance.

"I've never seen him this bad," Elias reminds me, worry swirling in his eyes, and my stomach drops like a rock. He gives me a long glance. "Who the fuck do we get to heal him? Witches? I've gone through all the potential contacts in my mind, but I doubt any have the solution we need."

I'm pacing across the room from the door to the fireplace, glancing outside to where the wind whips up dried leaves and shakes the trees. "Don't fucking know, but dragon's blood is magic itself. I know dragon blood to a fae is like venom and will kill them, but I have no clue what it will do to a demon."

"It's fucking killing him," Elias snaps back. "Did you see how drained he is? Cain bounces back from everything." He runs a hand through his long hair, his lips thin and tight. "We can't lose him, or we're stuck here for eternity."

I grit my teeth, well aware that there is no way we will be accepted back into Hell without our plan, and that means we need Cain. But it's so much more than that… "We stood by his side from the beginning, and we sure as damn hell are not letting him slip from us now."

A wave of desperation takes flight through my veins, and I'm pacing faster. Time is against us.

I have always been by Cain's side… always. The possibility of death haunts me, ramming phantom spikes through me each time I imagine him losing the battle.

Darkness glints in Elias's eyes. Cain's done a lot for him, too. For both of us.

He's always been the glue that held us together. Without him…

I didn't even want to think about it.

"We do whatever it takes to fix this. He's fucking bad right now. We both know it."

"There's no other alternative here. He *won't* die. I refuse to allow him to," I say. "So, I'll reach out to the local witch clan today. You speak to Viktor. The master vamp might know someone who can help. Try Antonio, too. He's been with fae long enough to maybe know something about their magic. We have Ramos for now. He should be able to do *something* in the meantime."

CHAPTER THREE

ARIA

*I*t takes a great effort, but I'm finally able to tear myself away from Cain's bedside and leave his room. I don't want to—the fact that I could lose him at any second is a constant worry on my mind—but I also know that simply sitting there won't do anything to help him. And that's what he really needs right now. Help.

I hover in the doorway, wondering briefly if I should say goodbye. Just in case. But the thought of uttering those words makes my throat thick with emotion.

I won't say goodbye. I won't. I refuse to.

My fingers touch the winged pendant, and instead, I whisper into the silent room, "Come back to us, Cain," before finally walking into the hallway. A male servant is there, an older gentleman, with a basin of water, towels, and what look to be bandages draped over his arm. He nods his head before stepping inside and closing the door.

At least Cain won't be alone. That makes me feel a bit better as I walk down the hallway to where I know Dorian's room is at the opposite end. The two bickering demons' voices are the first thing I hear.

"I've never seen him this bad," Elias says with anger and desperation, making his tone short. "Who the fuck do we get to heal him? Witches? I've gone through all the potential contacts in my mind, but I doubt any have the solution we need."

Oh no. Looks like they were having no luck after all.

I slow my steps and shift closer to the wall to stay out of sight.

"Don't fucking know, but dragon's blood is magic itself…" Dorian goes on.

"It's fucking killing him," Elias snaps back. "Did you see how drained he is? Cain bounces back from everything. We can't lose him, or we're stuck here for eternity."

Their words are like daggers in my gut. If Dorian and Elias are at a loss of what to do, then there's no hope for Cain. They are the ones who are supposed to *know* people, powerful people, and if they have run out of options, what does that mean?

Something soft and warm brushes against my ankles, and a purring sounds. When I glance down, I find Cassiel circling my legs and looking for some head-pets. I scoop him into my arms and stroke his little head to quiet him.

Where can a person go to get a cure for death? Is there such a place?

As I look down at him, an idea strikes.

If the demons can't find a way to help Cain, then maybe I can. I can't just stand around and wait. Elias said it himself. Cain's in rough shape. Every second counts now. I need to do *something*.

"You know what they always say, Cassiel," I whisper to the lynx. "If you want something done right, you have to do it yourself." He continues to purr as I stroke his neck. He obviously doesn't care what we do as long as I keep up with the soft pets, which he adores.

I turn and hurry down the hall on light feet. Down the stairs, in the foyer, I find Sadie coming out of the dining room with a tray in her hands with more bandages, a steaming teapot, and an array of jars with different herbs and tinctures. All things for Cain, if I were to guess.

"Where are you going, Miss?" she asks with a curious tilt of her head.

"I need a car, please," I reply but make sure to keep my voice low. I can't risk Elias or Dorian hearing and trying to stop me, and I don't want to argue with them if they disagree with my idea. I can sneak in and out before they know it, and maybe come back with a cure. Something.

"Will you be driving yourself, or should I have Holmes pull it around for you?"

Although the idea of taking one of the demons' sports cars out for a spin does sound tempting, I don't have a license. I haven't even taken my hour requirement for a permit. When it comes to driving, I am greener than green.

It's tempting, but at the same time, I'm not stupid.

"Holmes, please. I'd like to go to Storm's markets."

Sadie glances up the staircase. "Do the Masters know you're leaving?"

Shit.

I am going to have to lie.

"Yeah. Of course." I blow out a raspberry to fake confidence. "We're all doing our part to help Cain. I'm just going to pop in the markets, get what he needs, and pop out. Should only be a few minutes. Half hour, tops."

She eyes me for a long moment.

"I'm coming back," I assure her. "Cain knows I'm done with the frivolous escape attempts. I've learned my lesson."

The mention of Cain has her stiff shoulders easing some, and she turns to a nearby accent table to put her tray down.

"I'll call for Holmes," she says after some time.

I grin. "Thank you. I'll wait out front for him." And before she can pressure me further, I open the front door and step onto the driveway. I only have to wait a few minutes before a smaller white car pulls up. A Cadillac, from the looks of it. And I can't help but wonder how many cars these demons really have in that detached garage of theirs. It's like one for every day of the week at this point.

Holmes gets out and opens the back door for me and Cassiel. "Miss," he greets as I slide across the brown leather seat. *Swanky.* "We're off to the markets today?"

"Yes, please."

When he shuts my door and gets behind the wheel, I ask him out of good ol' plain curiosity, "What happened to the Town Car we drove before?"

"It's been sent for detailing," he replied.

Ah. That made sense. All the blood and whatnot.

Cassiel curls up in my lap as if he no longer has a care in the world.

Holmes pulls away from the house, and I glance out the back window, half-expecting Dorian and Elias to come bursting out at any second. But to my surprise, they don't. The house is eerily still, the windows dark despite people being inside.

I draw in a deep breath and let it out. I know I've decided to stick around the mansion, at least until Cain is on his feet again, and this little excursion is purely to help the demons—maybe even keep myself distracted, who knows—but I can't help but feel some anxiety with doing it all behind their backs.

But would they let me go otherwise?

More than likely, absolutely not. I just need to be quick, see what the markets have to offer, and then get out before anyone realizes I'm gone. Sounds simple enough when I say it that way.

It isn't long before we reach the known underpass and entrance to Storm, discreetly marked with a black painted umbrella. Holmes pulls up to the stone wall and revs the engine three times. A man dressed in rags stands from his camping chair and comes closer. He searches the street and waits for a passing car to drive by. When it turns the corner and the area is quiet again, the gatekeeper knocks on the umbrella symbol and the stones shimmer before dissolving before our eyes. We drive through.

The Cadillac quietly hums through the busy underground streets. Supernaturals of all kinds stride down the sidewalks, visiting stores and restaurants. Completely normal, minus the long furry tails, wings, and pointed ears.

When we get to a stoplight, Holmes hooks a left, and that's when I see the painted black umbrella on a lamppost.

Follow the umbrellas, as all supes know. Since the markets are never in the same place twice, that's the only way to find them.

Using the hidden black umbrellas as our guide, we weave through the supernatural city. They lead us to what looks to be an abandoned parking garage, and when we pull up to a closed bay door, a large black umbrella appears on it. This is it. The entrance.

Holmes eases us forward. Instead of the door

opening, the car phases through it, as if it was never really there at all. A magical mirage, of sorts.

On the other side, we stop abruptly. The wheels spin under us, but the car only sinks, unable to move an inch further. I peer out my window to see we're no longer on asphalt but stuck in soft red sand.

"This is where I must leave you," Holmes says as he peers at me through the rearview mirror. "I won't be able to go farther than this."

I nod, understanding. "I shouldn't be long."

"I'll be just outside on the street when you're ready to leave."

"Perfect. Thank you."

I pull Cassiel into my arms and open the door. Once I step outside, my sneakers instantly sink into the deep sand, and I'm assaulted with a suffocating dry heat. My throat parches, and I cough. Cassiel bristles, too, rubbing his paw over his little head, his ears twitching.

"Where in the world are we?" I ask him. The magic attached to the markets has always been insanely strong, able to transport the place and its patrons anywhere in the world, and by the look of it, we've been dropped in a desert.

Some distance away, mountains of sand rise in peaks. Above me, the sun hovers in a cloudless sky and beats down on me. Every inch of my exposed shoulders, face, and arms stings from the powerful rays, and sweat beads my forehead. Not a very smart place to put the market, but it's all the more reason to get what I need and leave.

The hazy image of tables and tents appears yards away, and for a second, I wonder if it's another mirage, a trick of the eye from the oppressive heat, but I can't just stand here sinking in the sand. Best to keep moving.

Every step is a chore, like walking through thick mud or cement. The sand is so soft and slippery that I almost lose my shoes multiple times during the trek. As expected, I'm drenched in my own sweat in seconds.

When I finally reach the market, I am thankful it is, in fact, real. Large colorful cloths and tents have been hoisted above the vendor tables to provide shade, and giant fans push the stale, hot air around in an attempt to cool visitors. It's not much, but after walking in the direct sun for only a few minutes and feeling drained, I'll take it. A table is set up with water bottles and piles of beautiful scarves, and when I glance around, I notice almost everyone is wearing one either wrapped around their heads or draped over their shoulders as a way to protect their skin from the rays. I grab one, lay it over my head, and tie it at my chest so that it covers both me and Cassiel. It's a stunning red color, woven with gold thread. Then I take two cups of water and offer one to Cassiel before draining my own. It's cold and everything I need right then. Grabbing one more, I start down one of the aisles and search the tables and wares for sale.

It's hard to believe that just a few weeks ago, I stole the supposed "Orb of Chaos" from Sir Surchion with the intention of coming here to sell it and create a new life for myself. So much has changed since then. Fate had laughed in my face and took a hard left instead. Then, just for funsies, she made a few loopty-loops and spun in circles to really mess with me. Now I was living with three very different, very dangerous demons and questioning my next steps. I had a way to get out of their soul contract, but it wasn't a clause I think I was ready to take.

I don't know. The entire thing is fucking nuts. More like nucking futs, but you get the idea.

Finding a table with a variety of potions, I slow down and creep closer. There are vials and vases full of colored liquids, all labeled with the ailments they're meant to cure. My gaze lands on one that says 'Regeneration' and is a silvery blue.

"Excuse me, sir," I call to the merchant behind the table. He turns from the box he'd been unloading and grins my way. He's a tall man with a round middle and a squirrely beard, but his smile is pleasant enough.

"Hello there. See anything you like?"

"Are you a sorcerer?" I ask. I know it's not the most PC thing to do—asking a person's supernatural type—but I want to make sure these potions were made by a powerful spellcaster, not an elf or someone with smaller, more limited abilities.

The man's grin widens. "I was at one time," he muses. "But 'warlock' is a more fitting title for me nowadays, I think."

Ah. Warlock. They are like sorcerers in that they're spellcasters, like witches, but warlocks have chosen to go down a darker path. They don't really follow the rules, so to speak, but they are powerful, which is what I need, but their magic always has consequences.

Right now, with Cain teetering between life and death, I don't give a damn about consequences. I'll deal with them when they come. I just need to save him.

"This regeneration potion... What can it do, exactly?"

"It can help with simple things like hair growth to the more extreme like helping with fertility or regrowing lost limbs, depending on the dosage you take," he replies. "Can even help with those poor souls who need help getting it *up*, if you know what I mean. But I'm sure the guys don't have any issues with a beauty like you around."

Gross.

There were so many things wrong with that statement, I didn't even have the time or the energy to mull it all over and correct him.

Back to the potion. "Can it help a person who's been severely injured? Like on the verge of death?"

His eyes narrow on me, his expression changing from playful to something much more serious. He leans over the table and lowers his voice. "Are you in some kind of trouble?"

His breath is rancid when it brushes across my face, making me flinch back. At that moment, Cassiel hops from my arms onto the table, knocking over potions and causing them to roll off the side of the table and shatter.

Shit!

"Hey!" the merchant yells and grabs for him, but Cassiel dodges his hands with ease and continues to hop around the table. "Come here, you mangy cat!"

Afraid the big oaf might hurt him, I try to snatch Cassiel too, but he leaps to the side, hitting into a shelf. A pitcher of green liquid spills over, drenching him in the gooey stuff. He hisses.

I seize Cassiel just before the merchant can get his hands on him. "I'm so sorry about this. I don't know what's gotten into him. He hasn't really been out of the house in a long—"

"You're going to pay for all this, I hope you know," the man growls as he picks up the shards of glass and takes in his ruined merchandise. "That fucking feline's just cost me months of work and profit."

Cassiel begins to lick at his paws, and I tsk at him to stop. Who knows what that goop really is and what it can do.

"Well?" the merchant presses.

I pat my pockets, only to discover I've made one

vital mistake. I've come to the markets without any money.

Come on, Aria. Really?

How could I be that stupid? I had been so worried about leaving without Dorian and Elias noticing, I forgot the most important thing. Money. And I have nothing on me to trade.

Fuck.

"I'll take that shiny necklace of yours," he says, reaching for the winged pendant between my breasts.

I quickly jerk back, heart pounding. "No way!"

His angry gaze lands on Cassiel. "Then I'll take the cat. Could prove useful for some of the potions that require sacrifices—"

"Touch him and I'll—I'll—" I press Cassiel closer to my chest, and the feisty little guy hisses at the merchant.

"You'll what?" he snaps and straightens to show his full height. He's almost as tall as Elias and three times as wide. I quickly swallow my threat back down, and Cassiel continues to hiss and snarl at him.

I consider making a run for it, to try to get lost in the crowd. There's a good chance he's not as fast as Elias, but a loud slap of metal hitting the table jerks our attention up. A woman stands beside me, dressed in a long purple skirt and off-the-shoulder blouse that shows off her flat stomach. Her hair is braided and woven with beads. She gives me a small smile.

"Miranda," the warlock quips, seemingly

surprised to see her. Honestly, I am, too. "What are you doing out of your tent?"

"Brutus." When she lifts her hand, she nods toward the velvet bag she's slapped on the table and slides it toward him. "For the mess the lynx made of your table."

He grabs the bag, opens it, and peers inside. "This will hardly cover all the damage," he says.

"So take this then. Your wife's been getting a little too friendly with your neighbor. Something you *might* want to look into before you end up having a fifth baby that unexpectedly looks just like him."

Brutus's eyes widen as the shock settles in. And to be frank, I'm just as stunned by her words as he is. Who the heck is this woman, and how could she possibly know something as intimate as that?

But he doesn't question her words. A second later, he's throwing whatever's left of his potions in the box and hauling it away, his face red with panic and anger.

"I'd also stay away from the fried foods for a while!" she shouts after him as he disappears into the mass of customers.

When we're alone, her attention turns to me, and I'm still too confused to move or say anything.

"Aria, right?" she asks, smiling down at me.

"Uh… yeah." How in the world does she know my name?

"The demons' Aria?"

I'm not too keen on that clarification, but still, I

nod. Maybe she's a friend? Man, I hope so, because I know all too well that their list of enemies far surpasses their list of allies.

"And you're Miranda?" I remember the merchant saying that was her name.

"Yes. Here, come with me." Before I can refuse, she presses her hand into my back and guides me through the wave of people. I'm wary since I don't know this lady, but she moves with me with such precision, we reach our destination within seconds. We stand in front of a huge tent strung up by ropes and decorated with Christmas lights. The sharp scents of different incenses assault my nose all at once, and Cassiel snorts in my arms.

"Let's go inside," Miranda coos and holds open the tent's flap for me.

I hesitate. "Uh, thanks for helping me back there, but I'm not sure…"

"You're looking for a way to save Cain, yes?" she asks, eyeing me.

I blink, her words taking me off guard. I hadn't said anything about Cain or about him being hurt. Even to the merchant.

"Don't worry. I can help you." She nods toward the tent. "Inside."

Glancing over my shoulder, I hope I'm not making a mistake here in trusting this stranger. But if she can truly help Cain…

I step inside, and what I see halts me in my tracks again. A massive circular room with a high, peaked roof, white columns, and floating lanterns. Obviously, it's been touched by magic to hold such a large space in such a seemingly small tent. The best part, though? It's much, *much* cooler in here than in that oppressive desert heat.

"So," Miranda begins, sliding further inside, "Cain's gotten himself into a bit of trouble, huh?"

"How do you know about that?" I ask, still marveling at the mystery of Miranda's place, and her as well. "Better yet, how did you know about the merchant's wife? Or my name?"

"Oh, Brutus? He's a bit of a bully, and his wife's known to be a… loose cannon."

That's a nice way to say 'cheater.'

"But everything you said was strangely specific," I said. "And I'm pretty sure we've never met before—"

"You'd be right. We haven't. Not in the traditional sense."

What the heck does that mean?

"Do you know Cain?" I ask instead, trying a different route with my questioning.

She grins, as if she's enjoying my prying to get to the conclusion myself. "I do. And Dorian and Elias."

Okay, then. So a friend?

"They were here not too long ago to get my help to find you," she goes on. "When you were taken by a dragon? Does that sound familiar?"

I shiver, unable to forget those terrifying moments I was fleeing Sir Surchion and running for my life down the mountainside. I'm not sure I'll ever be able to shake it, or the nightmares it left me with.

"I told them where to find you." Her honey-brown eyes meet mine, and I know she's waiting for me to put the clues together and figure her out.

She knew things about Brutus—specific things, things a normal person wouldn't know. She knew where to find me when I'd been kidnapped. She knew Cain was hurt.

"Are you a psychic or something?" I ask suddenly. That seems to be the only explanation I can come up with.

"Close enough." She reaches up, grabs one of the shimmering silks draped from the ceiling, and tugs so it falls free. Pushing it into my hand, she gestures to Cassiel. "You might want to clean him up, or he'll be too big to leash."

I stare at her, confused as hell. But if she is some kind of psychic and knows things I don't, it'd be smarter to listen to her advice than to ignore it. I rub the green goo off Cassiel's fur the best I can, making sure to get anything around his mouth and nose. When I hand the silk back to her, she tosses it on the floor with a disgusted curl of her upper lip.

"Warlocks," she grumbles, more to herself than me.

"So, you said you know what can help Cain?" I ask.

"It's not a what, exactly, but a who."

"What?"

"A *who*," she repeats. "To bring Cain back from the dead, you need a master of death itself. You need a necromancer."

"A... necromancer?"

"Is there an echo in here? Yes. A necromancer."

"They're real?"

She huffs a laugh. "Of course they are. Were you raised by wolves or something?"

"In foster care, so pretty much."

"Ah, well, yes. They do exist, but they're one of the darker supernatural types. You have to be when dealing with the dead."

That makes sense.

"But where can I find a necromancer?" I ask.

She holds up a finger and walks around the room. On the other side, she pulls back another curtain and disappears through it for some time. When she reemerges, she has a rolled-up piece of paper in her hand.

"You can find him in Cold's Keep." She hands me the paper.

Cold's Keep? I've never heard of such a place. I unroll the paper to see it's a crudely drawn map that's been photocopied many, many times. Most of the details have faded, but what I can make out is lots of trees. Like a remote town in the middle of nowhere.

"Is it close to here?"

"Here? No. Close to Glenside? Hmm... A few hours' drive, if I were to guess," Miranda explains.

Ah...

"His name is Banner," she continues. "A bit of a loner. Has an uncanny attachment to the dead."

I roll my eyes. "Of course he does."

"Bring this to the demons. It'll help you find him."

I roll the map up and tuck it into my pocket. "Thank you. I, uh, don't have anything to pay you with. As you saw with the warlock, I kinda forgot my wallet."

She shakes her head. "No need this time. But make sure the demons understand that time is not on their side. Cain is no use to me dead."

My stomach sinks. Her ominous words make my sense of urgency spike to an all-time high. I have to leave and get this new information to the demons. "Are you sure this Banner guy can help?"

She frowns. "He's the only chance Cain has."

Coming from a psychic, that means everything.

"Thank you… again," I say and turn to leave.

"Oh, and Aria," Miranda calls. I stop and look over my shoulder.

"Yes?"

"Unlike me, necromancers won't work for free. Make sure you don't bring anything you aren't willing to lose."

Unsure what she means exactly, I only nod. "I'll bring my wallet next time."

Then Cassiel and I leave the tent and head back into the overbearing heat.

CHAPTER FOUR

ELIAS

A snap of energy races up my spine, the kind that comes with a warning, a preempting of danger. I've felt this before, a primal instinct that has kept me alive more times than I can count. But my mind isn't on me... I glance over to the door.

Aria.

Fuck! I'm already striding across Dorian's room.

He's on the phone with Antonio, but by the sound of it, all we have so far are ancient texts on dragons with no guarantee there is any mention of saving a demon from a dragon's attack.

But right now, something else is wrong.

Determination blazes through me.

Growling under my breath, I burst suddenly out of the room and careen into the hallway, where a guard leaps out of my way. I thunder toward Cain's bedroom and drive open the door to find it empty of Aria.

Cain remains on the bed, bloodied, his breaths shallow. He's barely clinging to life.

I whip back out of the room and steamroll up to Aria's bedroom, only to find no sign of her there, either. A chill clings to my spine. The faster I charge through the mansion to track her down, the more my insides twist with the hard truth.

She's not in the mansion. I know it deep in my bones.

I should have known better than to leave her alone. I had seen the agony in her eyes, the hurt across her face. Dorian accuses me of jumping before thinking, but my little rabbit is ten times worse. And now I'm burning up with fury that she is doing something stupid that will put her in danger. I push onward and rush through the mansion, checking anywhere she could have gone, but I already know she's not here. Her scent is faint.

In the garage, I find the Cadillac and Town Car gone, and I sigh heavily. "What have you done?" I whisper.

I dart back to Dorian's room and shove the door open, storming inside.

"She's gone," I blurt as he ends the call on his cell.

When he meets my gaze, I see the fear in his eyes. He knows exactly what I'm talking about.

"Are you kidding me? She's run off?" The corners of his mouth pinch, his posture curling forward.

"Listen, you stay here with Cain. I'm going to find her and spank that sweet ass raw for pulling this stunt now. I can pick up her scent. She won't get far." My beast turns inside me, eager for release and to hunt down our rabbit, except this isn't only about fun. At this moment, I need her close and by my side. I need her protected.

Dorian glares at me, but I know he's furious at the whole fucked up situation we've found ourselves in and not at me.

"Fine, go bring her back," he snaps, and I'm already out the door before he can even finish the last word.

In retrospect, I should have known better than to assume she wouldn't do something stupid.

The wind bellows past, carrying her sweet scent, rousing my hound, who pushes forward.

She's mine.

I rapidly strip from my clothes while toeing off my boots, then I lunge toward the driveway. My body shudders as my hellhound tears out from me in mere seconds. The excruciating pain is nothing compared to the agony pounding in my chest at what Aria is up to.

The notion that she used this moment to run from us makes me nauseous. I refuse to believe she'd do this, yet the thought lingers on the back of my mind.

I shake my head, dislodging the worry and instead focusing on her faint scent in the air. My paws pound the earth, sprinting toward the gates. It isn't long before I leave behind the mansion and rush along the road, and there is only one way to go from here. Into town. I pick up my pace and dart forward until I reach the painted black umbrella near the underpass. My entry into the magical underground of Storm.

The gatekeeper, who resembles a hobo and is dressed in rags, stands from his lawn chair. The man looks me over in my hellhound form, sniffs the air, and wrinkles his nose. When he deems me safe, he turns and taps the painted umbrella with a hand. Suddenly, the stone face of the underpass glimmers and gives way to a ramp that takes me straight to the subterranean level. The passage is big enough to allow for cars, but today I'm on foot.

A quick look his way, and then I race inside. Within seconds, I find the first painted umbrella symbol to lead me to the markets. Aria's scent swings that way, too, and I follow both trails to an abandoned parking garage. Another black umbrella marks the entrance, and I'm about to race inside when I spot Cain's Cadillac and our driver, Holmes, parked on the side of the street.

Suddenly, the garage door dissolves as the magic relents, and a woman appears through the hazy glimmer.

Aria.

Tucking myself behind the garage, I pause to catch my breath, to wait for my drumming heart to slow, watching her.

What is Aria doing at the markets, anyway?

I recall my beast. My skin pricks, electricity

curling around my body as the change takes hold. Expelling a breathy grunt, I ride the pain as fur draws back into my skin, bones crack, and in moments, I'm standing as a man.

I step out from my hiding place. A small, crying gasp comes from my right, and I jerk my attention in its direction.

An older female in a red dress is staring at me, mouth gaped open, while her husband has her hand, trying to tug her away from me. Her long ears twitch while her gaze trails my body, stopping on my groin. Her mouth parts, her sharp goblin teeth exposed in a mating call. Except she's wasting her time on me. Goblins aren't my type because they are biters, and I'm the only one that's going to bite in a relationship.

Still, I can't hold back the smirk at her surprise, at her husband's jealousy. Everyone knows goblins aren't the most endowed creatures, while hellhounds... well, not that I want to brag, but we pack a fucking punch.

"Why are you still looking at him?" the man growls at his wife.

I laugh and keep striding, letting them bicker. A familiar, sweet scent on the breeze smothers me.

"Elias?"

I straighten my spine and whip to find Aria staring at me. A long, red scarf is draped across her head and shoulders, reminding me of an Indian princess. And she's holding Cassiel under an arm.

She took that furball with her shopping? Now, of all times?

Those piercing, dark eyes bore into me, and she is all I can think about now. Her beauty, her gorgeous figure… I swallow back the anger I want to throw at her, but when she glares at me, it all comes rushing back like a storm.

"What are you doing here?" I snarl, reaching for her.

But she's fast, and instead of grabbing her arm, I hook the scarf instead. It slides off her and onto the ground.

"Why the heck are you naked?" Her gaze dips, something I don't miss despite the anger warring across her face.

"I came to find you," I answer loudly. "And here you are again, running away like we mean nothing to you after we helped you. This is our thanks?"

"That's not fair." She looks around us and then behind her, but no one else is close.

I snatch her wrist and drag her closer, my anger getting the better of me. She moves fast—too damn fast. One minute she's holding Cassiel, the next, she's let him hop out of her arm and slaps me.

"Let me go!"

My cheek stings, but I can't deny she has me so worked up, I half contemplate throwing her over my shoulder and turning that cute ass red.

"Aria!" I lean forward, not to threaten her, but to make her aware of who is in charge here. My fingers squeeze her wrist. "What part of 'don't run away from us' don't you understand? Cain is near death, and you scared the hell out of me, vanishing like that. I can't have anything happen to you… not after everything else. Fuck, Aria!"

Frustration twists her expression, and flames seem to flare behind her eyes when she looks at me.

"I came to find a way to help Cain," she answers angrily, tugging on her hand to release herself from my grip.

Her response surprises me, and I pause when a sudden, sharp bite pierces my calf, and I howl from the stinging pain.

I snap around just as she rips free from my grasp, and I find Cassiel's mouth latched to my leg, teeth embedded into my flesh.

"Fuck! Dammit!" I grab him by the scruff and yank him off. "You are so close to becoming hellhound chowder."

He snarls at me, swiping the air between us, missing my nose. Why the hell did we take this thing into our home again?

"Leave him alone." Aria snatches him out of my hand and cradles him against her chest, peppering his head with kisses.

I growl under my breath. "Let's go home," I hiss, trying to calm myself, well aware my fury isn't directed at her. I'm so worried about Cain, so scared that I might have lost Aria. The tension is like a mountain on my shoulders, slowly burying me into the earth. "If you want to go anywhere, talk to us first. You scared the hell out of me that you were running away again."

She steps closer, standing toe to toe with me, even if she only reaches my chin in height. But she tilts her head back, not backing down, and damn but I love the fire in her. "For your information, I've made the decision to not run away anymore. I already told Cain."

Her lips pinch with a challenging look before she whips around and hurries toward the Cadillac.

When did she tell Cain? He would have told us. Wait… she's decided not to run away anymore?

I walk after her when I notice a small crowd of half a dozen people staring my way. *Yeah, get a good look.* I don't even bother with them and charge for the car, then grab the back door just as Aria starts to pull it shut.

"Hey!" she cries out. "Go to the other side."

But I'm sick of games, and I shove myself in next to her, nudging her over. She squeals as she shuffles over, still grasping onto the furball.

I shut the door and call out to Holmes, "Take us home."

"What the fuck is your problem?!" she demands.

I turn on her. "Don't ever pull a stunt like that again."

She draws her brows together. "What stunt?"

"Aria!"

"You didn't like that I went and found help for

ALL SHOT TO HELL

Cain, is that it? Or that I took control—is that what you don't like?"

"It's you being in danger," I answer, the words hissing through my teeth.

"Oh…kay… I think it's control you have problems with."

"Little rabbit, I have control." I swivel around to face her. "We are a team, so you need to tell us if you're going to run off."

"You're not the only one who is worried about Cain, so you don't have to be so aggressive. I heard what you and Dorian were saying, how dire the situation is. I'm not going to sit around doing nothing."

I run a hand through my hair, studying the way she blinks quickly, how her stiff posture screams to back off. Damn, she is stunning, and her anger just draws me to her more, but her stubbornness kills me.

"As I said before," I begin, "my priority is *you*. I won't risk losing you."

Silence.

She gnaws at her lower lip, looking me in the eyes. "I'm not used to that," she says, her voice almost timid.

"Someone caring for you?" I reach over and push a loose strand caught in her lashes behind her ear.

She half shrugs, half nods, and lowers her gaze like admitting it is embarrassing.

"Do you even want to hear what I found out that might help Cain?" She changes the topic, and I can't help but notice her vulnerability. I grew up without parents, put into a legion army from a young age. I never knew anything but commands, and it took me many decades to realize the strength of a tender word.

"Of course I do," I answer.

She sets Cassiel next to her and as far from me as possible, then twists to face me. We bounce in our seats as we drive over a rough patch of the road.

"I met with Miranda, the psychic from the Storm markets. At least I think so. She was kind of cryptic. Anyway, I told her about Cain, and she said she knows someone who can help us. She even gave me a map showing where to find him." She's talking super fast as she slides a hand into her pocket and pulls out a rolled-up paper. She undoes it and shows me a hand-scribbled map labeled with the main roads and directions and names. It looks like it's been photocopied a dozen times, as some of the print has faded.

I study the map closely but don't recognize the location, though it might make more sense if I compared it to a real map.

"And who did she suggest?" I ask, curious, as Miranda isn't necessarily our greatest fan after Dorian took her as one of his conquests then dumped her.

"Banner. He's a necromancer."

"Banner? That doesn't sound like a name for a necromancer. But if she says he can help, I'm willing to give it a try."

Necromancers are a different animal. To get the

magic they possess, their souls are dark. They're unpredictable, untrustworthy. But then again, we're dealing with a demon close to death, and what better person to help than a conqueror of the dead? I'll need to speak to Dorian and find out if he knows about this Banner.

Aria rolls the paper back up and tucks it into her pocket.

"Thank you," I say. We have a lead, which is more than Dorian and I have been able to find so far.

She turns toward me and lifts a hand to my face, placing it on my jaw, and tips her head closer to me. She kisses me deeply, and it's incredibly hard to keep focused when she kisses me so deliciously sweet. It makes me forget why the hell I was upset in the first place.

I cup the back of her head and leave a trail of kisses across her cheek before tucking my face in the curve of her neck. Kissing her, tasting the sweet taste of her with a hint of salty perspiration. I take a deep breath and inhale her scent, my hound ruffling within me with the reassurance she is ours and safe once again.

A low, sexy moan comes from her throat.

"You are always safe with me," I whisper in her ear. She relaxes against me, her hands looping around my neck.

"Why do you care so much about what happens to me?" she asks, the look in her eyes genuine as she looks up at me.

"You mean a lot to me," I answer truthfully and decide to open up a bit, to show her a sliver of the darkness from my past so she learns to trust. "I lost a lot in Hell. I was betrayed by someone I thought I loved, but everything she said and did was a lie. That was a hard pill to swallow. But what I see in your eyes is different. Someone who is passionate and so sincere. I want to believe you are nothing like her."

"That's awful, to have someone betray you. I kinda know that feeling." I sense her body hardening against me. "She sounds like a bitch for hurting you, and I may not know her, but she's definitely nothing like me."

I don't respond, and we stay quiet for a long while in each other's arms. "I'm glad you made the decision to no longer run from us."

"I didn't mean to scare you. I'm terrified we're going to lose Cain." Her wobbly voice fades.

She simply presses closer to me, her soft breasts crushed against my chest, and I hold her tight. She doesn't have to tell me why she changed her mind about staying with us, just as long as she keeps her word. Her breaths grow shallow, and it pains me to hear the agony in her voice.

It shouldn't surprise me Cain's injury has affected her so badly, but it does. Clearly, whatever they experienced on their recent trip changed the dynamics between them.

This whole time, I'd seen our connection as primal and animalistic. In her presence, my hound howls to claim her, to rut her. Everything comes down to sex, right? But I realize how wrong I've been with what I've been feeling. Hell.

Her hand lazily trails up my bare chest, and she stays in my arms for the rest of the trip.

Once we arrive home and head inside, we find Dorian in Cain's bedroom. The dhampir, Ramos, is there too, standing over Cain, who's been changed into a clean shirt and pants. Whispering something under his breath, Ramos tosses a handful of what looks like dust over the bed. But the particles float over Cain, connected by what looks like a transparent membrane that encases him.

"What is that?" Aria rushes across the room and to the bed, fright shaking her words.

"A magical shield that will hold him in a temporary coma," Ramos explains and steps back to give her space.

Aria glances at me, not trusting Ramos fully. I mean, he did take her from her home the last time she saw him, so I can understand her apprehension.

"Ramos is an expert in Kyusho Jitso and more... *non-traditional* East Asian medical practices," I explain, trying to give her some comfort.

Ramos dips his head in a subtle nod. "I managed to find a way to hold his illness in limbo and stop it from progressing."

"That's fantastic," she adds, stepping closer.

"It's only temporary," Dorian cuts in. "One week, right Ramos? That's all we have?"

The dhampir nods. "And after one week, his condition will deteriorate even faster."

A cold chill flares over my skin. "So we have seven days to find a way to help him or..." I can't bring myself to voice the rest of the words.

Ramos nods, and no one else responds. The unspoken words and trepidation hang in the air between us.

We fail to find a cure and Cain dies.

CHAPTER FIVE
ARIA

"Ramos, can you give us a minute?" Dorian asks. He nods, gathers up some of the dirty towels and water bowls, and leaves the room.

Once the door closes, Dorian turns to me. "I'm surprised by you, little girl. I didn't think you'd take the first opportunity to run. Especially after everything we've been through. And with Cain…"

He heaves a sigh, his shoulders slumping, and it's the first time I've ever seen him upset like this. Disappointed.

He thinks I bolted, and I understand why he'd jump to that conclusion. It wouldn't be my first time trying to escape, but the fact that this time I'd left to help Cain makes my chest clench with guilt. I don't want him to think I don't care. Because I do. Probably more than I should, given the circumstances.

I glance at Elias. He knows the real reason why I left.

"It's not what you think, Dorian," he says. "She wasn't trying to run away this time."

His head tilts to the side, and his gaze scans me over. "Oh?"

"I mean, yes, I did leave," I start, "but I had every intention of coming back. I only wanted to go to Storm's markets and see if I could find something that could help Cain."

Dorian's body eases. "And? What did you find?"

I pass over the map and wait for him to give it a good look over. "Cold's Keep? Where is this? What's there that can help us?"

"Not a what. A who," I reply, using Miranda's exact words. "A necromancer named Banner."

Dorian's eyes widen in shock. "A necromancer?" His gaze slides to Elias, and a slow smile forms. "Why, Aria, a necromancer might be exactly who Cain needs. Ha!" He claps his hands together. "We have to go to this Cold's Keep now and find this fellow. Who better to cheat death than a master of death himself!"

"That's exactly what the woman at the markets said," I add in as relief floods me. Thank God I've done the right thing here. "The psychic woman. Miranda."

Dorian freezes on the spot, and his face drains of all color. "I'm sorry. Who now?"

"Mir-Miranda?" I don't like the sudden change in his demeanor. Elias hadn't had nearly as strong a reaction when I'd told him about the psychic in the market. My gaze flicks between the two demons nervously. "She said she knew you guys."

Elias leans close to my shoulder and whispers, "Miranda is a Seer. And Dorian's ex-girlfriend."

"What!" I balk. She failed to mention that small detail during our meeting. I have no idea what a Seer is, but the second part of his statement was harder to miss.

"I don't have exes, or girlfriends for that matter," he replies quickly. "Miranda was a fling. A sexual conquest. That is all."

A tight knot twists in my gut, and jealousy stirs. Like with the over-friendly store clerk at Gracy's Groceries, the thought of any other woman touching my demons makes me prickle with rage. I know they had lives before I came along, but that doesn't mean I want to *think* about it.

Dorian brushes it off with a dismissive wave of his hand. "If Miranda gave you this map, that means it's legitimate. You heard Ramos. We're on borrowed time. We have to find Banner."

"Can we trust this chick?" I'm starting to have my doubts.

"She's a part of a very complicated deal with us, one she needs Cain to be alive for. She'll want to help him," he says.

A deal? Cain had made a deal with her? For what?

I don't like the sound of that. Not one bit.

"Let's throw some clothes in a suitcase and hit the road," Dorian goes on. "Meet you in the foyer in ten?"

He and Elias move to the door, but when they see I've stayed put, they both turn and look at me.

"Aria?" Elias calls. "You are coming with us. Right?"

I wrap my arms around myself. "What about Cain?"

We can't just leave him alone. Not like this. Even with Ramos's ancient Asian magic tricks.

"Ramos will stay with him. He's the best suited for stuff like this," Dorian explains. "And he'll have the staff's help and whatever supplies he needs."

Despite his words, worry still weighs on my shoulders. I know what has to be done to save him, but for some reason, leaving Cain to go on some trip feels just as wrong as doing nothing.

A heavy hand rests on my shoulder, and when I look up, Elias is looking down at me with a sympathetic smile. "He'll be in good hands," he assures me. "Ramos knows what he's doing."

"He's right." Dorian appears by his side. "And we have a week to make this work for him. That isn't much time."

That's an extreme understatement. We barely have any time at all. But I get what they're saying. As much as I don't want to leave Cain behind, doing so to recruit the necromancer is the only way to save his life. There really isn't any other option.

I heave a sigh. "Alright. I'll meet you downstairs then."

Elias gives my shoulder a light squeeze before the two of them leave the room.

Alone again with Cain, I rub my lips together and bounce on my feet. I hate this. Really, really hate this. Just the thought of leaving him for a few days has my insides all tangled up in knots. I grip the winged pendant, hoping it can somehow give me the strength or courage I need to walk out that door.

Now wearing a clean white shirt and pants and seeming to be frozen in time, Cain looks to be even more dead than before, and the image makes me ill. I'm terrified that I'll leave and somehow come back to an empty bed.

Holding the necklace tighter, I look at him one last time before forcing my feet to lead me out the door.

---

*A*fter plugging the town of Cold's Keep in the GPS and Google Maps only to come up with zero results, we're forced to use the poorly done map and what it can tell us. Which isn't much at all. Dorian pointed out that the main squiggle in the middle of the paper looks to be I-89, and that means Cold's Keep is north of Glenside, but that's all we have to go on, so that's where we're headed. North.

As we drive through Vermont in Dorian's sexy black Ferrari, I'm alone in the back while Dorian drives and Elias stretches out his legs in the front. I don't mind being alone back here, though. I'm a bit stuck in my own head, my gaze glued to the passing scenery of snowy treetops and mountain rocks. Outside, the entire world is painted in either gray or white, and there's a tranquility to it that combats the chaotic thoughts and feelings raging inside me.

Not having Cain here with us... It feels wrong. So wrong. I never thought I'd see the day when I would miss his twisted scowl or the way he would infuriate me, only to sweep me back up a minute later in his dark charms. Without his presence, things just don't feel right. There's an obvious emptiness filling his place, and I am sure Dorian and Elias feel it, too. We're all a bit lost without him.

"Hey, you okay back there?" Dorian asks, glancing at me through the rearview mirror.

Sucking in a deep breath, I say, "Yeah, I'm fine. Just thinking about what we need to do, you know? And how little time we have."

"I don't want you to worry yourself too much," Dorian says. "I've known Cain for a long time, and he's always been a fighter. He'll come out of this."

He glances at Elias for backup, and when he doesn't say anything, he throws him a sharp nudge with his elbow.

Annoyed, he rubs his arm. "What the fuck was that for?"

Dorian's gaze hardens on him, and he nods towards me. "*Right,* Elias?" he presses, waiting for him to get on board. "*Right?*"

Elias clears his throat. "Er, yeah, right. Exactly what Dorian said."

"Smooth," he growls at him.

"What?" Elias shoots back. "I said what you wanted me to."

Dorian shakes his head, knowing Elias is a lost cause. "*Anyway,*" he begins, drawing out the word, "here's my plan. We drive up the interstate for another hour, then we pull off, find ourselves a local supernatural, and ask them how far we are from Cold's Keep. Hopefully they've heard of it and can point us in the right direction from there."

"That's a terrible idea," Elias grumbles. "You want us to just stop and ask local strangers if they've heard of some magically hidden town in the middle of nowhere and pray they know what the hell we're talking about?"

"You have something better, genius?"

Throwing him a glare, Elias bites back. "Actually yes. I say we call one of the spellcasters on our contact list and have them do a location spell. Have them give us exact coordinates."

"That would be great *if* location spells worked like that." He holds up three fingers and counts them off as he speaks. "One. Location spells can only give us a general area. Not an exact one. Two. They can only be used to find a *person*, and only if the spellcaster has something personal from that person. So unless they have a lock of this necromancer's hair, you can forget it. And three, we tried asking contacts to do location spells when we were looking for Aria and Sir Surchion, and they weren't too keen on helping us then. I doubt that would've changed by now."

I blow out an exasperated breath. Well, there goes that.

"Fucking shit," Elias huffs. "We can't just drive all over the state and hope we stumble across it."

He's right. But maybe there's another way.

"Can I see the map?" I ask them.

"Sure." Dorian passes me the rolled-up paper. "Though I'd hardly call it a map. Looks more like a three-year-old found a pen and went to town."

He isn't wrong. Most of the lines look like accidental squiggles with no real purpose or pattern. As I examine it again, I can't find anything distinct or a landmark that could possibly help us pinpoint Cold's Keep's exact location.

I lean in closer and notice some faded markings at the end of the main line, the one Dorian assumed was the interstate. They appear to be letters, too.

Is that a *V*? Maybe a *U*?

No wait, a *C*?

Dammit, it's near impossible to tell for sure.

"Find anything helpful?" Dorian asks as he expertly weaves the Ferrari in and out of cars, going thirty over the speed limit.

"Does V-U-R-W-L-C-H ring a bell to anyone?" I ask, trying my best to make out the barely visible letters.

"Not in English," Dorian chuckles. "Is that supposed to be another language?"

"Ugh, there's not even enough vowels in here for it to make sense!" This is hopeless.

As we drive, we pass a large green sign with the upcoming exits listed and their distance in miles away. One of the names catches my eye.

Norwich.

I glance at the map again. Could it really say *Norwich*? Is that *V* actually an *N*? Maybe if I squint real hard and turn the paper slightly to the right. Yeah, I guess it could be an *N*.

And according to the sign, the town is coming up in half a mile.

Dorian is flying down the interstate, sliding in between cars and trucks, and earning a few middle fingers along the way. But with our exit coming up and him all the way in the left lane, we're going to miss it.

Moving to the edge of my seat and pushing my body in between Elias and Dorian's wide shoulders, I yell, "Take this exit!"

Dorian jumps, spinning the wheel all the way right and jerking us into the next lane without even looking. I'm thrown sideways, and the loud blare of a truck's horn has my heart climbing into my throat. He jolts the steering wheel again, narrowly missing the eighteen-wheeler's front end and slamming the gas pedal to the floor. I scream.

I don't know how he does it, but he manages to

cross us over four lanes of traffic and around the exit ramp without an accident. It isn't until we reach a residential area and the speed limit drops to twenty-five that my pulse settles down some. When Dorian eases us to a stop at a red light, he looks between me and Elias, breathing a little harder.

"Everyone okay?"

I swipe my disheveled hair out of my face. "Yeah, fine."

I peer over at Elias, who's been deathly silent this whole time. His entire body is rigid, muscles tight, jaw set. It's as if he's been frozen in time.

"Elias?" I poke his shoulder, and that's when his hand unlatches from the car door's handle and I notice the metal has the distinct indents of his fingers.

Well, shit.

Slowly, he turns to Dorian, his lips twitching with his building rage. "I HATE cars," he pushes through clenched teeth. "And I hate when you're driving them even more."

"Oh, come on now. It wasn't *that* bad," Dorian says, but when the light turns green and he eases off the brake again, Elias's hand shoots right back to the door handle to brace himself.

"What a baby." Dorian chuckles and then glances at me through the mirror. "But still, maybe a little more notice on the direction next time, Aria? What do you think?"

I nod. "You got it."

As we cruise down the streets of Norwich, I take in the sights. It looks like an older town, or at least vintage-inspired, with its red brick sidewalks, stone buildings, and gas lampposts.

We seem to have stumbled across a small shopping area, too, because all the restaurants and stores are bustling with customers. Wreaths, candlesticks, and Christmas lights decorate every door and window, even though the holidays are still a month away. But all the twinkling lights and the recent dusting of snow gives Norwich a very homey and welcoming appearance.

It is… quaint. Such a stark contrast to the dark reason we're here.

"Are you sure this is the right place?" Elias asks after he's finally relaxed some. He stares out the window at the patrons with a confused and slightly disturbed look. "It's like we've stumbled across Santa's workshop here. I even smell gingerbread and peppermint."

"I-I think so. Here. Look at the map and tell me what this says." I hand the paper over to the two of them and point to the faded words. "Does that look like it says 'Norwich' to you?"

Elias snatches it out of my hand and holds it close to his face. "That might be an *N*... or a *B*?"

"You see my problem," I mutter.

"I'm going to trust you and say we're in the right place," Dorian adds in. "Now, let's find a hotel to regroup for the night, and then we can go looking for Cold's Keep."

Elias passes me back the map, and after rolling it back up, I reach for my satchel on the floor to slide it in. My fingers brush something soft and furry, and I cry out. "What the—"

A soft mewing sound comes from inside, and my heart skips.

Elias's nostrils flare as he sniffs the air. "Are you fucking kidding me? No fucking way. He didn't."

"What?" Dorian asks, glancing around. "What is it?"

Cassiel leaps onto my lap, chin held high, as if he's proud of himself for keeping his secret for so long.

I laugh—I can't help it—and scratch the lynx's head. "You clever little thing."

He purrs in response and pushes into my hand for more pets.

"You brought the cat?" Dorian's voice rises in disbelief.

"No! Clearly he stowed away. I had no idea he was even in there."

"You expect us to believe that?" Elias snaps. "It's a *cat*. They aren't intelligent."

"Says the hellhound." I shrug.

"Hey, the hound is only part of me. And there was a legion of hellhound demons under my command. What does he do? Lick his butt and sleep all day? Woo-freaking-hoo."

"Ah, so the same thing as you, pretty much,"

Dorian chimes in, which earns him a hard punch to the arm.

Shaking my head at the absurd turn this conversation has taken, I lift Cassiel up and rub our noses together. They might not be happy about it, but I'm glad he came along for the trip. I could use the distraction.

"Don't listen to them," I whisper to him. "I'm glad you're here."

Cassiel gives the tip of my nose a little lick, and I hold him close again.

Elias grumbles under his breath and crosses his massive arms over his chest. "It's not smart to bring a pet with us on this trip. It could get dangerous."

As if he actually cares about Cassiel's safety.

"We can leave him in the hotel room," I reply. "He'll be fine."

"It's not like we can turn around now," Dorian says to Elias.

"We could just…" He makes the motion of grabbing something and tossing it out the window, and I gasp, clutching Cassiel a little tighter.

"You wouldn't fucking dare," I snap.

Dorian laughs, his shoulders bouncing. "Looks like we're stuck with the cat."

Elias bangs the back of his head against the headrest. "Fuck me."

After driving a bit more through the town, we stop in the first hotel we see. Like the rest of Norwich, it's a small, modest place, a brick-faced building with large lobby windows and an ornate Christmas tree inside.

Dorian sweet-talks the receptionist while Elias gathers up all our bags and heads for the elevator. I follow him with Cassiel tucked safely and discreetly in my satchel. You know, just in case they don't allow pets.

Once Dorian meets up with us, he hands me one of the plastic key cards.

"Were you able to get rooms near each other?" I ask him just as the elevator dings and the doors open. We all step inside. Between Elias's over six-foot height and Dorian's broad shoulders, there's not much room left for me in the metal box, but my card says Room 402, so that means we have four flights to go cramped like this.

"If you mean next to each other as in the same room, then yes," Dorian says as he waves his keycard with Room 402 written on it too.

"W-What?" I choke. My stomach does a cartwheel at the thought of the three of us all sleeping in the same room. Together.

A smirk lifts the corner of Dorian's mouth. "Is that going to be a problem?"

If I actually want to get some sleep? Probably.

"Don't worry, little girl. If Elias's snores get to be too much, there's always the pull-out sofa for him to be exiled to. Or a balcony."

Elias clenches his jaw. "You're fucking hilarious."

Ignoring his jab, Dorian goes on. "But, as much as

I'd love to stay for a few hours and get comfortable, we have a magical town to find, and the woman at the front desk is an elf, so after we drop off our stuff—"

"And the furball," Elias interjects.

"And Cassiel, yes—I'm going to compel her to tell us the location of Cold's Keep. That way, if she knows it, she'll have no choice but to tell us."

---

*A*s most plans go, Dorian's sounds good, but it doesn't work out so well in execution. Compelling the poor girl at the front desk only got her to say two things: Yes, she knew where Cold's Keep was, and, my personal favorite, "Go jump off a cliff." Those were her exact words.

Of course, Dorian is confused and not too happy to hear this, because the girl shouldn't have been able to say anything but the answer to "Where's Cold's Keep," and instead her answers tell us nothing of the sort. He's even worried he's losing his gift, or maybe being on this plane for so long is weakening it too much to be useful.

First I could resist him, and now this elf? I can tell it's disturbing him, and I wish I had an answer, but I am just as perplexed as he is about the whole thing.

After that small bump in the road, while standing on the sidewalk, we decide to look at the map again to see if we can decipher anything else from the faded shapes and scribbles.

On the paper, just northwest of Norwich is a star and the letters we *think* are supposed to spell Cold's Keep. Whoever made this map obviously didn't have the neatest handwriting, but if I'm reading the thing right, we should technically be close. Maybe twenty miles away? It's hard to tell.

"Are those trees?" Elias asks, peering over my shoulder at the map, too.

"I'm not sure…" I confess. "They look more like poorly-drawn clouds to me. Or just smudges?"

"If they're trees, maybe it's deep in the woods?"

"If I wanted to hide an entire town away from people, that's where I'd put it. Somewhere remote," Dorian says.

"I can always shift and search the nearby forest. See if I can find anything that way."

"That's a good idea," I reply. Not the best, but good.

We hop into the car and drive a bit until the houses and stores become less and less and we finally hit a patch of trees. Dorian pulls over, throws the car into park, and we all jump out. Elias strides straight for the dark tree line, stripping off his clothes with every step. The last thing I see is his naked ass before the shadows consume him completely. A second later, the sounds of an animal huffing and paws hitting the ground echo and then fade away.

"Didn't expect to see a full moon out tonight,"

Dorian teases and throws me a wink. I chuckle, more at his pathetic attempt at a joke than the actual joke itself.

Dorian turns to me then. "Maybe we should wait in the car. It's a bit chilly out here."

He's right. The wind bristles past us, and they got a lot more snow than we did in Glenside. Even in my thick coat, gloves, and scarf, I'm still shivering. Elias may have fur to keep him warm, but I sure don't.

I nod, and I'm about to walk over to my door when my pinky toe twitches in my sneakers, as if waking from a long sleep. The familiar tingling sensation that always follows races up and down my spine, pinning me in place.

"What is it?" Dorian asks, stepping closer to me out of concern.

"I…" Wondering if I imagined it, I wait a beat, but when my toe starts its strange wiggling and dancing again, I know for sure it's real. "I sense some very, very strong magic," I tell him. "Dark magic."

His brows rise. "Wait, here? Now?"

My toe continues to buzz, confirming it. "Yeah."

"Is it another relic? How? Here?"

"I can't say for sure..." I start hesitantly. "And the only way to know for sure is…"

His gaze swings back to the woods where Elias disappeared only seconds ago, and his entire body turns rigid. "To follow the trail."

CHAPTER SIX
ELIAS

The frigid wind whistles past my ears. Snow crunches under my paws as I thunder through the woods. The cold feels good combing through my fur, and for a brief moment, I forget why I'm out here in the first place.

That's right. I'm supposed to be looking for the magical entrance to Cold's Keep. What exactly that is… I'm not fucking sure, but hopefully my nose can sniff it out.

After speeding past trees and around a frozen creek, the sound of footsteps echoes in the distance. Head swiveling in that direction, I freeze, ears perked up, and listen. Two sets of feet, if I were to guess correctly, and they're closing in on me fast. My nostrils flare as I sniff the air and catch two very familiar scents wafting on the breeze.

Dorian and Aria?

They were supposed to wait for me by the car.

Uneasiness shoots up my spine, raising my hackles. If they've come in here, something must be wrong. With the tree coverage overhead, it's dark in here, but Dorian's brought a small flashlight to guide them. The spotlight shines my way.

"Elias!" Aria shouts when she spots me, and the two of them rush over. To my surprise, there's no panic on either of their faces, so I relax some. But only some.

"Are we still going the right way?" Dorian asks, coming to her side.

Confused, I tilt my head.

"Yeah," she replies. "It's getting stronger. We have to go up here further."

What the heck are they talking about?

Dorian takes a step forward, but I meet him to block his way. He shifts left and I stop him again, a growl low in my throat. No one is going anywhere without telling me what the fuck is going on.

"Settle down, Scooby-Doo. Aria's dark magic alarm is going off."

I glance at Aria, who nods. Does that mean she's sensing another relic? Here, of all places? How can that be?

"We have to keep going," she says and gestures deeper into the forest. Even though it's safer to let me lead, I step aside and let her take the front before taking the place directly behind her. It pushes Dorian further back, and he snorts in aggravation.

"Doesn't matter!" he calls to us. "I like it back here anyway! Better view."

I roll my eyes, but Aria chuckles.

We trudge on through the snow, the wind slowing us down some. As we come to the crest of a steep hill, I see the sharp drop before Aria does, and I snap her coat in my jaws and tug her back before she takes a final step that would've sent her tumbling yards down to her death. We both stumble back, colliding with Dorian.

"Oh my God," Aria gasps, her eyes wide with fear. "I didn't even see that drop."

Dorian holds her shoulders, appearing a little frazzled himself. "Neither did I." He turns to me. "Good catch."

I dip my head.

Cautiously, Aria creeps closer to the ledge to gauge the height of the ravine. She shivers. "I don't understand. My toe is still going bonkers, as if it wants me to go on."

"Maybe it wants us to find a way down?" Dorian suggests. "Maybe we can find a safer path."

She ponders that for a long moment and frowns. "I'm… I'm not sure."

A flicker of movement catches my eye. Gaze dropping, I see Aria's shadow stretching out, a black smear against the whiteness. I glance at Dorian, but he's not moving his flashlight at all. Nothing is manipulating the darkness. Nothing natural, anyway.

Muscles rigid and spine hunched, I growl.

"Oh no…" Aria breathes as she watches the shadow slink across the snow. "Sayah."

Sayah. The shadow creature?

We all watch in horror as the shadow crawls across the ledge, on and on, until its form lifts off the ground and keeps spreading outward, as if crawling along something we can't see.

"What is it doing?" Dorian asks.

"I think… she wants us to follow her," Aria answers.

Yeah, right off a cliff.

My lip curls, and another growl rumbles in my chest. I don't trust many people, and I especially don't trust a shifty dark spirit-thing possessing my girl.

To my surprise, Aria takes another step forward.

Is she barking mad? I quickly move in front of her.

"Aria, I don't think following that thing is a good idea," Dorian says hesitantly.

"I just want to see something." She brushes past me to the very edge. I hover nearby, just in case I have to snatch her again. Carefully, she pokes out her foot and waves it about. Then, to my complete astonishment, it hits something solid. Snow crunches underfoot.

Dorian runs a hand over his mouth in shock. "Well, I'll be damned."

The shadow found a hidden bridge that must've

been drenched in magic. One I hadn't even been able to sniff out myself.

Suddenly, Sayah zips back into Aria, as if pulled back by a yo-yo, and Aria's body twitches as they realign again.

Freaky. I've never seen anything like that before. It's still hard to believe someone as small as Aria could hold such great power inside her. And why the hell is that thing helping her now, anyway? What does it know that we don't?

"Do you think it's the entrance of Cold's Keep?" Aria directs the question to both of us.

"Has to be, right?" Dorian replies, a pleased smile appearing. "Now the girl at the front desk's directions make more sense. 'Go jump off a cliff.' Ha!"

Aria goes to take another step over the chasm, but I move in front of her to take the lead.

"Elias—" she protests.

"Let him go ahead. It'll be better if he's the one to fall. Maybe then we can see if he lands on all fours, like a cat."

I snort. Fucking Dorian.

Aria relents and lets me go ahead. Slowly, I take another step forward. When my paws hit more solid ground, I glance past them, seeing nothing but jagged rocks, trees, and the curve of the creek hundreds of feet underneath us. It's the most unsettling thing I've ever seen.

Another step, then another. My heartbeat is a

raging river behind my ears. Behind me, Aria and Dorian start to inch forward.

Only a few more steps, and I'm caressed with the invisible fingers of magic. It brushes through my fur and tickles across my skin. A shiver slides up and down my spine, but in front of me, the scene has changed dramatically. I'm standing in the center of a town with brick and wood buildings and cobblestone streets. Gas streetlamps burn low, their lights barely penetrating through the dense darkness cloaking the place. Everything seems to be tinted in gray. Muted. Quiet. Eerie. It's as if I've stepped through a portal and ended up back in time.

"Woah." Aria's voice chimes in behind me as they shift through the magical veil and enter the town.

"How... *dreary*," Dorian says, looking around.

"It's almost like we've stepped in a movie set."

Calling to my power, I push the animal back and let the surge take over my muscles and bones. The shift takes seconds, and when I straighten my spine and roll my shoulders, I'm instantly hit with the sting of cold air.

Aria reaches into her satchel, pulls out a bundle, and passes it to me. Taking it, I realize it's all the clothes I'd discarded in the woods before shifting.

"We grabbed them on the way," she says and looks up at me with a smile. "Figured there'd be a chance you might need them again."

The corner of my mouth lifts. "Thanks."

Dorian cuts in. "I, for one, wanted to leave you stranded butt naked, but she's nicer than me."

After pulling on my clothes, we all turn back to the town's center.

"Now what?" I ask. "Where do we go next?"

"I have no idea," she replies. "Do we ask someone?"

"Who?" Dorian swipes a hand toward the quiet and empty streets. "There's no one here."

"We can, maybe, knock on a door?"

"Demons showing up on your doorstep in the middle of the night? Might not get the best reaction."

"Hey, I'm trying here. I don't see you coming up with any ideas," Aria snaps.

"Does the map say anything else?" I ask.

Aria shuffles through her bag again and pulls it out. Dorian and I peek over her shoulder to get a look, too. Besides some squiggles that I'm assuming are supposed to be the forest, there's nothing but a star in the center, I'm assuming to mark Cold's Keep. Nothing about inside the town itself.

Sighing, she folds it back up and puts it away. "Nothing, like I thought." After a moment, she says, "Wait… Does this place have a morgue or something? A cemetery?"

"Why?" Dorian asks.

"Have you ever seen a movie? Creepy dudes always hang out in creepy places, and where else would a necromancer want to be than around dead people?"

"Seems a bit on the nose…" Dorian answers.

"What do we have to lose?"

"She's right," I say. "Can't hurt to check."

I scan the town's center and find a bunch of signs with arrows pointing the way to the town hall, tavern, oddity shop, and more. At the very bottom, it says 'Cemetery' and points down a smaller street on our right. I nod for them to follow.

The alley is cloaked in shadows. No lamps this way. Dorian swings his flashlight ahead of us to show us the way, and we follow the slender beam down some stone steps, around the corner to the back of some houses, and down a hill. It isn't long before we come to the tall metal gate. Beyond it, tombstones of all shapes and sizes rise out of the snow, dark reminders of a person's mortality.

I would've said 'a human's' or 'a supernatural's' mortality, but Cain's situation reemerges into my thoughts, how close he hovers on that line of life of death, and I know death is now a real threat to us, too.

The clink, swoosh, clink, swoosh of metal shifting through dirt sounds, making us all freeze. It's the first noise we've heard since we got here, and it cuts loudly through the silence.

"Sounds like someone… digging," I say, trying to make sense of what I'm hearing.

"Digging a grave, maybe?" Dorian asks, his brow lifting.

"Let's get this moving because Hell-beings and

cold don't go well together, and I'm freezing my balls off here without my fur." Without waiting another second, I push the gate open. It whines loudly against the rusty hinges, and immediately, the digging sounds stop.

"Way to keep inconspicuous, Elias," Dorian hisses.

"Who the fuck cares? It's a graveyard, full of dead people. I'm bigger and scarier than anything in this place."

"With the same amount of brain activity."

I glare at him.

Aria pushes past us and strides ahead. "Jesus Christ, how did Cain last a hundred years with you two?"

Her tone was light-hearted—the jab obviously made to be a joke—but the mention of Cain has us all moving a little quicker and quieter through the graveyard, reminding us of our true purpose here and the limited time we have to get this done.

"My toe is going crazy," she mutters to break the heavy silence. "Definitely wants us to go this way."

We stroll past smaller marble mausoleums and headstones, past fresh mounds of dirt over newly dug graves and ones that are sunken and covered in vines from age. The place is over-crowded and clearly has been used by the residents of this supernatural town for a long time. Some dates inscribed in the headstones even go as far back as the 1800s.

Once the sound of a shovel slicing through dirt begins again, we follow the narrow path towards it, hoping that whoever is digging around here can give us some direction or clue on where to find this Banner fellow.

Finally, we come upon a hole in the earth with a mound of dirt and snow beside it. Only the top of a man's head can be seen, and periodically, the glint of a shovel as he swings it over his shoulder to expel the dirt from the hole.

He must have heard us coming through the cemetery—we weren't exactly the quietest—but he doesn't acknowledge us at all or stop at his task.

Aria glances at the two of us, wondering what we should do next. Dorian only shifts closer to the hole, trying to look down.

"Um, hello?" she calls to the stranger. "Excuse me."

But he ignores her and continues scooping up the dirt and chucking it out of the hole, either too preoccupied with his job to hear her or simply not caring enough to answer.

Rubbing her lips together, Aria tries again. "Excuse me, sir? We're wondering if you could help us. We're looking for someone. A… Banner? We're wondering if you could point us in the right direction."

Nope. No luck.

I clench my jaw, my patience wearing thin. There's no way he didn't hear her that time, so his rudeness is clearly intentional.

Dorian crouches at the edge of the grave and

waves to try and get the man's attention. "Yoo-hoo! Hello! Anybody home?"

The man snorts but doesn't look up.

What the fuck?

My annoyance quickly transforms into anger, and heat prickles up my neck.

Okay, now it's my turn.

I trudge over, and the next time the shovel's head swings out of the hole, I grab it, yank it out of his hands in one swift move, and stick it into the pile so it's standing upright. It works, and the man's head snaps up.

Cloudy white eyes meet mine, catching the light of the moon above and glinting ominously. My hound recoils out of instinct, unsure what it is I'm being faced with. This isn't an ordinary man at all. Not even an ordinary supe, for that matter. His skin is deathly pale, with bulging blue veins pushing through his neck and forehead, purple lips, and dark patches around his eyes. At first glance, he looks like a reanimated corpse. A zombie.

Readying for a standoff, my muscles clench, and my animal rears up. The stranger puts both hands on the side of the hole and lifts himself out with ease. My arm swings out to push Aria back while Dorian backpedals, too.

When he stands at full height, I'm shocked to find he's almost as tall as me. It's something I should've expected since graves are meant to be six feet deep and he was down there with just his hair showing.

But still, it's something I don't expect, since not many creatures can look me in the eye, and this guy is staring at me with ones that are eerily milky white.

He wears a button-down shirt, jacket, and slacks, all covered in dirt and straining against his size. Thick shoulders, wide chest, and hunched back, he looks like one of Frankenstein's experiments gone wrong.

"What do you want?" He barks the question, his voice gravelly and strained, his mouth moving awkwardly to get the words out like it isn't used to the action.

Dorian and I glance at each other.

"Sorry to interrupt your... digging," Dorian begins carefully, "but we're looking for someone, and you seem to be the only one around here that we can find."

His head swings to Dorian, and he grunts. "I'm busy."

"Please," Aria pipes up from behind me. "We're trying to save our... friend."

Again, the monster-man's head whips around, finding Aria this time, and his jaw tightens. But she goes on.

"We need to find a man named Banner. A necromancer. If you could just tell us where we can find—"

"You found him," he says and pulls out the shovel from the mound of soil. "And I cannot help you."

Shit. This guy is the one we need help from? The

necromancer? Guess Aria wasn't kidding with the whole 'hanging out around dead people' thing.

"Can't or won't?" Dorian asks.

He replies by turning away and hopping back into his hole.

Dorian tries again, this time laying on the charm. "Look, let me apologize for us having interrupted your special me-time and for my bullish friend over here mishandling your shovel. But as the girl said, we are in dire need of your expertise. Someone we care about is on the brink of death, and we need you to bring him back to the land of the living."

Dirt flies out of the pit as the shoveling resumes. I grit my teeth.

"We'll pay you handsomely," Dorian goes on. "Whatever your fee, we can pay it."

Banner stops. Now we've got his attention. His head pops up again.

"I have no need for such societal constructs as money," he grumbles.

"Then something else." Aria comes to my side, her voice full of desperation. "Anything. Please, we don't have much time."

He pauses, his white-eyed gaze scanning us all over. Debating.

After a long moment, he grips the shovel's handle with both hands, muscles bunching. "Fine," he snaps. "Tomorrow. Midnight. At Banner Barrow's crypt."

"Can't we simply talk today? Now? We're here

already," Aria says desperately. "Like I said, we don't have the ti—"

"Tomorrow," Banner snarls viciously, reminding me more of a beast than man.

Aria leans forward, about to argue more, but I press a hand into her shoulder to stop her. We're lucky he's agreeing to help us at all, at this point. He's unstable as it is.

Dorian pulls his shoulders back and nods. "Tomorrow then. We'll be back."

Banner's gaze swivels to Aria once again, and his head tilts to the side, studying her with a bit more interest. The paleness of his eyes glows.

A growl vibrates through me, my hellhound not trusting Banner in the slightest. And for good reason. Necromancers are a different kind of evil, a kind that is unnatural. Unpredictable. Fickle. Banner may be powerful, but the dark magic he possesses seems to be ripping him apart at the seams. He's coming undone.

And he's the only one who can save Cain.

CHAPTER SEVEN
DORIAN

"Does it seem strange that we're looking for the Banner Barrow crypt, when clearly Banner is still alive?" Aria asks as we step through the graveyard's front gates.

An owl screeches from a nearby tree. Its boughs twist like contorted limbs, and the silvery hue of the moon falls on the dirt path we follow deeper into the cemetery. The land is covered in a jumble of old tombstones. Two tombstones we pass sit at an angle, like they are old drunken friends leaning on each other. The night is still, as is the wind, and a heavy, oppressive heat sinks into my skin.

A strange, familiar sensation fills me, and I can't help but feel a bit like being back home. I smile. It sure as hell beats the last twenty-four hours we've spent waiting to visit the necromancer in that Hallmark-inspired town that seems to insist it's Christmas all year round. Apparently, Aria loves the festive season. She dragged us into so many stores that, I swear, if I never see another bauble again, I will never complain about another thing, ever.

"Could be his father," Elias suggests, answering Aria, who flips out her flashlight and carves a beam through the darkness.

"Still strange," she answers. "Is he living in his dad's crypt? Crap, what if he brought his father back from the dead?"

A sudden squeak pierces the air, and Aria flinches right into Elias, who wraps an arm around her waist, holding her close.

I laugh at her over-exaggeration. "Does this place freak you out that much, babe?"

"Um, hello. We are in a graveyard in the middle of the night. This is where horror movies were born," she says, untangling herself from Elias's side, but despite her bravery, the fear on her face is clear. In fact, it's beautiful… I have a thing for gorgeous girls being scared. Call me a sadist.

"Nothing here to be scared of," Elias assures her. "The dead are forgotten, eaten away by earthworms."

"What about other creatures or spirits? Or, you know, zombies? They could be around here. We are going to see a necromancer," she murmurs.

"She's got you there," I tease and cut a stare at Elias, who glares at me.

"Want to hear a story I once heard about a graveyard?" I say to pass time, as this place is enormous, and I'm not seeing any signs of the crypts yet. They must be all the way at the back.

"Like a ghost story?" She gasps at me as if I've gone mad.

"Not a ghost story. But it is said that as you walk through a graveyard at midnight and start counting the number of gravestones, if you find your first name before you reach thirteen, the spirit of a demonic goat will haunt you for eternity."

She barks a fake laugh. "That sounds like a stupid urban myth." Then she rolls her eyes at me and keeps moving. "Goat, really? Is that what scares demons in Hell?"

I shrug.

"I heard that one," Elias pipes in. "One of the demons in the legion was obsessed with those stories and told them all the time. But the goat is more of a shape-shifting demon and not as playful as it sounds."

"Yeah, they are just stories and not real," Aria says, picking up her pace.

"Then why don't we give it a try?" I tease, gaining myself a try-and-I'll-break-your-arm look from Aria. A shiver of excitement races up my spine at the promise of her getting physical with me. "What harm will it do?"

"Ah… well, we might somehow summon a goat-demon, and we already have enough problems," she deadpans.

"You just said you didn't believe in the tale," I tease.

"You did say that," Elias adds.

"I thought you were on my side?" She gapes at Elias, who smirks in response.

"You two are impossible. I don't even want to be in a cemetery at midnight, let alone testing out urban myths. Let's find Banner, get this done, and then you can do whatever you want in the graveyard on your own."

"Sure," I answer and smile to myself. I have no intention of doing so, but I am enjoying seeing more and more of what scares Aria, what she enjoys and doesn't, and who exactly this girl wriggling into my life is.

Silence permeates every inch of the landscape. Farther ahead, the tops of the large, stone mausoleums rise into view, blacker than the night. A fog spills forward from behind them, crawling along the ground like a virus.

"Okay, so it has to be one of these," Aria says, her voice low like she doesn't want to speak too loudly.

We hurry closer to the mausoleum crypts. A pebbled path weaves like a serpent amid them. Aria sweeps the beam of her flashlight across the tops of the buildings, where family names are chiseled into stone. The land ascends, and medieval sculptures now flank the mausoleums we pass, mostly angels worn away with weather and time. It always amazes me, the power people place in angels, when really they are just as corruptible as demons. The only difference is they are protected under the shield of

Heaven to help bring out only their best, but we are no different at the heart of it.

"Wow, I think that's it," Aria suddenly says, drawing my attention to the set of broken steps leading up to a great stone building with a pointy roof, resembling a church. The location overlooks the cemetery below like a great gargoyle. Aria's beam of light travels across the arched doorway, the stone worn and partly covered in overgrown ivy. Then the names come to light.

Banner Barrow, etched into stone.

"This is us," Elias states and takes the lead up the chipped and moss-covered steps. Aria follows him, and I'm at her back.

We are alone out here, and suddenly I feel uncomfortable about taking Aria inside with us, unsure what to expect. But leaving her out here isn't an option, either.

Elias bangs on the door like thunder, and it pushes open, left unlocked for our arrival.

"Well, that's a good sign," Aria says, her voice brimming with sarcasm.

We step inside to a dark room that smells of earth and the heavy stench of decay. The flashlight illuminates the hollowed-out shelf against the back wall and the marble coffin nestled inside. The scrape of rat claws on the cement floor fills the silence as they scurry away from us.

"This is creepy," she says and throws the light

along the walls. She pauses on what looks like a door near the back corner.

"Let's go," I say, and we quickly move to exit the main part of the crypt. We find a set of crooked steps and take them. They lead us deep underground, where the air is suffocatingly hot. At the landing, we face a long, dark hallway and nothing else. The occasional rat darts ahead of us and vanishes into crevices in the walls and floor. There are so many of them. Vile creatures.

"It's so depressing down here," Aria whispers, flashing the light to guide our path where the floor is dotted in dead rats. "Gross."

"Maybe he's making himself a rat army," Elias says, laughing at his own joke, but it quickly dies short. He glances at me, and I know we're thinking the same thing in that moment. When it comes to a necro, nothing would surprise us.

When we turn a corner in the passage, a faint blinking light comes from a door sitting ajar at the end of the corridor.

The hairs on my arms stand on end, but I never back away from danger, so we follow Elias. Back in Hell, I'd often go on missions with Elias and Cain deep into the pits to hunt. There, no one watched, and no one missed the darkest beasts of Hell we fought.

He gives one knock and pushes open the door, light pouring in and stealing the shadows. We follow Elias, and I step over the cracked entrance. Unlike the rest of the crypt, the walls in this room are draped in black fabric, lights overhead reflecting off every surface. The shelves of books, the desk covered in small white bowls filled with what look like various spices, the vials of blood hanging from rope in a straight line over what appears to be a long wooden table used as an operating table for spells. It sits in the middle of the room, stained from what I assume is blood.

Aria sidles up against me, and I look down at the dread in her gaze as she eyes the table.

In the far corner of the room, Banner has his nose in a leather book, his wild hair throwing darkness over his face. Unlike the first time we saw him at the graveyard, now the guy appears… different.

He glances up, pushing up thick glasses that have slid down his nose, and shuts the book with a clapping sound. "You've arrived, good, good. Hope the dead rats didn't scare you. In my defense, they were dead when I arrived here tonight." He smirks, and I somehow don't believe him. But there is something so unusual about him.

He is smaller.

Meeker.

Nerdier.

He's wearing simple sweatpants and a black tee, and he's barefoot. And the corners of his mouth are orange. *Has he been eating Cheetos?*

I glance around, feeling like we've walked into the wrong necromancer's crypt and someone is pranking us. It definitely looks like Banner, but it's like he's had a transformation.

"I have a busy night planned," he announces and rushes around the room, searching for something under the books and in the drawers, even in the pocket of his coat hanging off a hook on the wall. "Ah yes," he mumbles to himself as he rushes past us and out of the room, vanishing into the darkness. I exchange confused looks with Aria and Elias, who are clearly thinking the same.

"What the fuck? He can't be the same guy we saw last night," I snarl-whisper and turn to Aria. How can he be completely different in a matter of hours? "I'm starting to think he's a con artist, not a necromancer."

"And if he is," Elias snarls loudly, "I'll rip him apart."

"Shit, keep your voice down." Aria shushes him. "Look at this creepy room. Of course it's him."

I blink at her, then at the strange decor. "Maybe we should head out. I don't like staying in here like one of his rats, waiting for the slaughter."

I want the upper hand in any situation. That's how you don't get killed.

"We aren't going anywhere," Aria hisses and pokes a finger into my chest. "We are here for Cain, and if that means dealing with a struggling necromancer with an identity issue, then we do it."

Identity issue? More like an extreme case of multiple personality disorder.

A crunching sound comes from our side, and we

both look over to Elias, who is in the corner with a plastic tub of Cheetos in his arms, helping himself.

"What the hell are you doing?" she snaps at him just as footfalls close in from the hallway.

Elias quickly returns the snacks to a shelf and wipes his fingers down his pants, leaving incriminating streaks of orange.

Aria rushes over and pats his pants clean, which only has Elias smirking for all the wrong reasons.

The door creaks open, and we all whip around. Elias smacks his lips behind us, and I jab an elbow into his ribs.

Thankfully, Banner doesn't notice as he steps over to the table and places a piece of paper and pen down.

"So, who do you want to bring back from the dead? Why else would you come to me, right?" he says in a rush. "I must know before we go any further. Before we can talk about payment."

Annoyance growing, I clear my throat and step forward. That's when I notice Banner's eye is twitching, and the nerve in his temple is dancing wildly, like he's barely holding himself together.

Something is very wrong with him.

ARIA

A rat scurries over my feet, and I jump in my own skin, refusing to scream and sound like a terrified girl. This place reeks, it's filthy, and why in the world does Banner look so different tonight?

Not to mention, the tingle in my toe is still going off the rails, worse than last night, from the moment we approached this town. It shouldn't surprise me that a necromancer uses dark magic, yet it sits on the back of my mind, a deadly reminder of who we're dealing with.

I glance at the vials of blood tied to the string dangling over the table. Skulls. Bundles of what look like hair. Various medical instruments... There is so much crap in this room, including a hurricane glass filled with soil up on the bookshelf. The glass seems to almost glint, which is strange. What the hell is it, anyway? How exactly are all these things used? I wince at the disturbing images flashing through my mind. Maybe I don't want to know. A shiver shoots through me. Talk about the heebee-jeebees.

"We need to bring someone back from the brink of death," Dorian explains, drawing my attention to him. "Multiple puncture wounds by a dragon's spiked tail."

Banner studies him, head to toe, the edges of his upper lip curling upward. "Did you bring something that belongs to the injured?"

We all exchange worried looks. It never crossed any of our minds to bring anything that belonged to

Cain, and in hindsight, we should have. Why hadn't we thought of that?

Feeling stupid, I twist back to look at Banner when my wing necklace shifts and pops out over the collar of my sweater.

The chain weighs heavily around my neck, and I finger the pendant, my thoughts swirling to the answer to Banner's question… the answer I don't want to give. But there's no other choice, is there?

My throat dries, and I still my irrational thoughts. Cain's survival trumps everything else.

I gingerly reach around to the back of my neck and unlatch the chain, then scoop it into a palm. I drop my head and stare at it, remembering Cain had it fixed for me.

"Cain gave me this. Will that work?" The voice isn't mine. It's shaky and filled with hesitation. It's not what I want, not when it meant so much to discover Cain went out of his way to get it back to me. My last moments with Cain rake through my mind, floating to the surface.

Banner reaches over and snatches the necklace from my palm, curling his fingers around it. A flare of anger surges through me, instinct nudging me to reach back and retrieve what's mine.

He shuts his eyes, placing his fist to his chest, silent for seconds. Darkness blurs his face, and the skin around his eyes and mouth trembles and bubbles. As if he's changing. When his eyes snap open, his irises and pupils are a milky white.

"So, the injured is like you two." He glares at Elias and Dorian. "A demon!" He barks the words like they're poisonous, spit flying from his lips.

A growl rolls past Elias's throat, and I look across my shoulder at him, to the shadows behind his eyes. "What difference is it if Cain's a demon? You deal with death daily here."

"I don't heal the damned."

"We'll pay you whatever you wish," Dorian says, fumbling for control over the conversation. "Name your price."

"I told you. Money holds no value to me."

Oh no. We're losing him.

Dorian must be thinking the same thing because he blurts out, "A favor then. A deal."

That makes Banner pause. Like last night, interest sparks in his gaze.

But unfortunately, it's snuffed out rather quickly, and he shakes his head. Greasy hair swings past his brow. "No. No, I won't work with demons again. Their deals never work out the way they're supposed to."

Again?

I pause. What does he mean by that?

"Was a demon deal the reason you're like this? Did you use one to gain your powers?" Dorian peppered him with the same questions I was thinking. "What was his name? Maybe we can help you get out of your contract—"

"I never said I wanted out," he snarls, the skin on

his face and neck shifting unnaturally again. Things were beginning to make more sense now. Banner must've made a deal with a demon, and that's how he became a necromancer. But something had to have gone wrong along the way. He wasn't all necromancer, because he wasn't *all* there to begin with. How much humanity had he lost in his trade?

An uncomfortable silence settles over the room. Banner's nose wrinkles, the paper on the table scrunched up into a ball in his fist.

Not sure what else to do, I clear my throat and step forward. "Have you lost someone dear in your life? Of course you have… we all have. I, myself, had to deal with loss too many times to count…"

I meant during my foster home days, of course. Not exclusively in death. But bouncing from home to shelter to another home made it difficult to keep friends. Anyone I got remotely close to could be gone in an instant, so that made getting attached at all a difficult thing. And when I did finally put my trust in someone, losing them became too painful for a multitude of reasons I'm sure a therapist would love to unpack.

That may be what's happening with Cain. As much as I don't want to admit it, I've let my heart get involved. Losing him too would just solidify what my entire fucked-up life's been trying to tell me.

That I don't *deserve* to be happy. That I don't *deserve* to have people who care for me.

"I'm going to be frank with you. I'm not good

with loss. I'm not. And I'm guessing you might very well be the same way. Why else get into the death business, other than to stop losing people close to you? Stop the pain that comes with it."

It's a stretch—I know—but when I notice Banner's muscles softening, I realize my words must have resonated with him. So, I keep talking. "Cain means so much to me. I can't lose him. I... can't."

He frowns, pushing his sliding glasses back up on the bridge of his nose.

Swallowing hard, I try not to think about what we'll do if he rejects us, fighting the panic rising through me. There's no 'plan B' here. Banner is our only hope. *Cain's* only hope.

Six days.

That's what we have left. The bright light overhead flickers.

Banner tilts his head to the side, studying me. "What is a normal girl like you doing with demons?" he asks out of the blue.

Dorian places a hand on my shoulder, a gentle touch, one that tells me I don't have to answer. Except I do, in my own way. "Sometimes, fate has other plans for us, and we can fight it kicking and screaming, or we can put our big girl panties on and tackle it head on. Fate's a lot smarter than we give her credit for."

Banner cracks a smile. "I like you. You get it, and well, there is something I do need that you may be able to get for me in exchange for this service... Something I can't get myself. We can call that your payment. You get me what I want, and I help your friend. Deal?"

Dorian and Elias step up alongside me like bodyguards.

"What do you want, and where is it?" Dorian asks.

Banner licks his lips, and his gaze dances between Dorian and Elias with a newfound excitement. "What I seek lies in Scotland. It's heavily guarded, but that won't be difficult for demons, now will it? No, it shouldn't be difficult for you at all."

A shiver travels up my spine. He is practically drooling, practically bouncing on his toes.

My stomach clenches with dread. I have a feeling that what he asks of us is a lot more treacherous than he's letting on.

"Scotland? Is that a joke?" Elias replies, his expression perplexed. "And why can't you get this thing yourself? What's stopped you before?"

"I have my reasons," he answers dismissively. "I have tried many times but failed."

I don't like the sound of that.

"How about you heal our friend, then we go on this mission for you," Dorian offers. "We don't have time to waste jet-setting around the world. We give you our word."

He barks a laugh. "You expect me to believe the word of a demon?"

The air thickens with tension.

"We'll sign it in a contract then," Dorian says.

"No," Banner snaps. "No contracts."

I chew on my lower lip. What he's asking for sounds worse by the moment. "Can we have some time to talk about it?" I ask.

"By all means. The hallway is yours." He waves a hand to the doorway.

The three of us don't waste a second and hurry outside, drawing the door shut behind us. I flick on my flashlight and point it to the ground as we gather in a tight circle.

"This sounds dangerous," I say. "But what if we have no other choice? I mean, we don't even know if he has a cure that will work for Cain." My heart is beating frantically as I weigh the options of leaving Cain behind or facing whatever evil this object possesses. We just battled a dragon and are still dealing with the repercussions.

"We can deal with it," Elias states.

But can we? Although I know so little about all things underworld that I have no choice but to believe him.

"You make it sound easy. And what do any of us know about Scotland? I know zero."

"We don't really have a choice," Dorian admits, his lips thinning with the truth of our predicament. "We have no backup plan to help Cain. So Elias and I fly out tomorrow, get it done in a couple of days, then fly home with plenty of time to spare."

"I'm coming," I butt in.

"You sure?" Elias asks. "Wouldn't you want to watch over Cain?"

I glare at him. "I will go mad waiting. I need to come for my own sanity. You are not keeping me out of this."

"So guess that's a yes then to Banner's plan?" Dorian asks just as something brushes against my ankle.

I confirm with a nod, as does Elias.

I flinch around and find a filthy rat, then point the flashlight to the other rats against the wall, previously dead, now crawling to their feet. Wretched little things. Bones snapping, decayed bodies, bones sticking out of sides, missing eyes. Goosebumps rush over my skin.

"Oh my God, they are waking up!"

We rush back into the room.

Banner is leaning against the table, inspecting my necklace, and straightens up quickly upon our entrance. "That's a yes, then?"

The way he says that with a wicked grin makes me wonder if he had plans for his undead rats if we turned down his offer.

"Yes, we accept on the condition you completely heal Cain."

"I agree to do everything in my power to ensure he lives."

Dorian runs a hand through his hair. "Then tell us everything. Where we go and find this object. I want details." He stands tall, all business, in a way that reminds me of Cain.

Banner pushes his glasses farther up his nose. "Well, here's the thing. The location of the object lies with the Night Shade pack of shifters. They own the territory and are secretive about what lies there. They refuse to share the location with me, but seeing as you have a hellhound on board…" he glances over to Elias, "…you will be at an advantage."

I want to ask how he knows about Elias, but at the same time, I just want the information and to get out of here. The longer we stay, the more my skin crawls.

"So, what are we meant to do?" Dorian asks. "Just fly into Scotland and go hunting for this pack?"

He laughs. "Oh, don't worry, they will find you first. Then get the details on the Black Castle and the treasure it holds. Return it to me along with your almost deceased friend, and I will take care of him."

Suddenly, the quick trip Dorian mentioned in the hallway doesn't sound so easy and fast after all, and we're all silent for a few moments as we take it all in.

Banner's nostrils flare, drawing in a deep breath. "Are you doing this or simply wasting my time?"

Elias steps closer, shoulders broad, hands fisted.

Banner doesn't back away, and a spark of electricity races up my spine. He's wielding magic.

"Elias." I grab his arm and pull him back, then turn to look at Banner. "Yes, we'll do this." I stick my hand out. "And I'll take my necklace back."

He lowers his gaze to his hand, staring at what belongs to me, then he turns to grab something from a drawer. Next thing, he's coming this way with a hand-held microscope and studying the necklace like he's trying to authenticate it. Except it isn't the gold that makes this piece so meaningful for me, but who gave it to me.

"I will hold this until you return and let fate do as she must." His eyes smile, and fury burns through me that he's used my words against me.

I don't move at first, my attention fastened on my golden wing. I want it back. I *need* it back. It could very well be the only piece of Cain I have left, and the thought of it in someone else's hands infuriates me. But I can't jeopardize Cain's chance at surviving. I care about him more.

Banner goes back to analyzing the necklace with his microscope, while I turn to leave, noting Elias has already left and Dorian has the door open for me. The reluctance is clear on his face. He knows how much the necklace means to me.

I swallow the fire in my throat and leave with my two demons. Before I change my mind, we hurry through the dark hallway, ignoring the screeching sounds of undead rats, and don't stop until we burst into the balmy embrace of night. Elias is already down the steps, eager to leave this place.

Outside, I can finally breathe easily, no longer stifled.

We have another challenge to face. Together. This is starting to become a new normal for us, it seems.

But being down one person and on a very tight timeframe, the odds are stacked against us.

Am I worried? Absolutely. For Cain, for us… But I know Elias and Dorian will do anything to bring Cain back to us. And so will I.

Elias and Dorian glance my way, the moonlight glinting in their worried eyes, and I smile to give them some reassurance that I'm ready for this.

Ready to face whatever comes our way to save Cain.

CHAPTER EIGHT
ARIA

"You stole the tub of Cheetos?" I gasp as Elias sits in the front of the Ferrari, digging his hand into the honey pot and stuffing his face. The crunch of his eating the orange balls floods the car. Dorian hops into the driver's seat and sticks his hand in the tub too.

"Wow, we are going to die because you stole a necromancer's snack. What a way to go," I continue. "Why would you take it?"

Elias looks over his shoulder at me, licking the crumbs from his lips. "He took your necklace, so I took something of his. Fair's fair." He hands me the tub. "Want some?"

"He has a point," Dorian adds. "That guy was a fucking prick, and if we're going all the way to Scotland for this mission, then giving up his snack is the least he can do."

I mean, when they put it that way... Collecting the

tub, I place it on my lap. If Cassiel was with us now, he'd be eating these like nobody's business.

"Banner seems the kind to take something like this personally." I start eating the cheesy balls. They're surprisingly pretty good but very, very messy.

Dorian roars the car to life, the front lights spraying against the trees. I fill my mouth with more puffs before Elias reaches over and steals the plastic tub back.

"He won't touch us until we get what he wants. Then we hold onto it until he cures Cain. After that, he's fair game," Elias says, smacking his lips.

Unease settles in my stomach from the whole thing. We came all this way to get a cure, and now we're going on another mission. And the whole time, my pulse races from the invisible countdown ticking in my mind.

Cain is running out of time.

Tick. Tock. Tick. Tock.

We drive down the quiet road. No streetlights, just woodland crowding both sides of the highway. I lean into my seat and stare out, wondering how we've gotten so deep in trouble.

"That was profound, what you said back there about loss and fate," Dorian breaks the silence. "Did you mean it?"

"Every word." I look up and meet his gaze in the rearview mirror, his eyes sincere and heartfelt. "Why does that surprise you?"

He shrugs and keeps driving for a while before he finally responds. "You surprise me in a good way."

I smile to myself to hear he admires something about me, and I curl in against the door, staring outside at the passing landscape. I grew up with no compliments, so I learned long ago that I didn't need anyone to tell me I'm great as long as I believed it. But to hear Dorian sound impressed by me fills me with a strange sense of pride.

On the way back to the hotel, we stop and pick up some food from a takeout burger joint. Then it's back to our room on the fourth floor.

Inside, we find Cassiel curled in the middle of the large bed, fast sleep. He lifts his head at our arrival, his fur flat on the side of his face he's slept on, and sniffs the air. In moments, he's on his feet, prowling closer, making mewling sounds as his gaze narrows in on the dinner in Dorian's bags.

"He smells food," I say, and we all get settled around the table with our food and half-empty Cheetos bucket. I grab the packet of boneless chicken strips and tear them into smaller chunks for Cassiel while Dorian heads outside our room to make a phone call. He shuts the door behind him as he starts murmuring into the receiver.

"You spoil the feline," Elias insists, drawing my attention.

"And is there something wrong with that?"

"Just an observation. He'll get used to it and expect it all the time. How will you control him when he's fully grown?" There's no mirth on his face. He's honestly worried about me.

"I am bonding with him now so he knows we are family."

I set the full plate of chicken on the floor near the back of the room and Cassiel dives in, then I flop down at the table and grab a cheeseburger. I don't realize how starved I am until I take that first bite. Sauce, cheese, pickles. Yum. The people who remove the pickles from their burgers are monsters.

Elias watches me as we eat, like he has something on his mind.

"What's up?" I ask.

"Just thinking about us, the four of us, and how this isn't something I expected to happen." He takes another bite.

I blink at him, trying to work out what exactly he's referring to. "Do you mean us stuck here and working with a necromancer, or Cain being sick, or—"

"That I am mostly okay with sharing you with someone else. Never thought it'd happen." He licks his lips and sits back in his chair. "As I told you before, my hellhound has connected with you, claimed you. I didn't want to admit it at first because it's uncommon for a shifter to find their partner for life amid humans. But the more time that passes, the harder it is for me to deny you are mine. Ours."

I swallow the food in my mouth, riveted by Elias's admission. "Are you sure?"

"I am certain, and I have no doubt you feel the same way. But to share you has been on my mind. We've spoken about it, but I can't stop thinking about it."

"Are you having doubts?"

"Hell no. Shifters don't normally share, and that's the thing. I accept that to have you I must share. Dorian, Cain, and I have an unusual bond for demons, but it works. They saved me, they stuck by my side, they offered me something I lost at a young age—a family. So if I am to share you with anyone, it would be them."

I watch the way his brow furrows. I hear his words, but it's obvious he's still struggling with the decision. This is new for me too. I don't have much experience when it comes to boyfriends, yet I've found myself simultaneously attracted to three demons.

"It still feels surreal to me that I even have three guys interested in someone like me." I laugh at myself. "I mean, look at you three and look at me." I reach for more fries.

Elias is on his feet suddenly and walks around the table to me, taking my hand. "Come with me."

I accept his offering. "Where are we going?"

He walks me into the bathroom and turns me by my shoulders to face the tall mirror sitting against the wall. He stands behind me, hands on my hips.

"What do you see?" he asks.

I look at him and those strong yellow eyes, the

strength of his expression, how incredibly gorgeous he is. And suddenly I feel more insecure about standing before him, looking frumpy in my sweater and jeans, my dark hair messy.

"I see a powerful man who is everything I didn't realize I wanted."

"Try again," he says.

I glare at him. I know where this is going, but I'm not good with this stuff. It's why I'm happy with my hair undone, wearing just jeans and a top. I'm not into makeup or fashion. Sure, a lot of that has to do with a lack of money, but I've always prided myself on my smarts more than my looks.

"I don't want to do this." I pull from him, but his grip strengthens.

"We're doing this now. What do you see?"

I grit my teeth and throw him my best furious look.

"I've got all night, Aria," he says firmly.

"Why don't you tell me what you see?" I toss back at him.

He laughs, throwing his head back, but it's all fake. "This isn't about me. I want to know what you think."

I shuffle to escape his grasp, but he loops an arm around my waist, another across the top of my chest, his solid chest against my back. Despite him forcing me to stand there, there is something so warming, so reassuring for this strong man to hold me against him. He towers over me, yet the way he holds me is filled with passion.

"You're so frustrating." I sigh. "Fine. I am just an ordinary girl with dry hair, eyebrows that need shaping, and no fashion sense."

"Aria, you are a beautiful woman with mesmerizing eyes, with kissable lips, with hair I want to tangle my hands in, a curvy body I want to claim over and over. You're intelligent, and I adore how hard you fight for what you want. You mean a lot to me, and I wish you would see yourself through my eyes."

I didn't expect him to say those words, and now I'm staring at myself... really staring at what he said, at how my dark eyes are shaped like almonds, how my cheeks have a glow to them, how maybe I am more than I thought I was.

My eyes prick.

"Talk to me," he whispers in my ear.

"Before you three, I never really had anyone tell me I was beautiful. I'm just Aria, that's all I've ever been." The girl Murray barely fed or talked to. The girl Joseline told her problems to. The girl who had no history of her family.

A nobody.

Had that been the problem all along, that I'd been happy to be in the background rather than wanting more? Was I too scared to aspire for something I never thought I could have?

"What do you see, Aria?" he asks me again, and

when he looks at me this time, it feels like he can peer into my soul.

I can't find my words at first, worried that if I try to respond, I'll end up crying. How the hell did he bring this out of me so easily, anyway?

"I'm not letting you leave without you knowing just how beautiful and incredible you are."

Unsure what to say or even how to feel, I just look at myself. Elias kisses the top of my head. I'm surprised this has come from him, a man who rarely shares his feelings. Emotions tug inside me in every direction, threatening to take me under where I'll cry uncontrollably.

"Why are you doing this?" I ask.

"Because I lost so much in my life, and even when I found someone to give my heart to, it turned out that I wasn't enough to be loved back. She betrayed me, rejected me, and it took me a long time to deal with that. Long enough to never be fooled again. So I don't want to see you hiding behind this mask. Embrace who you really are." He smiles, and my insides fill with warmth.

His words, his actions, belong to someone genuine, and I'm not sure how to respond.

"You belong with us," he adds.

I've always followed my gut instinct, and right now, it has me turning around and looking up at him. My arms wrap around him and I press my face against his chest, inhaling the musky scent that is all him.

"Thank you," I whisper as he lifts my chin and kisses me deeply, sweeping me off my feet. This is a side of him I haven't seen yet, and it's everything. I want to feel his naked body against mine, to have him take me, adore me, make me feel like I belong. The world fades away while we are tangled in a perfect moment.

"Since you've joined us, our house feels warmer, and I have no desire to spend days in the woods anymore. Do you realize what a big deal that is?" He leans down and presses his forehead to mine. We stay like that for a long while until his stomach suddenly growls.

I laugh.

"I don't know about you, but I am still starving." He grins, and I keep laughing, pulling away and taking his hand in mine.

"Well, let's go get some food before you waste away."

We're back at the table, and Elias tells me a demon joke about the chicken crossing the road in Hell. But I'm not really listening. Not when I can't help but smile. What we have between us feels slightly different now. Part of me is still hot with embarrassment that he put me on the spot that way, while the other part floods with assurance that he cares so much for me.

I finish my burger just as Dorian enters the room. I reach for the nuggets and sauce while Elias pushes another burger in my direction. The thing with Elias is that he eats a lot, so we got six burgers between him and me, plus fries and other sides. Dorian isn't a big fan of human food, but he might change his mind.

"Flight is confirmed. We need to be at the airport at eight a.m. for a nine o'clock flight." Dorian slides into his chair, and I can't help but look at him a bit differently, too. All this responsibility and maturity is Cain's thing. Without him, Dorian's seemed to assume the role. Exhaustion clings to his eyes, stealing away some of their natural mirth.

"This is happening so fast," I say and wipe my mouth with a tissue. "Scotland is on my bucket list, but it still feels surreal we're going there."

"I doubt we'll have time to look around and do tourist things," Elias says.

"Yeah, I know, but still. Part of me is excited." I stuff two fries into my mouth. "Will you two wear kilts?"

I don't know why I said that, considering it's not expected, but the more I think about the trip, the more I picture all the images and shows I've seen on the destination. Not to mention all those hunky men in kilts.

"Oh? Kilts, huh?" Elias eyes me, his gaze narrowing as his mouth curls upward into a wicked grin. The way he looks at me sends a delicious shiver down my spine. "Got to go commando, too, for easy access."

"I'm up for it," Dorian says. "But if we do it, we can't be the only ones not wearing *underoos*."

I laugh, and I love how good it feels to be able to do so when everything has been doom and gloom lately. "How did I know you'd say that?"

They both smirk, and I can already see the wheels spinning behind their gazes on this very topic. "Whatever. I just want to try blood pudding and haggis. I always see them on TV shows."

"If you're into it, I won't stop you, but it's not my delicacy," Dorian answers.

"Don't worry, rabbit. I'll join you. I love all food."

Suddenly, something swooshes past my face. Cassiel has jumped up on the table. He moves so fast—one second he's there, next he's bitten down into a cheeseburger and leapt away with the whole thing.

"What the hell?!" Elias jolts to his feet.

"Let him have it." I chuckle. "He's got an appetite like you."

Elias snorts his way.

Deciding to change the topic, I say, "Anyway, what do you think was up with Banner tonight? He wasn't himself at all… I mean, not only appearance-wise but the way he spoke and held himself. There was something very off."

"He obviously has something broken inside him, but as long as he fixes Cain, I don't give a shit if he thinks he's Big Bird himself." Dorian shifts in his seat.

"True. As long as he does his part and doesn't

surprise us with an army of zombie rats to reclaim his Cheetos, we are good."

Elias eyes the bucket. "I will destroy those rodents if they get between me and the Cheetos."

Dorian's head falls back as he lets out a booming laugh. I adore it, the sound coming from somewhere deep in his gut.

"You sure you don't want to try a burger, Dorian? They really are good," I ask, pushing a smaller one toward him. "I know human food isn't usually your thing."

His lip curls as he stares at it, but after a moment, he says, "Sure, I'll give it a go." After he takes a bite, Elias and I watch him, curious.

He just shrugs. "It's okay, just not fulfilling for me."

"Nothing like souls, right?" Elias says, chuckling to himself.

"Well, here's to an uneventful trip," I say to once again change the topic, lifting up my half-eaten burger in a makeshift toast. They do the same.

It isn't long before we are finished, and Elias is already in bed, naked and with the remote control, flicking through the channels.

Cassiel is on the sofa, snoring away, and Dorian emerges from the bathroom with only a white towel wrapped around his waist. His hair is wet from the shower, and rivulets of water streak down his chiseled chest and abs. He walks over to the bed, strutting like he's putting on a show, and looks my way.

I can't deny how easily he affects me, my nipples hardening, pressing against the fabric of my top, as I study his Adonis body. Specifically, on the bulge pushing against the towel for release. Suddenly, desire flares inside me like the strike of a match.

"Switch off the lights, little girl, and come to us," he commands. There's no power in his words, but the smolder in his eyes and the promise they hold has me moving across the room.

I flick off the light, and when I turn back toward the demons, Dorian rips off the towel and tosses it to the side. His erection is already at half-mast, and he climbs into bed, on the opposite side of Elias, leaving an empty gap between them for me.

He pats the middle.

Why am I suddenly so hot? I'm breathing faster, the swell of my chest rising and falling.

My feet seem to move on their own, but there's no magic involved. It's just me and the anticipation of what's coming next. Two sexy-as-hell demons sharing a bed with me?

Oh Lord…

Suddenly, what Elias said about "sharing me" has a completely different meaning. I swallow roughly.

"Um, excuse me." Elias stops me in my tracks. "You want in this bed, then the clothes must go."

I raise a brow and glance down at my sweater.

Dorian tsks. "She's overdressed for the occasion. Don't you think, Elias?"

"Absolutely."

My breath catches in my throat and my insides burn like I'm alight. It scorches me all the way down to the apex between my thighs. I'm not a fool; I know exactly what this is all leading to. These two deviants have one thing on their mind.

Don't get me wrong, I'm pulsing with a need for them, but I also have no intention of playing easy.

So I pull back off the bed and saunter over to join Cassiel on the couch, chuckling to myself.

Seconds is all it takes. The thunderous sound of them jumping out of bed, the footfalls closing in behind me.

I snatch the small pillow from the sofa and whip around, just in time to whack it across Dorian's chest. He grabs it and tosses it aside, staring at me like a wolf. Elias stands beside him, holding that damn bucket of Cheetos, grinning like the Cheshire cat.

"What are you going to do with those?" I ask.

"You're about to find out," he promises me.

Dorian loops an arm around my waist and draws me against him, our bodies pressed together. My heart is thundering as he grips my chin and tilts it up so I'm looking into his eyes. Spectacular green eyes. His touch is like liquid fire, and I fall for him so easily, so quickly. I tell myself that the way my body reacts to him has nothing to do with him being an incubus. I want to believe this is all me. All about the connection between us.

"You are stunning," he says and leans down. His mouth captures mine, and I desperately lean closer, threading my fingers through his hair, drawing him closer, needing more. My whole body trembles with unbearable desire.

We clash in a powerful kiss. His fingers dig into my back, and I'm up on my tippy toes when another set of strong, fiery hands settles on my hips.

Elias sweeps my hair off my neck, and his lips find me in seconds.

Their hands roam my body, and soon my sweater is being tugged up and over my head. My jeans are wrenched down, and somehow, Elias snaps my underwear right off me. I want to protest that I don't have an endless supply while we're on this trip, but the thought melts beneath their kisses, their attention.

Elias's hands glide around my body, cupping my breasts. He kneads them, tugging on my nipples.

Dorian inhales my moans as they sandwich me, two naked demons making sure to press their erections against my ass and lower stomach. Anticipation wraps around me as I stand nude between them, and Dorian looks at me with that devastating smile that has my knees wobbling.

I close my eyes, taking a deep breath as shivers of delight race up my spine.

He whispers, "Are you ready to dance with two devils?"

Elias's hands move to my thighs, sliding lower. His touch glides between my legs, finding me drenched.

"Gorgeous, you are so wet for us."

Dorian takes my chance to respond as his tongue plunges into my mouth, his hands holding the sides of my face, keeping me in place. I'm shaking with arousal while Elias runs a finger along my heat, parting my lips and inserting two fingers.

I moan, my legs buckling, but they hold me up. Elias leaves a trail of kisses down my back until I feel the scrape of his teeth on my cheeks, biting enough to leave a mark but not sting with pain. In that moment, they are my oxygen, my everything.

Dorian releases my mouth and bends down. He pulls a nipple into his mouth, suckling on me, while Elias spreads my ass cheeks. His tongue slides down between them.

Oh, hell! How can this feel so amazing? He's licking my behind, while his fingers keep playing with me.

My hips rock at the building pleasure. My breasts are pulled and flicked, my clit teased, my ass worshipped.

And just as the climax starts mounting, the two of them pull back like they can sense it.

"Why are you stopping?" I breathe the words, tingling all over.

In the next moment, Dorian leans closer, tucking an arm under my knees, the other at my back, and lifts me off my feet.

Then he walks us across the room, returning me to the bed where Elias has tossed the blankets aside.

I'm thrown onto the mattress. I bounce a couple of times, laughing at how incredible these two men in my life are.

Then I look over to Elias, who's again holding the Cheetos tub, and a flicker of panic hits me with their intention.

"Don't even think about it." I quickly roll away.

Dorian grabs me by the arm and hip, bringing me onto my back again and pushing himself between my legs, spreading me.

"Be a good girl now." He grabs my waist and hauls me so my ass is perched on the edge of the mattress.

"Are you insane?" I gasp, batting his arms off my legs.

Elias grabs a handful of the orange balls, crushing them in his fist before sprinkling orange dust over my body. The crumbs tickle, and they go everywhere. Before I can even protest, he's bent forward and licking them off my breasts with delicious, long strokes.

It's a strange sensation to feel so turned on you might explode while scared at the same time that Cheetos may not be a good thing on certain parts of your body.

But when I hear the crunch of more cheesy treats and look down to Dorian smirking as he smears the powder across the inside of my thighs, I realize I'm fighting a lost cause.

I wriggle to escape. Then he's on his knees, his

head between my thighs. He licks the orange treats, eyeing me the whole time.

He pushes my legs wider, his mouth devouring me.

Oh, yes.

His wicked tongue does incredible things, running up and down my heat, flicking my clit, then he gently bites on my outer lips.

Hot breath washes over my breasts from Elias, and a girl can get used to this kind of attention. I rock my hips in time with their tongues as a climax rises through me once more. I reach over and run my hands through Elias's hair and tug him closer. Our mouths clash in a passionate kiss that sends me soaring into the heavens.

His tongue plunges into my mouth just as Dorian pushes his into my pussy, and that sets me off. I shudder, unable to hold back any longer. They never release their hold on me as my orgasm claims me, thrashing through me.

Elias swallows my scream as Dorian takes me into his mouth. Desire bursts inside me as I come, caught in the arms of my lovers. I shut my eyes and let myself fall, lost to the beautiful sensation that has me floating.

Elias releases me first, and I collapse back onto the bed, smiling, my heart beating with the most glorious feeling.

Dorian rises up from between my legs, his lips

and chin glistening with my wetness. "You are fucking gorgeous in the glow of an orgasm."

"That was incredible," I say, while Elias throws himself on the bed.

I tilt my head up to see him upside down, calling me to him with a curl of his finger. Just the image alone has me turned on.

I roll onto my stomach and crawl over to him on all fours. He's inched himself down the bed so his legs are on the floor and his hips are positioned on the edge of the mattress.

Before I can ask questions, his hands are on my hips, guiding me to straddle him. "Fuck me, Aria," he demands. "Show me how your pussy squeezes my dick, milks me."

My nipples tighten at his words, and I settle over his lap, his erection thick and stiff. He's gripping my hips, adjusting me so I sit down on his shaft. I brace myself, sliding down, taking him into me. Elias is a very big guy when it comes to his size.

"That's it, baby."

I moan, taking a deep breath and letting him in. The excitement on his face, the groaning of his throat, are deviously divine. He feels incredible.

Dorian steps up behind me and touches my hair, sweeping to the side. I twist my head to meet the hunger in his gaze. His stare is of a man captivated, seeing nothing else but me. Elias's words about how he really sees me come to me, and the look in his eyes when he said them is the same look I now observe in Dorian's eyes.

"Are you ready for both of us?" he asks, his hand running down my back, leaving a trail of warmth and tingles.

"Dorian—" A buzz of excitement and trepidation shudders through me. But Elias shifts my hips, tilting them in a way that allows him to hit the right spot when he plunges himself inside. A newly found fire ignites within me, and I moan. "Dorian, I want you."

That smile, so alluring, so hypnotic, does things to me. "You are so wet, so beautiful."

As Elias continues to keep up our steady rhythm, Dorian steps closer, slides a finger into his mouth, and then presses that same one into my asshole. Slowly, he pushes it into me.

I groan. I've never been entered this way before, but with him gently sliding his finger in and out, coupled with Elias's movement, a strange cocktail of pleasure and pain erupts from down below. It's exhilarating and nothing like I ever expected.

Dorian massages me like that for a while, and suddenly, I'm needing more. I grab my own cheeks and spread them to let him know this isn't enough.

He chuckles. "I love how eager you are."

Glancing over my shoulder, I watch as he palms his dick, readying himself. A second finger presses into me next, making me suck in a breath. The biting pain is sharp but quick, immediately overcome by more blinding pleasure.

When he pulls away, Elias pauses briefly, and in the next second, Dorian's fingers are replaced by the tip of his cock. It pushes against my back entrance, slowly, deeper. Nothing that hurts, but the kind that brings with it heightened arousal. My head falls back, and my entire body trembles. I never thought I'd be someone who enjoyed anal sex before this, let alone two men at once, but here I am and loving every second of it.

"Fuck…" I gasp as he slides in deeper.

Elias looks at me. "If you want to stop, you tell us, okay?"

I nod, then find myself slowly rocking back and forth with both my men inside me. I lean forward, arms pitched on either side of Elias's shoulders, and he claims my mouth as our momentum picks up again. It's like an unspoken action, but somehow we all fall into a rhythm, and the pace intensifies, bringing with it an extraordinary arousal I hadn't expected so fast.

Their growls are the sexiest thing I've ever heard.

Dorian's hand is in my hair, twisting around it, and he pulls my head back slightly as he rams into me. The wet sounds of our slamming are like a beautiful song.

"Shit," Elias roars, his hands on my breasts, squeezing, pulling. And me, I'm the luckiest girl in the world, being fucked by two demons like this. I can't get enough of them plunging into me, again and again.

ALL SHOT TO HELL

I feel them sliding inside me.

It's intense.

Flooding me with ecstasy.

The air thickens, and sweat drips down my back, our breaths racing.

"You'll come while we're buried deep inside you," Dorian demands, leaning close to my ear. His power trickles over me, leaving goosebumps up and down my skin. "You're ours. Always."

Then they both fuck me, and any attempt to hold back is lost. Dorian's compulsion power may not work on me, but it doesn't need to. My body obeys all on its own. I let my body dance between theirs, let them claim me, and as promised, let them bring me to orgasm over and over all night.

The alarm clock buzzes so loud, I'm ripped out of sleep and jolt to a sitting position in bed. Faint light pours in from the windows from the rising sun, and I rub my eyes, knowing we have a flight to catch.

Elias snorts, and I look over to him and find Cassiel sleeping on his face. Before I can reach over to grab him, Elias awakens abruptly like he's suffocating... well, he probably is. Cassiel jerks awake from fright and leaps off him, but not before his back foot kicks back, meeting Elias's cheek. One long line forms across his face, and his nose darkens red as blood breaks through the skin, reminding me of war paint.

He shouts and wipes a hand across his cheeks, smearing the blood. But it isn't until I look at Dorian that I gasp.

"Sweet hell… You look like a carrot!"

He's orange all over. Covered in cheesy dust and crumbles.

That's when I look at myself, and back at Elias, to see we are all the same. The bed is covered in Cheetos, everything stained orange. "Oh, crap."

Dorian laughs. "But that was one hell of a night."

"I'm going to murder Cassiel," Elias growls, staring at the blood on his fingers.

"Come on, it isn't that bad," I insist. "A small scratch. It'll heal in no time. Besides, you're covered in scars already. Why not one more to add to your collection?"

"I don't know why you insist on defending him all the time," he grumbles, throwing off the blanket. "He tried to choke me while I slept. You both saw it."

"You're being dramatic."

"I vote for leaving him behind. It's not like they're going to let us take a wild animal on the plane anyway."

"I booked us on a private jet," Dorian says. "So we can bring him with us. We have no time to return home. The airport is in the opposite direction. Speaking of…" He glances at the clock beside the bed and grimaces. "We need to hurry this up and get out of here if we're going to make it."

I rush for the bathroom first, needing to un-orange myself. I don't even want to think what the hotel staff are going to say when they see the state of the bed.

By the time we are clean and sitting in the Ferrari going to the airport, a sense of giddiness has overcome me.

"This will be my first time leaving the country, you know," I say from the back seat of the car.

Dorian answers, looking at me from the driver's seat. "I'm glad we get to experience your first time with you, then."

I sit back and smile, stroking Cassiel's head as he lounges in my lap. Despite all the stress and uncertainty of what's to come, this morning I feel calmer. Maybe a round of Cheetos sex was exactly what the doctor ordered.

CHAPTER NINE
ELIAS

What do I hate more than cars? Planes.

Being contained in a metal box going 60-100 miles an hour on asphalt... No thank you.

Being stuck in a flying tin can 45,000 feet in the air going over 600 miles per hour... Fuck no.

I'd much rather be on all fours, but since I can't run across oceans, I'm stuck in a jet for over ten hours with Dorian, Aria, and one very lucky-to-still-be-alive cat.

Speaking of the little runt, he's meowed in Aria's lap the entire trip. I could tell from his tone and needy behavior that he was in distress. Probably from all the junk food he ate before we left. Cheese doodles and burgers aren't really vet-approved cat foods, so I wouldn't be surprised if he's given himself a wicked stomachache. Serves him right.

At least I wasn't the only one suffering during the trip. Misery loves company, or so they say.

The moment the wheels hit the tarmac in Glasgow, my stiff muscles loosen. I'm happy to be on the ground again where I belong. As it should be.

Once the jet is taxied and parked, the stairs are set into place and we walk down onto the tarmac. A sleek black limo waits for us, but first, we hurry under a nearby tent where immigration is waiting to check our IDs and whatnot. Aria excitedly grips her new passport we'd arranged for her.

When that's all out of the way, we waste no time throwing our luggage in the limo's trunk and climbing in. In minutes, we're off again for the hotel. Aria rests her head on my arm while Cassiel continues to mew. When I glance across the limo at Dorian, his one brow lifts in amusement. He doesn't say anything, though, only goes back to looking at his travel brochure that he snagged from the plane.

I shift in my seat, but Aria only scoots closer. When I glance down at her again, I find she's closed her eyes.

"That jet lag," Dorian whispers and throws me a wink. "It'll getcha."

I don't move for some time, but eventually, Aria's breathing slows and becomes more even, telling me she's fallen asleep. Every bump the limo hits stirs her a bit, though, and soon, I give up in my attempt to not touch her and drape my arm over her middle.

She snuggles in closer. Even Cassiel has stopped his annoying cries and has settled down for a nap.

I can't stop the smile that tugs at my lips. This woman has bewitched me, and even though I've tried to resist her at every turn, I've only managed to fall further under her spell.

As we drive out of the dense and busy city streets and into more of a hillscape, the darkness of the early morning really weighs in. There are few lights on the road we're on, and the limo's headlights struggle to penetrate anything that isn't directly in front of it. Between our battle with the dragon, Cain getting hurt, visiting the necromancer, and now this trek across the world, I don't blame Aria for finding a minute to catch some shut-eye. We've been through a great deal in such a short amount of time.

All of us have.

Exhaustion begins to settle over me, too, and I can feel the heaviness in my bones. It's been days since we've taken a soul and replenished ourselves, and it's starting to take its toll. Once we settle down for the day, I'm going to have to go out and hunt, like I used to.

The idea awakens my hound, but instead of excitement, I'm hit with a fierce feeling of dread. Warning. Danger.

I jerk upward, startling Aria awake. She jumps, causing Cassiel to hiss and leap off her.

My gaze snaps out the window just as a dark

shadow rushes along the roadside, keeping up with the limo's speed.

"Fuck." I whip around to Dorian. "We're being followed."

I catch another figure out his window running on all fours. An animal? No, a shifter. Has to be.

"What is it?" Aria gasps in fear.

"Not good." Dorian's already stripping off his sweater. The blue runes appear across his chest, and his hair lightens to a blonde, almost platinum, color. When his horns curl out of his head, I know he's preparing for a fight. My animal growls inside me, ready for my own change.

"Who would possibly know we're here?" Aria rushes, her eyes wild with panic. "We didn't tell anyone."

"We have a lot of enemies, little girl," Dorian says. "This is just another Sunday for us."

My body clenches painfully tight as the shift pushes for release. I grip the door's handle, about to shove it open and hit the ground running, but something large slams into the back of the limo hard enough to send us tumbling sideways and the car spinning on the slick road. My head hits the floor. Pain shoots through my temples, and Aria's terrified screams fill my ears.

Shit!

As I push myself up, we're hit again from the opposite side. There's a horrible screeching as the wheels slide and spin across the pavement.

"Elias!" Dorian barks.

Lifting my chin, we lock eyes.

He reaches for Aria, telling me that as much as he'd love to join the fight, he'll stay behind with her. Then he says the two words my animal's been waiting for. "Sick 'em."

My hellhound surges forward, tearing itself out of my body without mercy. It takes my breath away, the pain indescribable and all-encompassing.

Throwing all my weight into the door, I throw myself into the darkness.

ARIA

The limo stops abruptly, rocking up on its wheels. My teeth are still rattling from whatever hit us, but at least the spinning has stopped. The back door is wide open, and the frigid air rushes inside. Elias may have disappeared into the darkness, but his vicious snarls ride on the wind. I shift closer to Dorian, Cassiel at my feet.

"Elias is a big boy. He can take care of himself," Dorian whispers against my hair.

Behind us, the opposite door is thrown open, and rough hands seize both of us and yank us backward. Another scream tears out my throat. Dorian grabs for me but misses as we're both tugged away in opposite directions. The last thing I see is Cassiel in the limo as the doors shut him inside.

My ass hits the pavement. I thrash against the assailants grabbing for me, but it's no use. They manage to pull me onto my feet and jerk me away from the car. It's hard to see anything but dense, moving shadows in the darkness, but just ahead of me, I catch a glimpse of Dorian's silver hair. He's putting up a good fight on his own in his demon form, and even manages to knock one of his opponents out with a single punch to the jaw. But there are too many shadowy figures around him. Too many people to fight off at once. Soon, he disappears behind the circle of bodies, and my heart freezes in horror.

I glanced around in a panic. *Elias! Where's Elias?*

I can't see him anywhere. The terrible snarls and yelps of animals fighting are softer now, as if he's been led further away.

Throwing an elbow back, I nail one of my captors in the stomach. He lets out a loud *oomph*. "Get off me! Let me go!"

My elbows are jerked behind me, my arms pinned in place. Inside me, Sayah stirs awake, sensing the danger.

"Stop your fighting!" the man holding me barks. His Scottish accent is so thick, it's almost impossible to decipher his words.

"Bring them down to the cave," another shouts from somewhere in the darkness. "Lachlan is waiting for them."

Cave? Lachlan?

Oh man. I really don't like where this is going. I glance back to the limo, mentally praying Cassiel hides and is alright.

Against my wishes, I'm swung around and shoved forward. I stumble over my own feet, but the man's grip is brutishly tight and keeps me moving. Even with the sky littered with stars, it's too dark here to see past my nose. I have no idea where I'm going or how these assholes know where to step, but soon the pavement gives way to rocks and a hill, and I'm half-tripping, half-sliding down with only a stranger to keep me upright.

When we hit level ground again, my sneakers sink into soggy mud, and instantly, they're full of cold water. I yelp.

It's freezing!

The sounds of more people splashing around me remind me I'm still not alone, and whoever these people are, they have full advantage over this situation right now. And me. If I am going to find a way out of this alive, I have to play it smart and wait for my opening. Even if I did manage to find a way to wrestle myself out of capture, I would be running blindly in the dark. And with no Elias or Dorian as backup.

As much as I hate it, I need to stay calm and plan my escape.

Dorian's familiar voice echoes ahead of me, and just hearing it gives me a smidge of hope. Even if it's him cursing like a madman. Still no sign of

Elias, though. Even the growling sounds have silenced.

We push on through ankle-high, icy water. It isn't long before we reach Dorian's voice, and the echoing magnifies all around us, reverberating loudly against my eardrums. There's the sound of water running, too, which makes sense since I'm standing in the stuff. But I'm also being dripped on from above.

So much wetness. So much cold. I can't stop trembling.

After my encounter with Sir Surchion in a cave, I'm starting to see a pattern with captors bringing me to caves. Something I'm not loving.

The soft glow of lamps flicker in the distance. Every so often, shadows move in front of the light, making dark shapes dance along the rocky walls.

Yep, definitely a cave. Dark, moist, and creepy as hell—a place where a monster might like to hide.

Or a gang of monsters, since we've been ambushed by a mess of them.

When we round a sharp corner, I find what I've been looking for. Dorian, standing in the middle of the water, the low lamp lights barely penetrating the thick darkness. He isn't being held, like me, but there's a pretty long and sharp looking sword against his throat, and the bone-skinny man holding it is wearing a grin that says he can't wait to use it and lop off his head.

His eyes snap to me, and his mouth quirks into a smirk. How he can be calm in a situation like this is beyond me. My heart is beating so hard, it might just pop out my chest at any moment. But he said they face these sorts of problems on the regular, so my only hope is that he has a plan somewhere under all that silver hair of his.

"Oh good. You've joined the party," he says to me jokingly. "I was just about to tell my friend with the sword here that it isn't polite to threaten people's lives. Especially so soon. We haven't even been introduced properly."

The man with the sword shifts on his feet and grits his teeth.

"I'm Dorian," he says, as if he's pretending to make friends. "And you are?"

"Do you ever shut up?" the man snaps.

What in the world is Dorian doing? Egging him on? Not a good idea.

"Actually, as an incubus, there are only two things I'm good at," he goes on. He's completely relaxed. Almost looks bored. "Sex." He glances at me for that one. "And talking."

Can you not inflate your ego right now? I want to shout, but unlike him, I'm too afraid to say anything.

"Drop the sword." A seemingly simple command, but not in the least. Power radiates through the three words, the magic skittering across my skin, making the fine hairs rise.

A second later, the sword drops into the water, making a loud splash.

So this is his plan... His power of compulsion.

Clever.

The men—and women, I realize now—around us shout in protest, but the skinny one can only gape at the water in confusion.

"Good lad," Dorian says with a mocking Scottish timbre. "Now, turn around and walk straight out of the cave. And keep walking, on and on into the lake, until the water gets deeper. And once it's past your head and your lungs are full, only then can you stop."

On cue, the man spins around and starts to trudge through the darkness, toward the mouth of the cave. Most only stare in horror, while others try to stop him, but his feet are determined to enact Dorian's orders, and he pushes past them all.

My stomach clenches painfully tight. Holy shit. He's going to drown himself.

Once the sound of water sloshing about fades away, Dorian turns to the men by me.

"Let her go." Again, his power brushes over me, and the strong grip on both my arms disappears.

Dorian's eyes flash menacingly in the dancing firelight. "Step away from the girl."

They do.

Around the room, every face has gone pale with shock and fear. He grins.

"See? That wasn't that hard, was it?" He waves for me to come over to him, and I hurry to his side as fast as the calf-high water will allow.

Wrapping a protective arm around me, Dorian

mutters, "Stay close." No power woven in his voice this time, just reassurance. I nod.

Then, lifting his chin, his gaze scans the crowd. "Unless you want to end up like your friend out there, I suggest you let us leave. Now."

No one moves, giving us our answer.

With a firm hand on my back, Dorian guides me through the water. As we round the corner, a large, dark figure blacks out the entrance to the cave. We freeze in place.

"I suggest you keep your fucking mouth shut, or you'll both end up like your fucking dog here," a thunderous voice bellows.

The shadowy figure moves, as if throwing something at us, and a huge splash rains over us, soaking us to the bone.

But when I see the flash of familiar amber eyes and dark fur, my brain automatically shuts down.

Oh no... Elias.

CHAPTER TEN
ARIA

A black hellhound bursts out of the murky water in front of me, splashing all of us as a growl deepens on his throat. Elias is pissed, and I don't blame him. That's when I notice the rope dangling from around his neck, and my insides ice over. These bastards hunted and captured him before dragging him back here like a dog.

A trail of blood rolls down the side of his head and drips into the water, tainting it.

Anger surges through me that these—whatever shifters they are—rough-handled my Elias. They choked him. It makes me sick to my stomach to picture him treated this way, and my earlier silence is now taken over by my fury.

"What do you want with us?" I sweep my gaze on the dark, large figure by the entrance, knowing without a doubt that we're dealing with the Alpha, but all I care for now is Elias. I slosh through the water, making my way over to my hellhound, who's shaking his head vigorously to remove the corded rope.

"I've got you," I whisper to him.

He pauses upon hearing my voice, and I quickly fiddle over his matted fur, which is now tangled around the rope. Loosening it, I shove it over his head, freeing him.

He settles down after that, but his chest is still pumping furiously for air. I keep my hand on his back to help calm him, though his gaze is locked on the kidnappers, and a threatening snarl rips from his throat.

"Come at me, hellwolf," one of the guys calls out from about ten feet away, slapping his bare chest. He's only maybe five-foot-five, round and broad, with legs thick as tree trunks. His golden-orange hair sticks outward in every direction.

I suddenly feel like I'm in a *Mad Max* movie.

Dorian's laughing, the sound boisterous and fake, and I seriously don't believe he's scared. "Listen here, oompa loompa. Unless you want to join your friend in the lake, answer the lady's question. Why the fuck are we standing in your pee water?"

That makes the guy more furious. His lips peel back, and his eyes shift right before us... widening to perfectly round discs, his dark pupils expanding, swallowing up the whole irises. They are bulging out just like... *Oh, are you kidding me? He's a goldfish shifter?*

Dorian continues to laugh and laugh. I, however, don't want to take my eyes off the darkened shadow of the alpha. The way he just stands there gives me the creeps.

A sudden surge of static energy rushes up my arm from Elias's body, followed by sharp sparks of electricity. I draw my back my hand.

He's transforming.

The fur vanishes in seconds, his body shuddering, water sloshing wildly. In no time, he rises out of the water as a gorgeous man, utterly naked, ripped with muscles, water trailing down that tempting body.

Yeah, I went there. Even in the situation we're in, I'm eyeing him all over.

Blood trickles down his shoulder and over his chest from where they'd hit him at the back of the head. Assholes. That was the only way they'd overpower a hellhound. Though Elias doesn't seem to notice the wound and growls at the short man, his threat echoing against the stone walls.

"You fucking enter our territory unannounced and mock us with your laughter." The Alpha's deep, raspy voice floods the cave with a strong Scottish accent, much like Sean Connery.

He steps forward where I can better see him. He's a burly man who is close to seven feet tall, large in size. Energy ripples off him. His short silvery hair is wet and combed off his face, his loose white shirt and black and green tartan kilt spotty with water.

I didn't need to be a shifter to understand the

threat behind his words. All shifters are damn territorial, and probably have the biggest egos of any supernaturals.

Dorian comes closer, the water around his ankles rippling outward. "I think we got off on the wrong foot."

The Alpha snarls, his face warped with anger. "Your arrival is a declaration of war against my pack," he bellows, and at his words, his shifters close in around us. "Kill 'em all."

Immediately, his pack creeps closer, tightening the circle all around us. Elias grabs me by my waist and draws me against his side. My heart slams into my chest.

Is he insane?

"As I said," Dorian reaffirms. "This is a misunderstanding. And before any of us do something we'll regret, let's start again." His tone is commanding and intense to the point where everyone stops moving.

"My name is Dorian, and these are my fellow travelers, Aria and Elias. We came a long way from the United States to seek your help on the good advice of Banner, our friendly neighborhood necromancer."

The Alpha's mouth twists with repulsion, and he spits in the water. Now I'm certain there's also pee in here. *Eeww.*

"Do not speak that shit-weasel's name," the Alpha snarls.

My curiosity is piqued.

"He mentioned he'd come here previously," I say.

"If you mean sneaking into our territory after we'd told him he wasn't welcome, then yes, he did. And I will personally slit his throat if he dares ever cross my path again."

A bit harsh, but whatever. I hold no allegiance to Banner and just want him to fix Cain and give me back my necklace. Then the shifters can have him.

"He implied you would know we were arriving. We assumed he had advised you," Dorian explains, deliberately stretching the truth.

"We have no interest in your territory," Elias says through clenched teeth.

"As a shifter, you should fucking know the rules of a shifter's land," the Alpha responds, pinning his glare on Elias.

I wince. I'm all for cursing, but for some reason, every time this guy does it, it hits the ear wrong. It's like a punch to the gut.

Elias is about to respond, but Dorian beats him to it. "As I said, we assumed this had already been sorted out. Our apologies, as it seems Banner has put us in a compromising situation."

I glance from Dorian, who has the best poker face ever, then to the Alpha and his men. Each of them seem to be in a strange, frozen stance, looking at us like with the smallest command from their Alpha, and they'll tear us apart.

Even the goldfish guy is trembling with fury, his face reddening, his skin starting to yellow, scales pushing out from his flesh. *Crap*, they are all bordering on the edge of a shift.

"Why are you here?" the Alpha barks, his shoulders pulling back, a darkness slithering behind his eyes. This man doesn't trust easily, and I doubt we should lay any trust in him.

The goldfish lunges at us when the Alpha unleashes a sharp, ear-piercing whistle. "Back."

I'm frozen on the spot, my eyes bulging at the spectacle. Goldfish-man halts feet from me, and I can see the battle warring across his face, like pulling back takes every inch of strength he has. That's when I realize all the men have a similar look. Whatever is wrong with them, it gives me the creeps.

"Come on. Out with it then," the Alpha urges us.

Elias and I are still glued together, side by side. Dorian starts to lay it all out for the pack. Cain on his deathbed, Banner confident he can save him, but only if we retrieve something for him from the Black Castle. "Time is running out, and this is our last hope to save our friend," he finishes.

His voice cracked each time he spoke Cain's name, and I swallow the thickness in my throat. There are so many *'what ifs'* in our plan. So many risks.

Heaviness fills the air, smothering us while Dorian and the Alpha remain in a stalemate. Neither man says anything for a long time, and my insides wind tighter and tighter in the silence.

"Please," I blurt out, unable to take it anymore. "There are no other options for us. We *need* to visit the Black Castle. We *need* to save our friend. All we're asking for is directions. Then we'll get what we want and leave. In, out. Quick and easy. You won't have to worry about us in your territory ever again."

Dorian looks over at me, his expression blank, but the intensity behind his eyes screams for me to back off. I tense all over and clench my jawline. Elias squeezes me closer to him.

"Does the human speak for you, demon?" the Alpha asks.

He swings back around. "I prefer Dorian. But what she says is true. We only need to be on your territory for a little bit of time and that's all."

The Alpha's gaze hardens. "To fucking steal something from our land."

Well, this is going just swimmingly, isn't it?

Under my skin, Sayah rustles impatiently. It's been so long since I've felt her present with me like this, front and center, and I know it's because she senses the danger we're in. The danger *I* am in. Having her so close to the surface, worrying about me, is somewhat comforting. Almost like old times. But it also makes me more annoyed that we're still arguing like this. Like her, I'm growing tired of the back and forth with these shifters.

"Look, if you feel so fucking strongly about it,

you can come with us. Make sure we don't piss on a tree or whatever it is shifters do to mark their lands." The curse just slips out, but it does the job. Everyone's eyes are pinned on me now—Dorian and Elias's in worry, the shifters' in shock, and the Alpha's in disbelief and anger. Maybe being around him is rubbing off on me in the worst of ways, but I'm in this deep, so I keep going. "We just need to go to the Black Castle. We'll pay you for the object, if it means that much to you. We don't care. But either way, we're not leaving here without it. We offered you this deal to be civil and respectful of your pack. What comes next is up to you."

"Aria," Dorian whispers, but it's not in a scolding tone, as I expect. It's in a deep rumble, and he looks impressed. Turned on, even, from the smirk curling his lips. Glancing up at Elias, I find he's wearing one as well.

The veins across the Alpha's face seem to be bulging, almost as if he's about to shift right there in front of us. He shakes his head, trying to keep control over himself, and droplets of water spray about. Why are all the members of this pack so ready to transform in a moments' notice?

After a few more moments, he grinds out, "If we allow you to enter the Black Castle, there is something there we will also need."

Wait, what?

The first part was unexpected, but what we'd

wanted to hear. But the second? They need something out of the castle, too?

"Can't you just go there and pick up whatever you need yourselves?" I ask.

"Obviously, if we could, we would've by now," he replies, still struggling. His muscles are all bunched and tight, and his eyes are glowing an eerie yellow.

"They can't control their animals," Elias mutters so only we can hear. It only confirms my initial guess about this pack. For whatever reason, their animals are dominating their human sides. Even now, they're all teetering on the verge of the change.

What are we getting ourselves into?

"Is there something we should know?" Elias pipes up. "We're going to need more details than that."

"Lachlan," a man standing near the wall, shaking his head, calls in warning. He's tall, on the thinner side, but toned. Brown hair runs across the top of his head, the sides shaved short.

So that's the Alpha's name. *Lachlan.* I remember someone mentioning it before.

Dorian interrupts, drawing the group's attention. "If you need our help, we need to know what we're dealing with here."

Lachlan purses his lips, frustration washing over on his face. "Meet us back here tomorrow night."

The man I assume is a Beta moves closer to Lachlan, whispering something too low for us to make out. But when they're done, he rolls out his stiff shoulders and turns back to us.

"We invite your hellhound to join us tomorrow night for a pack run," Lachlan says. His words take us by surprise. "As a sign of... brotherhood."

Now he wants to talk about peace and brotherhood? When he confesses he needs our help? Typical.

"A... run." Dorian's lips press into a hard line.

"Only shifters. You understand."

Elias straightens, seeming unamused. "I'm busy. Gotta wash my hair."

"What he means to say is that he'd love to." Dorian swipes an arm at Elias to shut him up. "What time and where?"

"Excellent." Lachlan looks anything but pleased and peers at his Beta, then back at us. "My second will collect him from your hotel at three sharp."

"Three a.m.?" Elias gasps.

"Do you take us for fucking savages? In the afternoon, ya bampot." Lachlan shakes his head. "You'll be taken to your hotel now."

With that, he turns and trudges through the water before vanishing around the bend in the cave. Most of his pack slide out after him, leaving us with his second and another pack member. Mr. Goldfish himself.

"Let's go," the second says and nods toward the cave's entrance.

Dorian goes up to the goldfish shifter and throws an arm around his shoulders. "No hard feelings there, right, Dumpling?"

I cringe hard at Dorian's insistence on having the last say.

The man sneers and shoves Dorian's arm away before marching out to catch up with the others.

"Fuck, man," Elias grunts under his breath. "Thanks for throwing me to the damn wolves."

"I kinda have to agree with Elias here," I add.

"Think about it," Dorian whispers, leaning in closer to us. "They want our help, which means they won't harm any of us for now. So this is your chance to do some sleuthing while on the run and find out what the fuck is up with this pack and the Black Castle."

Elias gives Dorian his best deadpan expression. "You don't seem to understand what a pack run means, do you? We aren't sitting around sharing tales of licking our balls while drinking cups of tea." He growls the last few words.

"Then make it happen. And besides, you could use some more friends." Dorian slaps him on the shoulder. "And smile once in a while, will you? No one likes a miserable old grump."

Elias snorts at him, his lip curling to show a fang.

By the time we emerge from the cave, it's still darker outside. We follow the shifters down a dirty track to the limousine, which is waiting for us near overhanging oak trees. I am eager to get the hell out of here. Just when we thought things might be simple for us, *nope*. They just become even more complicated.

I exhale loudly and can't help but take in the lake glistening beneath the silvery moonlight. Now that it's bright enough to see it, the water glistens like a treasure chest of jewels. Farther on the other side, a mountain rises high, covered in pines. This location is exquisite.

As the guys reach the limousine, I catch movement farther down by the water on a rocky ledge that juts out from the cave. I easily recognize Lachlan at once. His height and silver hair give him away.

Suddenly, he's stripping down to nothing.

I stiffen, knowing I need to look away. But it all happens so fast. Another pack member is there and collects his clothes, then the Alpha dives right into the water.

He doesn't surface for what seems a long moment. The guy sure can hold his breath for a long while. Then a ripple appears in the middle of the lake, and there is no way he swam that distance in such a short period of time.

A small head breaks the surface, followed by a large, long neck. Next thing, a couple of humps protrude from the water behind him... from his body.

I can't move, can't breathe.

My jaw drops open, and I rub my eyes, certain I'm imagining things. Images I've seen of the myth circle on my mind, and I still can't believe what I'm seeing.

"No way," I mumble to myself.

He's the fucking Loch Ness monster?

"Aria, you coming?" Elias calls out impatiently and Cassiel leaps out, bounding toward me. My heart soars at seeing that he's safe.

But my mouth is still hanging open. I swing toward the limousine and run toward the open door. "Oh shit… You are never going to believe what I just saw."

CHAPTER ELEVEN
ARIA

"Can you believe we're in Edinburgh?" I murmur, mostly to myself as we stand on a sloped sidewalk, curving sharply downhill. Buildings stand flush against one another, each just as lofty as the next and painted in various colors. It has a Jack-the-Ripper kind of feel, splashed by a rainbow.

My stomach bursts with excited butterflies. Scotland has been on my bucket list forever. Hell, I never thought I'd leave Glenside, let alone Vermont. And now I can say I've traveled across the world.

"It says on the map that this street might have been the inspiration for Diagon Alley," Dorian explains like it's no big thing.

My heart suddenly goes through tiny palpitations, and I might have just squealed.

"Should I guess you are a Harry Potter fan?" he asks, amused.

"Aha." The sound drips from my mouth as I bounce on my toes.

"There are a lot of strange mentions on this map of places to visit, and I can only assume they are related." Dorian studies the map further. "Only thing we can do is visit them all, I guess."

"Oh my, hell yes!" Despite everything we went through last night, I begged Dorian to take a few hours to just pretend to be normal. You know, do the touristy stuff and sightsee the city. After we woke up from a much-needed nap to regain our energy, Dorian agreed, seeming more eager to make my dreams come true than to actually explore. A disgruntled Elias had already left to join the local shifters for the pack run, so it's just Dorian and me wandering around Edinburgh.

I'm already strolling down the cobblestone sidewalk, imagining myself in Harry Potter, staring into quaint cafes, at bookstores, and into every shop. Most are decorated to match the popular series, adding to the magic feel of the space. How the hell did I not know about this before?

Behind me, Dorian still has his nose in the map, while impatience burns a hole through me. "Come on, we don't have much time. Let's walk as you read the map. I want to see everything."

Spotting one of those famous red phone booths, I hurry over. "Camera?" I ask, waving at Dorian. In the rush to get here, I hadn't brought my phone.

Smiling, Dorian passes over his. As much as I look like a tourist, I don't care. I start snapping photos.

Dorian laughs at me.

We've spent the past four hours wandering through Edinburgh, exploring everything, and having high tea, much to Dorian's protest. We even got to pat an owl owned by a sweet couple for more Harry Potter inspired pictures.

Even with so much excitement, we make sure to save the best for last. Finally, we make it up to the spectacular Edinburgh castle located at one end of the city, high enough to overlook the surrounding land.

"I would love to live here," I admit to Dorian. "Everything I need is within walking distance, and it's magical to stroll through the city and feel like I'm in a fantasy land. Plus, I need more of those shortbread cookies."

"If you squint and imagine flames and demons coming out of that castle, it isn't too different to the castles in Hell," he explains.

I laugh at him. "Right, there are castles in the underworld."

"Where do you think those in charge live?"

My mouth opens, but no words come out. I never really thought much about what Hell contained. Monsters and fire? A big black pit? I never really thought about people *living* there, somewhat normally. It's a bit bizarre to wrap my head around.

"So, you all lived in castles, hey?" I ask, curious

more than ever now. We follow the group of tourists through the grounds of the Scottish palace.

"Me? No. I traveled a lot, so I never really had a place of my own. That was before Cain asked me and Elias to share his home. It has 500 bedrooms."

"Holy crap... oh oops. I mean, sweet hell. Cain had his own castle?"

"Still does," Dorian says. A frown tugs at the corner of his mouth.

Sympathy tugs at me. As much as he likes to pretend being away from home doesn't bother him, it's obvious he still misses it.

The sun starts descending, adding an ominous feel to the stone building ahead of us. Other tourists are making their way in the same direction, and all I can picture is Cain sitting on a throne in Hell in his own castle.

Dorian takes my hand and brings it to his mouth. "It may be difficult to believe, but there is beauty in Hell. Maybe one day we'll get a chance to show you."

Hopefully no time soon.

I don't know what to say. The notion of going to a place of death terrifies me. Yet I've let three demons into my life, so it's not like I can say 'never.'

"Maybe one day," I answer as we arrive at the entrance gate and walk through to a store selling tickets to enter the castle, which half-dilutes the whole fairy tale and makes it feel more like an amusement park.

Dorian releases my hand to go and get us tickets. I

slip into the gift shop, tempted by all the Scottish goodies, from stuffed highland cows, to sheep shaped shortbread cookies, and even kilts. But I drift to the back where I find an array of books and pick one titled *Castles of Scotland*, and flick to the index. I look through the names, searching for the Black Castle.

Nothing.

Hmm. That's odd.

I pull every similar book off the shelf and search. Still zilch. Too bizarre.

"Want me to grab you some highland cow cookies?" Dorian asks over my shoulder, his hands falling to my waist.

"Is it strange that none of these books mention the Black Castle? Does it even exist?"

"I don't know, but I wouldn't be surprised if it was hidden from humans by magic. If the shifters couldn't enter it for some reason, it'd make sense. We are in the land of leprechauns and the Loch Ness monster, after all."

I twist and look up at him, my gaze narrowing. "You still don't believe what I saw with Lachlan, do you?"

"That's not what I said."

Disappointed, I push the book back between the others on the shelf. When I told him and Elias about what I saw at the lake last night, I'd been teased endlessly. I didn't find it funny. I know what I saw.

"You didn't need to. It was in your tone."

"Hey."

He's in my face the moment I turn around, trapping me against the bookshelf. "I would never doubt you. If you say you saw something, then fuck, it happened. I just wished I could have seen it too." He gives me a lopsided grin, which I don't know what to do with. Is he mocking me or just saying something to placate me?

"So that's what all the mockery back in the hotel was when I told you? You were jealous?"

He shrugs and pulls back. "Let's get moving." On our way out, he grabs two packets of shortbread cookies and pays for them before stuffing them into my backpack with all my other souvenirs from Edinburgh.

I smile to myself that he really does pay attention to what I like, that he is trying to make an effort.

He touches my elbow, dipping his hand down my arms, fingers interlacing with mine. I look over at his grin as he leads us through an arched stone entrance. He leads us down alleyways, this way and that way in the castle. We drift away from the crowds, and I can't help but focus on us holding hands like we're a couple. At the way his thumb runs small circles on the back of my hand. He's so tender sometimes, so unlike a demon.

Are we… *together* together? What about Elias and Cain? I'm not sure what exactly we have going on, aside from the burning desire between us, plus the fear of losing them. I'm not sure what to make of it.

I won't deny my attraction to them is crazy wild,

or that my body reacts to them in a way that still shocks me. The pull I have to each of the three demons is the main reason I decided to stay by their side rather than make another attempt to escape.

I'm not sure when our relationship progressed to this level, but there is definitely something deep inside me that needs them.

The longer I glance at Dorian, at his sharp cheekbones, the shadow on his jawline, the kissable lips, the quicker my heart beats. It's only when I trip over an uneven stone on the cobblestone path that I realize how long I've been admiring him.

"I got you," he says, swiftly swinging around and tucking an arm under my knees. I'm off my feet in a fleeting second, my breath rushing past my lips.

"Whoa," I gasp. "That's really not necessary." I instinctually glance around us, feeling like we'll draw everyone's attention, except in the small courtyard, there is no one around. Night slides across the heavens, shadows spreading, and the single spotlight attached to a wall barely illuminates the building.

"If my lady is having troubles walking, I shall carry her," he teases in a fake royal voice that makes me laugh and roll my eyes.

"Alright, Silver Knight. Put me down."

He gracefully does, but not before stealing a quick kiss, and when I meet his gaze, the wicked look he gives me reminds me of our night in the hotel with the Cheetos. My cheeks blush, and I doubt I'll ever be able to get over that night where both him and Elias claimed me at once, in the best possible way, of course.

"We better hurry and go inside to check out the castle before the place shuts down," he instructs, taking my hands, and we're off again. Everything about him is overwhelming. He's like a storm sweeping into my life and turning everything upside down.

But I don't want to stop it, which is nuts.

I worry that I'm losing my ability to think logically when it comes to these three demons. Up is down. Left is right. Things are so squirrely with them around.

As we enter the threshold into the castle, the lights running along the wall reveal narrow corridors, and soon we emerge into a grand room.

Red walls are all I see at first, wooden beams overhead, and what must have once been a regal ballroom or enormous dining area. Shining armor made to look like knights stand against the walls, leading the way to an oversized stone fireplace. Most of the room has been partitioned off by a red rope, except for the center, so I rush forward to the fireplace that sadly sits unlit. We are alone, and I spin on the spot, imagining what it might have been like, living here in ancient times.

"Do you have a room like this in Cain's castle?" I ask.

Dorian nods, studying me, his head tilting to the side. "Numerous rooms, bigger, grander. But in the guide, they mention an old library in the castle. Feel like seeing if we have any luck on tracking down information on the Black Castle?" He pulls a folded-up pamphlet from his pocket and flattens it out in his hands.

"Why didn't you mention it earlier?" I take quick steps toward him.

He shrugs. "I was enjoying seeing you explore the place."

"Well, where is it?" I glance down at the back page displaying a small map with points of interest to visit within the castle. With no idea if it will hold the answers we seek, I'm eager to find out.

We both head back out of the main room and follow a simple path, left, left, and right. Stone walls, a cold breeze on our backs, and only the sound of our steps echo around us.

"Where is everyone?" I ask, glancing over my shoulder into the eerie silence.

"Gift shop. Did you see how many people were in there? It's all about showing others where you went rather than experiencing the moment. Or the history."

"You're not a fan of tourist places, I gather." We follow the hall to another corridor that leads us to a set of stone steps.

"Is anyone really?" he answers.

"Hard to say, as I haven't been on vacation anywhere, but you want to know the truth? I want to see all the tourist places so badly," I admit. "I want to experience what everyone talks about. Pyramids in Egypt. Eiffel Tower in Paris. Opera House in Australia. The Great Wall of China. Machu Picchu. You get the picture. I know it's lame, but I want to do all the lame things, because, well, it was never possible before. Only a dream."

His gaze fills with admiration and a pinch of sympathy. My upbringing offered me no such luxuries like travel. I just want to do what others have done, to say I experienced a place, to just somehow feel normal. Except living with three demons who own my soul is the farthest thing from *normal*, isn't it?

"I've been to all those places," he brags.

"No you haven't," I shoot back.

He raises a brow. "What do you think we've been doing on Earth all this time? Twiddling our thumbs in the mansion?"

"Maybe." Which I know automatically sounds naive of me. "But it's kinda hard for me to imagine you three sightseeing like this. Like vacationers."

"Hm, maybe not like that exactly, but we have traveled a lot for work and for relic hunting." He glances back down at the map and up toward two passages that aren't roped off, then he takes the right turn, and I'm on his heels. "I'll gladly take you everywhere you wish one day."

Has he just offered to take me on a world trip? That leaves me giddy. If we so easily came to Scotland, why not other places, right? Once Cain heals, it might be something I bring up with him as well.

"So why did you settle down in a small town in Vermont, of all places? Why not Valencia, Spain, by the water, or Aspen if you like mountains. Maybe Hawaii or a Greek island? You guys have the money."

Dorian is watching me, his stare hypnotic. "We settled in the most convenient location to help us find more relics. It's secluded, quiet. And with the Storm markets, it made sense to have connections to other supernaturals. To have an ear to the ground and all that." He points down a dimly lit hallway, the ceiling made of arched stone, and only every second light on the strings hanging off the walls are lit up. "This way."

He steps into a room at the end of the corridor, and I join him, immediately hit by a strong smell of stuffy mothballs. Then my mouth drops open at the sight.

Two walls of floor to ceiling bookshelves, everything made of dark wood. The chairs, small round tables, the wooden food trolley.

The window at one end reveals the last threads of sunlight.

Old crystal chandeliers dangle overhead, too clean, too modern to be from such a long time ago. I wonder if the whole room has been updated completely? I approach the bookcase, held at an arms' reach by the red rope, and read the titles, scanning them for the word *'castle.'* Most of the leather spines

ALL SHOT TO HELL

don't have any words on them, or they are in a different language completely. Dorian has taken the other wall, studying the books as well.

"My dream is to one day have a library of my own, like the one Belle found in *Beauty and the Beast*."

Dorian doesn't say a word, and I half expect him to, so I keep talking. "How are we supposed to reach the top shelves?" I ask, surveying the room for a ladder and coming up short.

"You can get on my shoulders, gorgeous. I would never say no to having your legs wrapped around me." He chuckles to himself, and I don't even have to look his way to know he's staring at me.

"You're so predictable," I say.

"Is that so?" he answers from behind me while I shuffle down the length of the room, searching for anything remotely useful for us on the shelves. Part of me can't help but wonder if these aren't real books at all and just staged. That would make more sense if everything else in this room has been remade.

Unable to help myself, I lean forward and against the rope that pulls against my thighs, limiting my reach. Taking a quick peek to the doorway and seeing no one, I step over the rope and grab the first book my fingers grasp. It's an encyclopedia-style book, and I flip it open, but it's blank. Nothing but white pages.

"Crap." Disappointment pings through me. I shove the book back onto the shelf and randomly select another and another. All the same. Blank. I put them all back. "What the hell?"

A shadow suddenly falls over me, and I spin around, my heart clattering in my chest that a staff member walked in and found me breaking the rules.

Except it's Dorian. He cups my face, the other hand leaning against the bookshelf behind me, giving me his addictive smile. I soften against his touch, unable to resist him, so why fight it, right?

"Surprise."

"If you're trying to prove that you're not predictable, I've long moved on from that conversation." I laugh, throwing my head back, but then manage to whack it against the books and cry out from the sting.

In that instant, I'm losing my balance and falling backward. Dorian lunges after me, his arms around my back, but he's too slow to stop me from tumbling over, and instead of saving me, he tips forward, too.

Darkness closes in around us.

My heart kisses the back of my throat, my mind panicking. Then we hit a hard surface, Dorian taking the brunt as he squeezes me against him so we land on his side.

With heavy breaths, we stare at each other, then back into the library, where our legs still poke out.

"What the hell?" I whisper.

"Well, would you look at that," he says, glancing up at the darkened room we're now in. "I think you triggered a secret passage with your head, babe."

CHAPTER TWELVE

ARIA

We untangle ourselves and climb to our feet, both of us glancing deeper into the darkness we've just fallen into.

The light from the library reveals wide, stone steps with a railing heading downstairs into a pit of darkness.

"This looks ominous," I say. "Probably a place where the royals snuck into to escape."

"Or a place to fornicate with their mistresses."

I cut him a stare. "Did you just use the word 'fornicate'?"

"Trying to stick to the times."

"I'm pretty sure they didn't use that word. By the way, can I borrow your cell phone?"

He grabs it out of his pocket and hands it to me. I hit the light button, then sweep the beam across the stairs.

The light cascades down the staircase curving

toward the right and completely out of sight. The walls are stone and bare, giving off that cult type of feel as I imagine people in robes going down there to sacrifice a virgin.

"Here's a fact for you," Dorian begins. "In Ancient Rome, prostitutes would often wait for their clients under vaulted ceilings or arched doorways. And, well, the word 'fornix' means arch, which soon turned into a euphemism for brothels. So the verb 'fornicare,' *to fornicate*, began referring to a man visiting a brothel."

I give him a strange look. That's got to be the oddest thing he's ever said, yet it's strangely interesting.

"I am a wealth of information, especially when it comes to all things carnal pleasure." He cocks an eyebrow, seeming rather proud of himself.

"Okay, Mr. Walking Encyclopedia. Any random knowledge on where we are now?" I turn to exit when the toe of my shoe catches on something. I stumble forward, my pulse spiking, arms flailing outward like a pinwheel. What the hell is up with me and staying on my feet?

Dorian catches me once again, his arms looping around my middle, sweeping me off my feet and back toward him until I'm flush against his chest.

He breathes heavily like he might say something, but in that exact moment, the secret door swings shut too fast for us to react.

Darkness smothers me, and a whimpering sound

slips past my throat. Somehow, I'd managed to switch off the light on the phone, and fear clamps around me.

"No!" I rush forward, Dorian by my side, my free hand slamming into the shut door. Frantically, I fiddle with the phone, my heart pounding. The darkness feels like a noose around my throat, and my skin crawls like something is going to reach out and grab me.

"It's okay, Aria, I have you. Nothing will touch you." He holds me tighter, his tender lips on my ear. "I'll always keep you safe."

I grip onto the phone with my life. Fiddling with it, I'm finally able to switch the light back on. Suddenly, I can breathe again, though my chest is rising and falling furiously.

"What was that all about?" Dorian asks softly, unraveling me from his arms and twisting me by my shoulders to face him.

I shrug, pointing the light to our feet so that it doesn't blind us. Instead, it casts shadows over his face. "I'm a klutz?" I glance over to the door.

His gaze hardens on me. "That's not what I'm talking about."

I don't want to be in here a second longer if I can help it, so I'm honest with him. "Look, after everything I've been through in the past couple of weeks alone, I don't trust what I can't see. There are too many things that go bump in the night."

I manage to pry myself free from his grasp and

turn to the secret door. Using the light, I search for a hidden handle, lever, or a button. Something that can get us out of here. But there's nothing as far as I can see.

"There are plenty of things that torment the day as well," he says. "Humans can be just as cruel and devious as Hell creatures."

Oh, I know. Personally. There were plenty of human foster parents and kids I knew who could out-evil any supernatural.

"To be fair, I barely trust what I *can* see anymore, too," I retort. "It all kinda goes hand-in-hand."

I sense his presence behind me, the warmth of his body, but I'm feeling so agitated, and my skin crawls. "Let's just get out of here, then you can go all shrink on me."

He steps in front of me and studies me, his expression not angry, but he's looking at me with sympathy again, and I don't like it.

But instead of saying anything, he begins looking for a way out with me, patting the stone wall, and I appreciate that more than he realizes. When nothing else works, he attempts to grasp the edge of the door to pry it open, but he can't seem to get a good enough grip.

"Crap, I don't want to be locked in here. What if there are dead people down there?" I'm drawing in shallow, raspy breaths, hugging my middle, the light beam swinging toward the stairs. All I can picture are monsters or something rushing up toward us. I loved horror movies growing up, but now they are tormenting me to eternity and back.

"Um, Aria," Dorian says just as a familiar icy prickle slides across my skin.

I turn around slowly. *Please no zombies. Please no zombies!*

"Why is your shadow out?" he asks.

My insides go cold. Okay, not zombies, but pretty bad. I hadn't summoned her at all.

Sayah is sliding out of me, gliding down the stone steps and vanishing around the corner. Just seeing her has my stomach dropping through me and to my feet, while my chest tightens to where I can barely draw a breath.

"Fuck," I mumble and try to retreat, but I bump into Dorian.

Why do I have zero control over her? I used to be able to tell her when to come and go, and she'd listen without a fight. Now it's like she's her own entity entirely. I've seen what she can do, what she can become.

I shudder, and my breaths come heavier. "What is she doing?" I gasp. "Why can't she just stay inside me?"

Dorian whispers in my ear. "She is part of you, and that means you have sway over her."

"No, I don't. Have you not seen all the times she went haywire? That wasn't my doing. I had no control over her."

"Listen, babe. Breathe deeply, just like me. I want you to try it." He's taking slow breaths in and out.

I only stare at him in disbelief. He can't be serious, right? Sayah is a shadow monster, a monster that lives inside *me.* And he thinks taking some calming breaths is going to tame her? Make her listen?

"Do it," he commands, and I feel the silky webs of his compulsion power cascading over me. Goosebumps rise, and I rub my arms to shake it off.

"Stop that," I snap. "I hate when you use your power on me."

"Then stop fighting me and breathe," he says. "It might help."

Even at the risk of looking stupid, I give in and follow his guide in calming down, matching his slow, deep breaths. In and out. In and out.

This might help if I were going into labor or something, but I just can't see how it will help me get control of her.

"Call her to you now," he tells me with the confidence I lack.

I close my eyes, focusing on Dorian's hands on my arms and the feeling of my chest inflating and deflating in a calming rhythm.

Sayah, come back, I order in my mind. I repeat the words over and over, my hand gripping Dorian's arm to ground myself. I hate feeling so weak, so trapped.

But with Dorian there beside me, silently cheering me on, every chant of the words brings me closer to believing I can do this. Maybe it could work. It's not like it can make it any worse.

I open my eyes a crack to find Dorian smiling at me.

His gaze trails down my body, to my feet, then to the stairs beside us. I lower my attention, finding Sayah is no longer stretched out of me. Her dark shadow is gone.

My heart hammers in my chest as I desperately scan the area with Dorian's phone, just to be certain.

"She's gone," Dorian confirms. "I watched her retreat back into you."

Even the tingling sensation is gone.

I turn to face him, my head lifting to meet his eyes. "Do you think she *actually* listened to me?"

"I want to hope so. Either way, for now, I say we dub it a win." Dorian collects me into his arms, his lips on my brow. "You are so much stronger than you realize, Aria. But you can't let fear rule you."

I press myself against his chest, relieved and content just to be held by him, and the fear I felt only moments ago fades away the longer we stand here together.

I can't help but feel that tonight, there's something so much more going on between us. I never once thought I'd find a guy in my life, let alone three. I mean, I've always been a loner, terrible with relationships, and really, it had been easier to push everyone aside.

But with Dorian, I can feel his intense protectiveness over me. It's easier for me to believe he won't be like the others in my past and abandon me. And that means everything. He takes me to a place where I'm safe, comfortable, and where I forget how horrible the world can be.

Before I know it, words slip past my lips. "I'm scared of Sayah, and I feel weak for even saying that out loud. I mean, shit—you're a demon, and nothing scares you, while I'm over here admitting I'm terrified of my own shadow."

I lift my head to look at him, expecting to find sympathy and pity scribbled all over his face, but instead his expression is firm and hard. "Don't ever be afraid to tell me anything, no matter what it is, understand? That doesn't make you weak, Aria. And I think you're looking at this all wrong. What you just admitted makes you fucking strong."

"W-what do you mean?"

We stand in the darkness with only the faint light from the phone pointing to our feet, the rest of the pitch black around us feel like a beast licking up the back of my legs. It covers me in shivers. I want to have this conversation outside, not the hell in here.

"I know you're afraid of her taking you over," he tells me.

"You know how scary it is to feel like I might lose myself to her? That each time she appears, that might be the moment she turns on me?"

"And yet she's saved you a few times… We don't

know her true intentions. Is it simply the unknown that is scaring you?"

"I… I honestly don't know."

"We're not invincible ourselves, you know. You should have seen the three of us when we first arrived on Earth. We were a fucking mess. Elias vanished for months at a time, coming back bloodied and beaten, pushing himself to cope with our banishment and Serena's betrayal. Cain lost himself in his office and rarely came out or spoke to us. And I… I lost myself in as many lovers as possible. But all that did was delay the inevitable pain of facing the truth. We'd lost our home and everyone we'd ever known."

I chew on my bottom lip, hearing his words, knowing what he's saying, but there's so much more unrest in my mind. "I can't even begin to imagine being ripped out of your entire realm… I get what you're saying, but I've always followed my instinct, and right now, it's off the charts when it comes to Sayah. Something is wrong."

"Sometimes we all have to push ourselves to a place of discomfort to face the truth." He pulls away from me and starts heading down the steps.

I stiffen, my heart suddenly banging against my rib cage. "Dorian, what are you doing?"

"How often do we get to explore a secret lair? Now, are you coming?" He throws the question off his shoulder, while I'm pointing the light from his phone against his back. I know exactly what he's doing, forcing me to face my fears and all that bullshit.

"I thought we were trying to get out of this place?" I call after him, but he swings around the curve of the stairs, vanishing into the darkness. Only the clap of his feet striking the stone steps echoes against the walls. I want to scream at him.

A shiver clings to my spine. I take another look behind me at the sealed door, cursing myself for not running out the moment we fell in here. Then I swing back around and quickly rush after Dorian, not wanting to be alone.

Damn him.

"I really hate this game, just so you know. This isn't funny at all." I make quick work of the steps.

Following the natural curve of the stairs, a room comes to life under the phone's flashlight. The whole place looks like a secret whiskey room for stuffy old kings and princes. From the marble flooring, to the oversized stone fireplace on one wall, more bookshelves, and brown leather couches facing the hearth, it all screams underground bachelor pad to me.

"See, there's nothing dangerous down here," Dorian says, flopping down onto a sofa, sending a faint cloud of dust into the air.

"Only to your health." I skip down the rest of the steps and join him, then I turn on the spot in a small circle, taking in the room with my light. Dusty war shields hang off the wall, along with crossed swords.

Everything else looks bare, like someone's come in and stripped it of any personality or portraits.

Dorian's hand is tapping the leather seat next to him, and as much as I want to sucker punch him for being right, I swallow my pride and cross the room to join him. Setting the phone on a nearby end table with the light pointing upward, I dump my bag on the floor and flop down next to Dorian. The cushions beneath him bounce, gaining me a lopsided smile.

"Fine, you proved your point," I say while I glance around at the darkness in the corners of the room and back up the stairs.

"I give you my word that I will help you find a way to control Sayah."

I pull a bent leg underneath me and turn to face him. "You know, Cain said something similar to me. That he was going to help figure out what Sayah was…"

"Good. Then there are two people working on it at once." He chuckles. "You know what? Throw Elias in there, too. I'm including him, whether he knows it or not."

My lips quirk.

"Are you still bitter that I forced you to come down here on your own?"

I huff, blowing the loose strands of hair out of my eyes, trying to put on my best peeved face. "Maybe."

He laughs at me, and if he didn't sound like liquid candy, I might have thrown something at him. Though the only things close enough are his phone and my bag, and I don't want to damage either of those things.

"I love that you admit to holding grudges. You're adorable," he murmurs as his gorgeous eyes focus on my mouth like suddenly it's captured his interest.

When he raises his gaze, something sharp and intense slides behind his eyes. "Remember how I told you a while ago that I used to travel the world with my parents back in Hell, then decided to move in with Cain at his castle?"

I nod while saying, "Yeah."

"There's no easy way to say this but to come straight out. My parents are assassins, and those trips we took were them going on missions. I tagged along when they were ready to integrate me into their business, something they've been trying to do since I could walk." His dark eyes hold my gaze, and I don't quite know what to make of his revelation. "I flat out refused, and when they had enough of me saying no, they disowned me."

"That's a huge overreaction on their part," I whisper. Sure, being an assassin on Earth isn't considered a virtuous job, but I wonder how it is in Hell.

"My family's business targets humans and drags them into Hell for those who've requested them."

I freeze. "Wait, so like, without a demon contract? Your family would basically kidnap and take a person to Hell even if it wasn't their time? Then hand them over to the highest bidder?"

He doesn't answer right away, his lips thin, and I

watch the pain and the anger as it crosses his features.

"Yes. My family is sickeningly wealthy because of it. But there's a reason I'm telling you this, Aria." His voice is soft but firm, despite his obvious discomfort with talking about his past.

I try to keep on a passive expression to show him it doesn't bother me, but I'm utterly shocked to hear about his family. Here I just assumed they were demons like him. Maybe super sexually active. Not some elite assassination team.

Dorian always is so happy and laid back, but it's obvious this part of his past bothers him and has influenced him greatly.

I reach over and place a hand on his arm, slightly squeezing so he knows I'm there for him.

"Why are you telling me this?" I prompt.

"It took me a long time to trust anyone. But one thing I'll say for Cain... he's a tenacious sonofabitch who never gives up. Months later, after insisting I move in with him rather than live on the streets, I did it. But not before I confronted my parents and told them why I didn't join the business, how I loathed them for what they did. That didn't go well, as you can imagine."

"And?" I hang off his every word, lost to his tragic story, looking at Dorian with a very different light. Sure, he's still a powerful demon who can command his power and stand up to anyone, but nothing is ever the same when dealing with a broken family.

It takes him a long moment to respond, and I watch the wave of emotions dance over his shadowy face. "It shattered me when my mother said I was a stain on their bloodline. She did nothing when my father beat me, breaking three ribs and fracturing my skull before knocking me out. I could've fought back, defended myself, and sometimes I wish I had, but it was my father. So, I just took it. I woke up in the middle of the road, tossed away like garbage. That was what those fuckwits thought of me, their son." A tremble traces his voice, and he lowers his gaze. "They threw me away, and I was only equivalent to fifteen, maybe, in human years."

The heartache in his voice squeezes my chest, but I don't say anything right away. I want to let him have time to deal with the feelings he's awoken.

After a long moment, my fingers tighten a bit more around his arm. "That's fucked up."

It may not be the best or most comforting thing to say, but at least it's true.

He lifts his head, the pain on his face shattering through me. "I don't regret facing them, because I don't fucking kill innocents."

I'm numb and completely lost for words. This isn't what I had expected Dorian to tell me, but I love that he opened up and told me something so personal. And so heartbreaking.

Leaning forward, I wrap my arms around his neck and press my cheek to his, holding him tight. "I'm so sorry your parents did that to you. It makes me so angry that anyone would treat you that way. You deserve so much better."

"Maybe that's one of the reasons Cain and I get along so well. Fucked-up parents." He lets out a strangled laugh in an attempt to lighten the mood. "Although Cain may have me beat with Lucifer as a father."

His thumb slips under my chin, and I pull back to face him. "And just so you know, so do you—deserve better, that is. For a long time, fear crippled me, and as terrifying as it is to face terror directly, you might come out of it wounded but better for it. Plus, you've got us three by your side, and we would never allow Sayah to take you from us. Or anyone else, for that matter."

My mind is frazzled, and I want to cry at hearing his tragedy, which he brushes aside. He's had so many years to get over it, while to me, his story breaks my insides like shards of glass. That's when I realize there is so much more about the three demons in my life I still don't know about. It's something I intend to rectify, because I can't deny I'm falling for them, fast.

"We're in this together." His voice is confident, and something thickens in my throat. He's right, and I can't believe I've let myself fall so deep into fear.

My eyes prick, but I also don't want to fall apart so easily, so I do the next best thing to distract myself. I lean in and press my lips to his. Once we connect, a spark zips through my body, and he feels it. I know he does by the way his body curls around mine. He kisses me with devotion, with eagerness. His hand lifts to my chest, grabbing a breast, squeezing it. His fingers pinch my hardened nipple until it's painfully delicious, and then he releases it, which is torture in itself.

My hand skims down his stomach and strokes the erection in his pants.

"You keep teasing me, babe, and I'll strip you down and fuck you right here."

I gasp when I try to reply, which he grins at, gaining the response he wants. In a heartbeat, he's on his feet and has me lying on the couch on my back. I'm brought back to the moment we first met, when he'd pinned me on his couch in his room, and all the intense feelings I'd had for him then.

I'm feeling them now, but not because of his power. This time, it's all me.

His hands snake past the waistband of my pants, finding my underwear, which he wrenches to the side.

I gasp, then laugh, turned on so badly with all his quick movements and what they promise.

His fingers are on my pussy, inserting two fingers into me so fast, I arch my back and cry out.

"Fuck," he grinds out. "You're on fire."

I'm drenched, my legs parting for him further, and I moan as I stretch an arm out toward his belt. "Take it off," I command.

His guttural groan is interrupted by a faint robotic voice coming from inside the library.

"Edinburgh Castle gates will close in five minutes. Please quickly make your way to the front gate."

I freeze and look up at Dorian, his pants half unzipped. "Shit, we need to get out." I'm on my feet in seconds, adjusting my clothes, while he tucks himself away. Snatching the phone and bag, I run up the stairs with Dorian on my heels.

"Crap, crap, crap! How do we get out of here?" At the top of the steps, I start searching the wall again, pushing against the stone, slamming it with a fist. "Open the fucking sesame up! We only have three packets of shortbread cookies if we get stuck in here. That won't last the night."

"Calm down." Dorian takes my hand in his and draws me a couple steps back. "When we fell in here, we both stood around here, and then you tripped going for the door. Give me the phone." He takes it and points the light to the floor, and I understand.

I scan the floor and practically scream, "There!" the moment I spot a small button in the floor, perfectly camouflaged into the rock.

Dorian presses it with his shoe, and with a faint hissing sound, the door opens.

"Yes! I thought we'd be stuck there all night."

He takes my hand and we dive out, stumbling over the rope, then scramble for the exit. We run for our lives along hallways, left and right. My breaths are racing, and my leg muscles are smarting from how fast Dorian is dragging me.

Finally, we burst outside where a cool wind blows, and we speed across the courtyard, retracing our steps. When we finally come into view of the front gates, partially closed, I release a breath of relief.

A staff member is standing by the gate, glaring at us, unimpressed.

"Sorry," I offer as we swoosh past the guard and right out of the gates. Then I'm laughing at how close we were to almost spending the night in a secret cellar room.

We don't stop running until we are halfway across the open stone yard leading away from the castle. The wind flutters past, driving through my clothes, but the cool breeze is refreshing when my skin is still on fire from what we were doing before.

"Now, to finish what we started before…" His hand instantly falls between us, rushing past my pants, grabbing my pussy.

I squeal and flinch back. "Hey, we're in public."

That devious smile returns. "Just how I like it."

I believe every word.

"Are you insane? Not here. There are buildings around the yard, and they must have cameras out here." I recoil from him, because Dorian would get off on being watched.

But when he shows no sign of backing down, I do the only thing possible. I sidestep right past him and bolt away from him and the castle. My small satchel is bouncing against my back with each rapid step I take. I make a direct line for the cobblestone road leading into the heart of Edinburgh and thank the heavens the land is sloping downward.

I glance behind me, and Dorian's chasing after me, determination on his face. Giddiness envelops me, and short of screaming with excitement, I push myself faster, already spotting a cab farther down the street.

Waving like crazy for the driver to spot me, I sprint forward and jump into the back seat. My breaths are rushing, and the driver gives me a strange look.

Seconds later, Dorian gets in on the other side, both of us gasping for air. The driver twists his head to face us, and he has the bushiest white eyebrows I've ever seen. "Hou'r ye?" he asks, and I smile back, trying to catch my breath.

Dorian gives him details of our hotel, and we're driving off in no time.

I watch my demon, who turns his greedy gaze on me, darkness and hunger behind his eyes. My body hums, and I can't help but squeeze my thighs together to deepen the pulse buzzing deep at my core.

"You are in big trouble once we get back to the room," he promises me with a grin.

"Is that a threat or promise?"

"Whatever you want it to be. I'd say... *both.*"

I don't even know how long it takes us to reach our hotel, but the moment we come to a stop outside the front doors, I jump out. Dorian is paying the driver, and I'm running like a mad woman across the lobby and to the elevators, smashing my finger into the button.

"Come on."

I glance back, and Dorian is a beast, bursting in through the revolving door. He spots me and comes for me like he is the devil himself.

My knees shudder because the chase is both exhilarating and leaves me shaking. The doors open and I dart inside, then hit the 'close' button.

The doors begin to slide shut just as Dorian jams his arm inside, forcing them to bounce back open.

I gasp loudly, making his lips curl upward.

"You can never escape." He steps inside while I retreat into the corner.

"Cheater," I call out, but my body betrays me. I'm trembling with need.

"I can taste you on my tongue, smell how much you want to be fucked."

I shiver and bite down on my tongue to control myself. When he talks that way to me, I melt.

"You're all talk," I rebut, which may have been the worst thing to say to him.

He slaps the stop button on the elevator and comes at me like a tornado.

We clash, our bodies, our mouths, and I've never felt so wild, so desperate before.

His groan sounds strangled, like it pains him to not just plunge into me. I wrap my hands around his neck and hold him against me, kissing him like I'm starved, pushing my tongue into his mouth. His hands roam over my whole body, finding skin under my clothes, pushing my pants to my knees and cupping my ass. A finger finds the path of my ass crack, and I whimper against him.

Without warning, he presses his finger into my ass. I gasp against his mouth, my heart beating frantically.

He rewards me with a wicked gaze that burns through me, my body quivering with urgency, while this predator has his sights on claiming me right here and now. When he pushes his finger deeper into me, I moan, my body shuddering and my core tightening. We've barely started and I already feel the build within me, racing toward an orgasm.

"I have a surprise for you, gorgeous," he whispers, his voice deep and almost animalistic, while his free hand goes for his buckle.

My gaze flips up directly to the camera in the corner of the elevator, and panic spikes through me like barbed wire.

"Wait, no, not here," I rapidly say, placing my hand on his to stop him from unzipping his pants.

A guttural sound falls past his lips as if I've asked him to take a cold shower. He leans in, pressing me to the corner, still fingering me. The moan that falls from my throat has his eyes glinting with pleasure.

His chest rises and falls like he can barely think straight.

"Fuck!" he grinds out and pulls out of me. He fixes my clothes to cover me before turning to the elevator's buttons. He hits one and we're up on our floor in seconds.

Gasping, I can barely walk straight from how wound up I feel, how drenched I am.

He takes my hand and we're out of the elevator, flying down the corridor. I make the mistake of asking him, "So, what's the surprise that you mentioned before?"

As we reach our door, he unlocks it and hauls me into his arms. We haven't even crossed the threshold before he's kissing me roughly, a snarl rolling in his chest. The erection in his pants feels enormous against me, like somehow he's so much bigger than before.

I'm both terrified and excited.

I fist the fabric of his shirt, lifting myself to my toes to reach him better, to return the passion. Next thing, I'm off my feet and he's carrying me inside while we still kiss. Before he even kicks his foot back to shut the door, he's tugging my clothes off so fast, so barbaric, my entire body shakes.

"Off," he growls, eyeing my bra, then turns to lock the door.

Not wanting him to rip it since it's my favorite and the most comfortable one I own, I quickly unlatch it at my back and let it fall down my arms, then fling it across the room onto the table. Then the matching panties.

Dorian stares at me, the hunger in his eyes is devastatingly handsome.

His gaze traces the length of my body, and he drags his lower lip between his teeth, a reaction that leaves me utterly vulnerable. A shiver of excitement dips between my thighs, adding to an already burning inferno.

He tears his shirt up and over his head as he toes off his shoes, tossing them all aside. His jeans are tented as he unbuckles his belt, then pops just his top button. My gaze is trained on his pants, eager for him to release his erection.

I'm completely hypnotized by his perfect body. Muscles everywhere. He's toned, and my eyes can't help but naturally keep following up and down his chest, following the faint line of blond hair running down the center of his abs. I never knew such guys existed in real life, aside from the models in magazines, until I met my three demons.

He closes the distance between us in one long stride, and I'm back in his arms, floating into another plane of existence, one of pure carnal pleasure.

There is no stopping either of us now, no self-restraint. His hand spears through my hair, tugging my head back as he licks my lips and moves down over my chin before kissing my neck. Every kiss is rough and starved. His fingers slide over my breasts, pinching my nipples. I moan and arch against him, the buzz his touch evokes engulfing me.

His hand falls lower to between my legs and finds my clit, circling a finger over it slowly at first, driving me completely wild. My hips rock back and forth, needing so much more.

"Please, Dorian, stop teasing." I breathe the words heavily, while the build up inside me billows too fast for me to even contemplate stopping the orgasm.

"Scream for me," he whispers in my ear, fire leaping from his heated breath across my flesh as his power mingles with his words.

The wave of euphoria crashes through me rapidly, so much harder than I expected. I drown beneath its force, my knees quivering, buckling as I scream. Pleasure rips through me, tearing me apart.

I don't even know when Dorian lifted me off my feet, but I moan as my body bursts like fireworks are going off inside me.

"Fuck me, you're so beautiful when you come."

He lays me on the bed tenderly as though he struggles with releasing me from his arms. Just as quick, he's parting my legs and tugging me toward him.

He unzips his pants and drops them and his boxers, stepping out of them.

I'm on my back, smiling from how incredible I feel, how I wish I could float on air with the hum of an orgasm for hours. I crane my neck up to take in all of Dorian, and when my gaze lowers, I freeze.

My mouth drops open.

Dorian has two cocks, both growing from the same base, stacked on top of each other like a double-decker bus.

"What the fuck is that? You never had…" I shuffle back up the bed, glancing up to meet his eyes again. His hair has changed to more silvery strands, and runes appear across his chest—his demon coming through. "You have two dicks?"

He laughs and leans forward, snatching my ankles before dragging me back toward him, keeping my legs wide.

"It's something some incubuses are born with, a double lucky dip for the girls."

"But…"

I can't find words or stop staring at his two members, thick and erect, both tips moist with precum. And I'm not a fool, knowing exactly where they will be going and why he had gone straight for my ass in the elevator. To get me ready.

"No, you're too big, too much." I'm struggling to breathe.

"Don't worry, gorgeous. I'll fit easily. You'll see. You're so wet and ready for me."

The way he says that and looks at me, I'm starting to doubt where exactly he plans on putting those two dragons.

"You're not going to try putting both together in one…" I look down my body and back up at him.

He reaches over, his fingers on my pussy, and I

moan at how smoothly he glides the pads of his fingers over my heat, moving deeper and finding my ass. "Today we'll take it slowly."

I half-gasp, half-whimper at the implication that he will try to put two into my pussy another time.

"How come I never realized you had two before?" I'm still bewildered by the whole thing.

"It's part of my demon form. I can manifest one or two, and I had to make sure you were ready before I revealed myself completely to you."

He steps over to the head of the bed and grabs a pillow. "Lift that sexy ass for me."

I do as he asks, and he slips a pillow under me, lifting me in a perfect position, and when he spreads my legs open, he smiles. "I love seeing you dripping wet like you're made for me."

Before I can respond, he's pushing himself closer, the tips of his cocks on my slick. I bite on my lower lip, tingling with arousal, while my stomach twirls with nervous butterflies.

"You will enjoy this. Are you ready?" He grabs hold of his lower cock and has it sliding between my ass cheeks, covering me in excited goosebumps.

Who would have thought I'd enjoy anal sex so much? Slowly, he pushes into me, letting me get to the point where I'm relaxed. Then he pushes himself even deeper.

He groans despite my initial resistance, but with the building friction, a spark of electric desire shoots through me. He is only partly inside me when he guides his other thick member into my pussy. The sensation is exhilarating, intoxicating.

I gasp the deeper he moves into me, and the more my muscles tighten, the more Dorian grins, loving every second of claiming me.

I'm breathing hard by the time he's fully buried in me.

His chest is pumping for air, a haze over his eyes, as he's clearly lost to arousal. "I wish I could just stay inside you like this."

But it doesn't take him long to start sliding out and back in. He takes my legs and hooks them against his chest, my feet hanging over his shoulders. I'm at his mercy, and it's exactly where I want to be.

He may have started slow, but he's speeding up, riding me like a demon. My hands spread out and I clasp the sheets, pulling at the fabric as he pounds into me over and over. He fucks me unrelentingly.

My cries of pleasure entangle with his gravelly growls, my heart slamming into my chest just as fast.

"Dorian." I breathe his name, barely able to manage that.

"You're mine!" he snarls like a beast, and the way he looks at me is filled with such possessiveness, such devotion, a crazy thought crosses my mind that maybe part of what he feels is love.

He never pauses, and I'm lost in him completely. His hands on my hips are tender, like somehow he worries about breaking me, which is the opposite of the way he's taking me, making me cry for more.

Every emotion flaring over Dorian's face in that moment is ruthless, dominating, and powerful.

Each time he slams into me, I moan, arching my back, the whole bed groaning under us. The headboard whacks into the wall banging loud, and apparently that was just the start as Dorian picks up speed.

With it comes an unbelievable tightness across my core, my legs starting to tremble, my insides throbbing.

"That's it," Dorian coos. "Come for me, squeeze down on my cocks."

It doesn't take but just those few words, because as he thrusts into me, I scream with the most incredible orgasm, loud and fierce. He grunts just then too, his fingers digging into my hips. He roars his own climax, our bodies trembling with the most beautiful feeling.

When finally the arousal dims within me and Dorian calms down, we're both breathing heavily.

"Shit, that was crazy. So good," I say.

He slides out of me, smiling widely. "Are you okay?"

"Fuck, I am still floating on clouds. You were that amazing."

He chuckles and makes his way to the bathroom as I shuffle up the bed, my inner thighs and muscles a bit sore.

"That's how I want you to feel every single time I fuck you." He comes back and parts my legs to clean me, which has to be the most beautiful gesture ever.

After cleaning himself, he returns and jumps into bed alongside me. Suddenly, a loud creak erupts from the frame, and the whole bed drops beneath us.

I yelp at first, both of us bouncing on the mattress, then I burst into laughter. "Oh shit, we broke the bed."

He's howling with laughter and drags me into his arms. "A broken bed is a sign of a fantastic fuck."

Curling into his arms, I can't stop smiling. I close my eyes, never wanting to stop feeling like everything in my life is perfect. Exhaustion rattles through me faster than I expect, and my last words before I let myself fall asleep are, "Don't ever let me go."

DORIAN

A cool, light breeze sweeps into the dark hotel room from the open window. My beautiful girl is curled up with her back against my side, sleeping, her breathing deep and heavy. She had been fucking incredible, even when I took her far more roughly than I intended. Everything about her consumes me.

Her last words before falling asleep refuse to leave my mind. I turn to look at her, her legs spread out and taking up most of the broken bed.

"I will never let you go," I whisper.

Silence.

I wonder when Elias will come back from the run.

Although, if I were to guess, I'd say it'll be early morning. Shifters are all about their moons, after all. But that's fine with me. The more time I get to spend with Aria alone, the better.

A heartbeat later, a wave of power races up my arms, lifting the hairs. The smell of sulfur leaks into the room.

I grit my teeth and sit up, staring into the dark room for the prick. My sight lands on a silhouette out on the balcony across the room from the bed.

I quietly slide out of bed, careful not to wake up Aria. Barefoot, I pad across the floorboards of our hotel room, completely naked, my fists curled at the intrusion.

Sliding the glass door open, I step out into the brisk chill and shut the door behind me. I abruptly turn to Maverick, who stands near the railing, one arm propped on it, the other in his pocket. He's wearing a smirk that aggravates me deeply.

Some people just want to make you shove your fist into their face from their mere presence. That is Maverick for me. The sonofabitch is a slug.

"What the fuck are you doing here?" I hiss. My initial instinct to hurl him right over the balcony is a strong one. Sure, it won't kill him, but it would make me ridiculously happy.

"Nice to see you too, Dorian." He straightens, lowering his arm from the railing, and stands tall.

"Fuck you and formalities. You're a weasel who only shows up when you want something… something for Lucifer. That is, when you're not too busy with your head up his ass."

He rolls his eyes at me like I'm an insufferable child.

My arms flex, my fists tighten. His gaze turns to the glass door behind me, to where Aria sleeps. It's clear to me he's been out here for a while, watching us sleep like the creep he is. I'm usually a lot more patient with him, but to have him appear now, of all times, bothers me greatly. There is no such thing as coincidence when it comes to demons.

Licking his lips feverishly, he says, "You've been keeping a secret from me."

I scrunch up my nose with zero tolerance for him. "What the hell are you talking about?"

"Come now, don't act coy," he says in a playful tone.

"Fuck off!"

"So is this your big master plan, then? Is she supposed to be your secret weapon?" His gaze flickers into the room and back.

Aria. My shoulders stiffen as my demon side rises to the surface, its fire licking across my nape. Is he referring to her ability to track down relics? Maybe her shadow?

"Stop wasting my time. Go rifle through some garbage or something, you traitorous rat," I snap.

His earlier grin diminishes, darkness gathering in his eyes. "Lucifer knows about her power, by the way." He spits the words, glaring at me like he's sending death right after me. And as soon as the last word leaves his lips, he pops out of sight.

"What power?" I rush the question, but all that's left is a dusting of black mist that stinks of sulfur. "Fucking asshole."

CHAPTER THIRTEEN
ARIA

The rental car Dorian chose this time isn't as fancy as his usual M.O., but after our last run-in with the Night Shade shifters and how easy it'd been to run us off the road, Dorian figured we were better off in something more reliable on the country's vast hillscape. A Jeep Grand Cherokee. The most expensive, souped up model, of course, but not Dorian's typical hotrod of choice.

Since Elias came back from his run early the next morning, we waited for him to catch up on some sleep before heading out to meet the Night Shade pack again. We drive to the lake where we first met them, and the whole time my mind flickers back to last night and how we broke the hotel bed. Something Dorian insisted he'd address with the hotel manager. My body tingles all over from the memory of his hands on me, his two cocks inside me at once, expertly raising the pleasure with every touch and stroke. It's something a girl just couldn't forget.

Cassiel stirs in my lap, mewling over and over. I try shushing him, knowing Elias already didn't want him to come on this trip, but he hasn't been acting like himself lately. He looks bigger, feels a bit heavier, and he's been crying most of the day. At first I thought he might've eaten something funny, but now I'm not so sure. I'm worried about him and don't want to leave him alone. So he's joining us at the Black Castle tonight. Despite Elias's protests.

When we arrived at the bend in the road where our limo had been hit, we climb out. Soon, we're greeted by two familiar faces. Lachlan climbs up the hillside, wearing a gray knitted sweater and kilt, his hair wet and slicked back from his face, and beside him is the hard-looking, overly stiff Beta. I don't know too much about shifters—not enough to know what kind he is—but his gaze is so piercing and unyielding, I doubt it's something soft and fluffy like a mountain hare or squirrel.

"We're here," Dorian calls to the shifters and claps his hands together. "Let's get the ball rolling."

Lachlan's gaze falls onto Cassiel in my arms, and his lip turns up but he doesn't comment on it. "Unfortunately, I won't be joining you tonight," he says instead, which surprises us all.

"What do you mean?" Dorian asks.

He turns to his Beta. "Tavis will be guiding you to

the castle and giving you any information you might need to be successful."

Elias nods, a smile creeping in. When Tavis steps forward, Elias grips him by the shoulder like a friend, and his hard exterior cracks. Looks like the run went well enough that Elias and Tavis created a friendship of sorts.

Lachlan glances over his shoulder at the full moon reflecting off the lake behind him, and the cords in his neck bulge. The skin around his face ripples from the change again, and I can't help but wonder what the heck is really up with this pack. I've never seen shifters so out of balance with their animal and human sides.

"Why aren't you coming?" I ask Lalchan, which snaps his attention back our way.

The Alpha rolls his shoulders, as if trying to relieve some of the tension building there. "My pack needs me tonight more than other nights. Tavis will take my place. He knows just as much as I do about the workings of the castle."

I eye him suspiciously. What is he hiding?

Well, besides being the Loch Ness monster, of course.

"Let's get a move on then, Tavis," Dorian says, gesturing toward the Jeep. "Lead the way."

"We'll be going on foot," Tavis replies. It's the first time I've heard him talk, and his voice is much deeper than expected.

He strolls past us, up the hill, expecting us to

follow. We glance at each other briefly before trudging along in his wake. Dorian and Elias catch up with no problem, but I struggle a bit. Especially since the incline is so sharp and the ground is muddy and slippery. My sneakers can't seem to get traction. I'm forced to use my hands for support. Cassiel cries, not liking the bumpy ride.

Maybe Elias was right and I shouldn't have brought him along.

Even though the men have gained some distance ahead of me, I can still overhear their conversation as we near the crest.

"So, Tavis. What does a jolly ol' lot like you need from the Black Castle?" Dorian asks, attempting another Scottish accent. It sounds more like a mix of British and Southern American somehow. A bad mixture, and I wince in embarrassment. I'm not sure if he's trying to be offensive or funny.

Elias looks unamused.

Tavis hesitates. It's clear he's unsure how much to tell us, but once we all reach the hill's top, he slows down. "There's a lot you don't know," he begins cryptically.

"Obviously," Dorian cuts in. "That's why we're asking."

Tavis holds up a hand to quiet him. "There's a lot you don't know and that we don't even understand," he goes on. He continues to walk through the darkness without even bothering to look where he's going. "We think we've been cursed."

Elias's brows rise in surprise. "You... *think?*"

I'm with him. How could you not be sure of such a thing? How does that even work?

"We had a run-in with a pretty powerful witch around six months ago, around the spring equinox," he begins. "We found her snooping around our land and in the Black Castle, and when we stopped her and forced her out of our territory, she swore to us that we'd pay. At first, we thought nothing of it. Lachlan wasn't fazed. As the most powerful pack in Scotland, we get threats all the time, but then things started to change. *We* began to change."

"What do you mean?" I peep up. Tavis's head swings my way, and his eyes widen as if he'd forgotten I was even there. He clamps his mouth shut.

"She's with me," Elias assures him with a quick smile over his shoulder.

Somehow that's good enough for him, and as we continue through tall grass, Tavis starts again.

Shifters, man. They live by their own secret code.

"We're losing our humanity. That's the only way I can describe it. Every day, we inch closer to the animal and farther from the man. Some of us have lost the ability to change at all. They're stuck as their beast."

My chest clenches with dread. They're losing their ability to shift? I can't even imagine such a thing. To slowly lose yourself... becoming trapped in the mind of an animal forever… it's a thing of nightmares.

Elias stops in his tracks, the severity of what Tavis said hitting him hard. We all halt.

"Cursed," Tavis says with a solemn nod. "It's the only explanation we can come up with."

"Can a witch even *do* something like that?" I ask. I think of Joseline and how most of her spells had always been mild. Docile. The most complex one I'd ever seen her perform was an attempt to roast a chicken once when we lost power. Let's just say the thing exploded and covered every inch of the kitchen.

"The witch must've drawn on the magic from the equinox for something like that," Dorian puts in.

"Or something darker," Elias says.

"How about you?" I ask Tavis, wanting to know more about this. "You don't seem to be struggling like the rest of them."

Tavis begins walking again, and we continue to follow. "I was away the day the witch was cast out," he says. "Lalchan had me meeting with our neighboring pack to the west for a few days. But I'm still feeling the curse's effect. I just think it's hitting me slower than the others."

"Are you a Loch Ness shifter, too?"

Elias snorts a laugh, and I glare at him. He and Dorian may still think it's funny, but I know what I saw.

"No, that is just Lachlan. He is the last of his kind,

which makes him all the more eager to find a way to reverse the curse. It's up to him to find a mate and produce an heir in order to save his species. I am an eagle shifter."

"Wait, what?" Dorian blinks rapidly, then glances at me. I grin so wide my cheeks hurt. He may have said they believed me before, but it's clear they still had their doubts about it. Well, nothing to doubt now.

"Oh, you heard him," I say, a hand on my hip. "He said I was right."

Dorian looks at Elias and chuckles. "Well, will you look at that... Our little Aria was right all along."

That puts a pep in my step.

We pass long stretches of farmland where goats and cows graze, trekking up and down more muddy hills and patches of tall grass. The night air is thick with the stench of manure and hay. Now I see why we couldn't take a car to the castle. There are no roads here to drive on. No signs of people. Not even a tower or black stone from a castle that's supposed to be out here. Just a whole lotta nothing with a heaping side of diddly.

After some time in silence, I finally hurry my steps to catch up with the men and ask the question I'm sure is own the demons' mind too. "Where is this Black Castle anyway?" I am starting to believe it doesn't exist.

He stops again and waves in front of us. But there's nothing there.

"Uh…"

Shaking his head, Tavis lets out a soft laugh. "It's here, just under our feet."

Whoa.

"Really? How?"

He beckons me over. Dorian and Elias creep closer. Then he points to a patch of tall grass just a few feet away.

At first, I don't see a thing, but when the wind blows and the weeds shift, the wood of a cellar door peeks through.

Talk about a killer hiding place. If it wasn't for Tavis's guidance, we would have walked right over it.

He pushes the stalks aside and wrenches open the door. It looks extremely heavy and makes a terrible, ear-grating sound as the hinges work.

Elias, Dorian, and I peer inside. My stomach somersaults. There are only some old and questionable-looking stone steps leading into more infinite blackness…

"This is where I leave you," Tavis says, which surprises us all.

"Leave us?" Dorian asks. "Aren't you supposed to be leading the way?"

"I cannot pass the threshold to the castle. It is why we need you to retrieve the cure for us. The curse prevents us from getting inside and retrieving what we need to break it."

A magical object for the necromancer. A magical cure for the Scottish pack. We're starting to become a carrier service here, apparently. Or like Oprah, handing over these things like they're prizes.

"And what is it that we need to get, exactly?" Elias narrows his eyes on him.

"We believe the cure resides in a flower. A rare one that only grows underground, can be found in the castle, and is densely saturated with magic. It's called the Night Queen Blossom."

Dorian huffs. "Again you are unsure?"

"The Night Queen flowers are what the witch was searching for before we caught her," he explains. "When we forced her off our land, she threatened us, mentioning that we would now need the very thing we wouldn't let her have. We assume it's the flower. After doing some research on the Night Queen, we found it's popular in most counter curses, and—"

"You put the puzzle pieces together," Dorian finishes. Tavis nods.

"We tried retrieving it, but whenever we step further than here, the ground quakes. We're afraid it'll cave in and be lost to us forever."

"And that's why you need us," Elias goes on.

"Why not get any old Joe-schmo off the street to do it for you?" Dorian asks. "They could've helped you."

"The Black Castle has always held many secrets," he says, voice lowering to an ominous tone. "Ones it doesn't like people to uncover."

A shiver snakes up my spine. "You talk as if the castle is alive or something…"

Tavis looks over at me with a grimace, and my pulse picks up. That wasn't exactly a no.

This is becoming more complicated than it was supposed to be.

"Don't worry, Aria," Dorian begins, snaking an arm around my waist and drawing me close. "It's nothing we can't handle."

Elias edges closer on my other side, boxing me in. "Nothing will happen to you while we're around."

But I'm not just worried about myself here. I'm worried about them. Maybe even more so. The entire ordeal with Sir Surchion had been my fault to begin with. I'd brought that psycho dragon shifter into our lives, and he nearly killed Cain. I don't want to risk losing them, too.

I want to say all these things, but I keep the thoughts to myself and only nod. We have to go into the Black Castle anyway for Banner's object, whatever the fuck it is. We still don't know. But I'm the only one who will be able to sense the dark magic in it, so my fears will have to be put on hold for tonight.

It's time to suck it up and do this thing. For Cain.

Unfazed, Cassiel leaps from my arms and saunters down the stairs, disappearing into the darkness as if it's no big deal.

We all exchange looks. The earth doesn't quake under our feet. The walls don't cave in.

All good signs, right?

"Well, looks like the cat knows what to do," Dorian says and takes the first step down. He pauses, waiting to see if anything magical or deadly happens, but all is calm and quiet. Shrugging, he turns to me and offers his hand. "Shall we?"

Still wary, I slip my hand into his and let him guide me into the thick blackness. Dorian's form is instantly swallowed up by shadow, and I can't see a thing, but I hear Elias's heavy footsteps thudding behind me.

"I'll be right here when you get back," Tavis calls down to us as we descend. "Be careful, my friends."

ELIAS

Within seconds, my eyes adjust to the dense darkness underground. The air turns earthy and stale, and I wonder just how long that door has been locked and this place forgotten. The only creatures that I smell nearby are rodents, which isn't too surprising. Mice, bats, rabbits... Nothing that could harm us in the slightest.

Oh, and one whiny lynx kitten, one who shouldn't be here with us at all.

Dorian clicks on a flashlight, forcing me to squint against the sudden brightness. He turns on a second one and hands it to Aria. Their beams sweep across the stone floors and tall archways. Twisted roots crawl down the walls and along the ceiling, while a layer of dirt coats the floor. Whoever's idea it was to build a secret castle underground, they must have liked their privacy. Or they were hiding something extremely important. And since both the necromancer's special object and this Night Queen Blossom are supposedly down here, I'm guessing the latter.

Cassiel's meows echo ahead, as if he's beckoning us to follow. I clench my jaw. Damn kitten thinks he's the alpha in this hierarchy. Ha, I don't think so.

I push my way past Dorian and Aria to the front of the line. "I should lead," I say, meeting Cassiel's glowing yellow eyes. "I can see, hear, and smell any danger before we reach it."

"Good idea," Aria says.

"Then I'll take up the rear... *again*." Dorian flashes a wicked smile, obviously enjoying his double innuendo there.

Color stains Aria's cheeks, and she stammers, "Y-Yeah. R-Right," before clearing her throat.

I stroll ahead, making sure the lynx falls back in line. He hisses at me, like usual, but Aria is quick to scoop him back up in her arms, and that's enough to silence him.

Pathetic. He's becoming as spoiled as a house cat. As fat as one, too.

After going down more stairs, we enter a grand, circular room with tall domed ceilings and many darkened doorways. Old woven tapestries eaten away by moths hang from the rafters, the colors and pictures faded. A chandelier hangs lopsided at the center, covered in cobwebs and rusted. It reminds me of the entrance hall in Cain's castle back in Hell, only smaller and with the main staircase leading to lower levels instead of rising to upper floors. This place is a bit trippy, like a negative imprint of something that should be above ground.

"Which way do we go now?" Dorian asks, his voice echoing in the massive space.

"I'm not sure," I reply.

"Tavis didn't really give us much direction," Aria adds, but then hesitates. "Uh, hold on."

"What?" Dorian asks. "Is it your dark magic toe magnet again?"

Her eyes close, and she stands there, rigid, for a few long moments. Then her eyes snap open and she nods. "I do feel something... Something very dark, deeper in the castle." Her gaze whips around, taking in all the doorways. "Through there," she says finally, pointing at one across the way, near the steps.

"Do you think whatever it is, it's what Banner wanted?" she asks.

"I can put money on it," I reply.

"And what if we're wrong? What if we get all the way back to the U.S. and find out we grabbed the wrong thing?"

"Then he saves Cain or I shove it down his throat. Take it or leave it."

She doesn't seem satisfied with that answer, so I add, "It's his fault for not telling us exactly what it is. He's lucky we don't bring him back a paperclip and call it a day."

"A paperclip?" Dorian arches a brow. "Do you expect to find a paperclip in this place?"

"You know what I mean," I growl. I wave them all forward. "Let's just go."

We walk on, following the instructions from Aria's dancing toe. It leads us around a sharp bend, down some very questionable stairs, and to a landing that drops off to nothing but more questionable blackness.

"A pit?" Aria scoots around me to get a better look, and I quickly grip her by the shoulder and haul her against my body. Don't need her stumbling and taking a dive. "It's a dead end."

Dorian turns to her. "What is your magic toe saying, Aria?"

"It definitely wants us to go on." She shines her light across the way to find the other half of the landing several yards away. "And that's too far to jump."

"Maybe for you," I say and push them to back up some and give me room. "Watch and learn."

I give myself enough space for a running start, ready myself, and rush forward, throwing all my weight and power into the jump. I'm flying through the air, soaring over the unknown, the animal in me elated by the thrill of it all. I land with my feet teetering on the edge of the other landing, and I'm forced to windmill my arms to try and regain my balance. My heart falters.

"Elias!" Aria screams in terror.

Finally, I'm able to catch myself and regain my footing. The momentum has me stumbling forward, but I brush the hair out of my face and wave at them to show them I'm okay. "See," I say, a bit breathless, "nothing to it."

"Elias, you asshole!" Aria yells at me. "You almost gave me a fucking heart attack. You're lucky you're all the way over there or I'd kill you!"

I bark a laugh. I don't know why, but I love when she's feisty like this. Just thinking about her trying to land a swing at me has my cock twitching to life. Maybe it's the hellhound in me, but I'd love to wrestle her to the ground and make her submit to me, one way or the other. The more of a fight she puts up, the more fun it is for me.

"Brilliant idea, Evel Knievel," she continues to shout. "And how are we supposed to get over there now?"

When I look at Dorian, his hair's already changed color, his horns are out, and his nails have grown to deadly claws. He grabs Aria's wrist, yanks her and Cassiel into his chest, and tells her to hold on tight. Without hesitating, she wraps her legs around his waist and her arms around his neck. Then he leaps onto the stone wall like an oversized demon monkey. Aria's head peeks out, and when she catches a glimpse of the pit below, she shrieks.

"Fuck, fuck, fuck, fuck!"

"Hold on tight!" Dorian instructs and leaps again, his claws imbedding into the cracks in between the stones. One more go, and he's close enough for me to reach over and pry Aria's grip off him. And I say *pry* for a reason. She had been holding on for dear life.

I pull her and her pet onto the safety of the ledge. The moment Dorian hops on, his demon recedes, but the mischievous grin stays planted on his face. Aria whirls on us and punches us each in the arm as hard as she can, which isn't hard at all. I resist the urge to laugh. Dorian makes a good show of it, rubbing his arm and wincing, but she glares at us both.

"Both of you... you, you..."

"Yes?" Dorian purrs only to egg her on.

"You suck!" She whirls on her heel and stomps away.

I snort a laugh. *Women.*

Dorian gestures that we should follow her. We do, walking through another archway and down some more winding stairs.

When we all reach the bottom and what seems to be solid ground again, Aria halts midstep, and her body grows rigid.

"What is it?" I ask, sniffing the air. I don't smell anything different. Well, besides fresh water, and considering we're so far underground, that's not too surprising.

Slowly, she turns. "We have to go through there," she begins, pointing to another hallway at the end of ours, "but Sayah is warning me about something..."

The shadow creature can communicate with her? That's unsettling.

"Warning you? About what?" Dorian asks the questions for me.

She hesitates, her brows knitting together in thought. "I'm not sure…"

"You're not sure?"

"It's not like she can talk to me," she snaps in annoyance. "Not with words, anyway. It's not that easy."

"Then what *are* you feeling?" I ask. "Talk us through it."

She sighs heavily. "A strong sense of anxiousness. Foreboding. Like something dangerous is around the corner."

The worry on her face makes my chest squeeze. I don't want to put too much merit into an unknown, untrustworthy shadow that's possessing my girl, but at the same time, Aria believes it, and it's frightening her. So I won't ignore it.

"We'll stay close to each other," I say and take her small, dainty hand in my much larger and calloused one. "Come on."

I lead her through the hall with Dorian hovering at her back. The sounds of rushing water become louder with every step, like someone left all the faucets running in the rooms nearby. But there are no signs of water anywhere. Even the walls are bone dry.

I may not have some supernatural spirit inside me to warn me of danger, but the hairs on the back of my neck are standing on end now. I slow down, making Aria bump into me.

"Wha—"

I shush her sharply, listening. Smelling the air. A trickle of alarm zaps through me, but before I can say anything, the stones under our feet begin to shake. Dorian snatches Aria by the waist and hauls her back just as the ground splits a hundred different ways. Suddenly, the solid ground I was standing on is moving, bobbing in a pool of steaming and bubbling water. The heat coming off it burns my eyes and saturates me in sweat.

"Dorian!" I shout over to him. He and Aria are standing on their own rock-boat that's just big enough to hold them both but appears to be dipping in the water a lot faster than mine. They push against each other to avoid any deadly splashes. "We're going to have to leap across! These stones won't hold us for long!"

He mouths something to me, but the rushing water underneath us drowns out his voice. I can only hope he heard me and knows the immediate danger we're all in. The entire hallway has been reduced to only a few floating rocks.

Glancing back at Dorian and Aria, I see that he has her piggyback with her arms around his neck. Cassiel's little furry head pops out of his sweater's collar, and he nods at me, signaling that he's ready to roll.

A bubble near my shoes bursts, spraying searing

hot water across my sweatpants. The pain in my legs is instantaneous, but I can't let it slow me down. I hop to the closest rock. The thing swivels as I land, and I almost lose my balance again and meet the water. A hand seizes my shirt and wrenches me upright, and once I'm stable again, I see Dorian there, perfectly perched on his own stone, his lips twisted in a playful smirk.

How he can balance while carrying Aria and Cassiel and then snatch my ass before hitting the water face-first is remarkable to me. I used to think incubuses were just sex-fiends without any useful talents besides finding the next way to get their dick wet, but Dorian's gifts are nothing to scoff over.

"We have to work on your landings," he says as he lets go of my shirt. "You need a bit more grace to them. Less of an oomph."

Of course he would be making jokes right now. At the worst possible time.

Ignoring him, I jump for the next passing stone, but again, I can't get good footing and slip. My momentum sends me forward, and I have no other choice but to use it to propel myself to another stone.

I land on this one stomach first, my face hanging over the side, dangerously close to the water. The heat is so intense, my eyes water and my skin prickles all over. I scramble to my knees. Across the way, Dorian's on safe ground at the very end of the hallway. He puts Aria down on her own two feet and hands the lynx over to her.

Then, to my surprise, he comes back my way, leaping onto a nearby stone.

"Come on, you big oaf," he says as he holds out his hand. "No more playing around. Let's get you across."

"What do you propose I do? I'm not getting on your back, if that's what you're suggesting."

He laughs. "Uh, no. But I can help throw you. Give a bit more heave to your ho." Without waiting for me to do anything, he snatches my wrist and tugs me to stand. "That's it. Now, on the count of three…"

He wants me to jump. I get it.

"One… Two… Three!"

He wrenches me at the same time I jump, and our combined power catapults me over the water and through the archway to safety. I tuck and roll, narrowly missing colliding with Aria, before hitting the wall, hard. I groan.

Aria is quick to my side. Her hands touch my face, her eyes roaming over me for any injuries. "Are you okay?"

"I'm fine." And to prove it, I turn over and get up in time to see Dorian's made it back, unscathed. He doesn't even look out of breath.

"As soon as we get back home, I'm signing you up for ballet lessons," he says. "You're as graceful as a moose. No, worse than that."

I roll my eyes.

"Not to mention you could use some culture."

"Get off it, okay? We need to keep moving," I growl.

"Maybe we should turn back," Dorian suggests. "With all these traps, I'm starting to feel like I'm starring in an *Indiana Jones* movie."

"But what about Cain?" Aria quips. "And the pack's 'flower?'"

"I'm more worried about you at the moment."

The ground shakes violently again, and Aria braces herself against the wall. Behind us, the stones that had sunk in the pool of boiling water rise back to the surface, moving and shifting until they join together like an elaborate puzzle. Within seconds, the hallway appears completely normal again, any indication that we were almost just cooked like lobsters gone.

"What in the world…" Dorian murmurs.

"I'm starting to think that what Tavis said about this place being alive might not just be a tall tale," Aria says, looking grim. And I'd have to agree. The Black Castle doesn't seem to like visitors.

Suddenly, Aria's head snaps to the left, down the darkened corridor, and her eyes widen.

My muscles tense. Is it Sayah again? Another warning?

"What's the matter, dear?" Dorian asks, voice low. He's shoulders are curled forward, too, the blueness of his runes shining through the threads of his sweater as his demon hovers close to the surface. On alert. "What is it?"

Slowly, she turns to us again, expression still a conflicting mix of fear, confusion, and disbelief.

Maybe I'm still on high alert after that last fiasco with the water, but my anxiety gets the better of me. "What's wrong? More danger?"

"I..." she starts and then licks her lips. Even stranger is that her head tilts as if she's listening to something. Something only for her ears. "I... hear music."

CHAPTER FOURTEEN
ARIA

*M*usic... A piano being played in the distance. The notes seem to reverberate off the walls and echo all around me, the notes short and urgent, making my heartbeat gallop to match its pace. To make this even weirder, my toe is bouncing wildly in my shoe, wanting me to go down the hallway and follow the phantom song.

When I look at Dorian and Elias, though, they don't seem to be hearing anything at all. They're both looking at me like I've sprouted an extra head, with concern and fear, and that makes me panic all the more.

If I'm the only one who can hear it...

A relic? Could it be?

But my dark magic senses had been tingling before—when with Banner—and I'd seen no relic with him. Then again, there had been no music, either. The music only seems to appear when one of the harp's pieces is close by.

But here? In Scotland, of all places?

"Fuck, Aria," Elias barks at me, making me jump. I had been so lost in the music and my thoughts, I'd already forgotten I'd left him and Dorian hanging in the wings.

I shake my head, trying to focus on them and not the erratic banging of the piano keys. "I'm sorry. It's just… I hear music again. You know, *music*. And my pinky toe is going berserk."

"I'm not quite sure I follow," Dorian replies.

"You can't hear anything, right? No… random piano solo?"

Elias blinks. "Piano? No."

If his words didn't confirm it, the dumbstruck look on his face sure did. Only I was hearing the song.

"Remember when I told you that I was able to track the other relics because they called to me in a way? Through song?"

"And you hear it? Now?"

I nod. "I thought my toe might've been leading up to one before in Cold's Keep, but I had forgotten about the music. And if you can't hear anything…" I glance between them again, and they both shake their heads. "It's the only explanation I have."

Dorian grins, but Elias's gaze darkens, as if he's extremely concerned.

Then it hits me. Why he'd be worried about

finding one of the harp's relics here.

"It's not a coincidence, is it?" I speak my thoughts aloud. "The object Banner wants is the one we need, too."

Instantly, Dorian's smile vanishes. "Shit."

My belly fills with nerves. "If we're right and that's the case, what are we going to do? We can't just give up the relic. Then you can't get back to Hell. But if we don't, Cain…"

"Let's not worry about that now," Dorian says in a rush. "Let's just get what we need and get out of this death trap. We'll figure out the rest later."

I know what he's saying is true. There's no need to panic when we don't even know what's at the end of that hall, but I still feel sick.

"We need to be careful." Elias strides ahead of us, disappearing into the darkness again. Dorian lifts his flashlight and places a hand on my back, signaling me to go on. On high alert, we walk in Elias's footsteps, scoping out the area for any more surprises. With every step, the music grows louder and more aggressive.

We follow the curve of the wall until the corridor suddenly opens up. A strange, pulsing blue light spills from the room beyond.

Dread coils around my spine. This can't be good. I don't want to know what other deadly secrets this castle has hidden in its walls.

Elias stands at the doorway, peering in. He's a dark silhouette against the bluish light. "You're not going to believe this," he says and waves us over. Cautiously, we creep closer.

My fear is quickly turned to wonder as I peer inside. A room covered in creeping vines—creeping across the floor, the walls, and ceiling—and covered in tiny blue bell-shaped flowers. They blink slowly, lighting the room in a magical, almost fairy tale-like way. My mouth hangs open at the sheer beauty of it.

"It's like something straight out of a damn Disney movie in here," Elias says as he scans the room in awe.

"These must be the Night Queens Tavis was talking about." Dorian flicks one of the flowers, and the light beats faster from his touch. Moving closer, he studies it. "How… peculiar."

"Well, let's grab some and go already." Elias reaches up and rips a handful of vines off the ceiling. The lights instantly dim and die out as he stuffs the flowers into his sweat pants' pocket. Dorian takes some from the wall. I put Cassiel down and do the same, filling my satchel as much as I can. The room grows much darker with the missing Night Queens, but once we've grabbed what we hope is enough, we move into the next room.

In here, the phantom piano music is so loud, it pounds against my brain. I wince as pain hammers through my skull.

Dorian's hand presses into my shoulder. "Aria, are you okay?"

"It's… so… loud here." I struggle to even form

words.

"We must be close," Elias says and sniffs the air. Unlike the Night Queen room, this one is consumed with blackness. Dorian's flashlight roams around, finding another circular space with a domed roof and no other exits.

His beam lands on the far wall, where something white gleams. As he moves closer, Elias and I follow, and I realize what the pile actually is. Bones.

A full skeleton—skull, ribs, femurs, feet… It's all there.

Bile rises in my throat. Had this poor sap been trapped down here? Or did one of the Black Castle's traps claim his life?

That's when I see the shallow scratch marks in the stone, the dark red streaks, and…

I choke. "Are those… fingernails?" I cover my mouth. I'm going to throw up.

Unbothered, Elias touches the grooves.

"Animal?" Dorian asks.

"You'd think so, but no. Human."

"Was he trying to get out? Maybe escape something?"

"I'm not sure. I can't tell from the marks alone, but they seem random. Sporadic. I'm not sure what it means."

As if someone has slammed both hands onto a piano's keys, an eruption of noise blares through my head, and I scream, covering my ears.

"Aria!" I can barely hear Dorian through the thunderous *bang, bang, bang.* Over and over. I feel it in my chest; it's crippling, and I drop down to my knees.

"Aria! What can we do to help?" Dorian shouts.

"The relic," I croak out, unable to control the volume of my voice. I'll go deaf at this rate. "It's here... Somewhere!"

The noise is coming from in front of us. From the bones. I point. "There!"

Elias kicks over the skeleton, quickly ruffling through the different bits and parts. He grabs what looks like a spine, with sections of vertebrae, but it's coiled in a spiral, more like a serpent.

The music stops abruptly. In the sudden silence, relief rushes over me. I fall back on my butt, gasping for air. The migraine that's brewing is going to be a wicked one.

Dorian's eyes are alight with excitement. "The spine! It's the spine!" Laughing, he punches the air. "Holy shit! The harp's spine!"

I rise to my feet. "Thank goodness, because it was about to blow my eardrums out."

"We got everything, so let's blow this popsicle stand." He turns to Elias, who hasn't moved a muscle since finding the spine. "Elias?"

Still, he doesn't respond.

Dorian snorts. "Elias? Come on, we need to go before the ceiling opens up and this place starts flooding with man-eating beetles or something else melodramatic."

But when he gets no reply again, anger coats his

tone. "Fuck, man. Wake up!"

Elias's head snaps our way, and we both leap back. What we're staring at isn't Elias at all. His eyes are the brightest shade of yellow, almost neon, and they glow menacingly at us. His mouth is full of sharp teeth, and he flashes them all as he snarls. The skin around his face ripples like he's on the verge of shifting, and black fur sprouts from his neck and shoulders.

He's turned into some kind of beast. A half-hound, half-human beast.

"Oh shit." Dorian steps in front of me and holds out his arms like a shield.

"What's going on?" I gasp, fear seizing my chest. "What's wrong with him?"

"He's gone feral or something. Like the pack."

The curse… Has it somehow gotten to him, too?

Saliva dripping down his chin, Elias lets out a guttural growl. Dorian starts to backpedal, causing me to do the same.

"But he wouldn't h-hurt us… right?" I ask, gripping Dorian's shoulders.

His muscles flex under my hands, and his hair starts to change before my eyes. He's getting ready to fight. Not a good sign. "Something tells me he isn't thinking very clearly at the moment."

On cue, Elias lunges for us. I scream. But before he can reach us, a blur of gray darts across the room and leaps onto Elias's face, hissing furiously. It takes me a second to realize it's Cassiel, and he's clawing at

Elias's face and sinking his fangs into his forehead. Roaring, Elias bucks, throwing himself sideways. He claws at the lynx, trying to throw him off, but Cassiel holds on, slashing, biting, and fighting fiercely.

I don't know what to do. I'm frozen in place. Dorian, on the other hand, rips off his sweater and throws himself into the commotion. Using his speed, he snatches the spine out of Elias's grasp, using the sweater to wrap it up without touching it directly.

Instantly, the piercing color of Elias's eyes softens and his body slumps. The fur recedes, and his mouth returns to normal.

Leaping off him, Cassiel runs straight for me and jumps into my arms again. He feels much heavier now. Bigger, too. But besides that, there's not a mark on him.

Elias, though, is covered in blood. The gashes across his face and neck are bleeding profusely.

He sways a bit on his feet, blinking rapidly as if waking from sleep. When he rubs his face and looks at his palm covered in blood, he curses. "What the fuck?"

It definitely *sounds* like the Elias we know, but I'm still wary.

Elias's gaze lands on Cassiel, and he growls, trudging toward me. "That's it. That little shit's going to pay—"

Dorian slaps a hand onto his chest to stop him. "Woah there, big fella. Reel it back in. You just went rabid on us."

He pauses, glancing at Dorian with blood trailing down the sides of his face. "I, what?"

"It's true," I say, my throat tight. "If it weren't for Cassiel, you would have killed us."

"Oh, come on," he says and rolls his shoulders. "There's no way I would've—"

"It sure looked that way to me, too," Dorian replies firmly.

As if stunned, he snorts and shakes his head. Then he searches our faces again, as if to see if we're pulling his leg. When he finally decides we aren't, he steps back. "But I… I don't remember doing anything like that."

"What *do* you remember?"

"The skeleton. The spine. Then…" His forehead wrinkles in intense thought. "Cassiel clawing my face."

"Yeah, you're missing some parts."

"Shit." He leans back on his heels, unsure what even to say.

Dorian holds up the spine that's safely wrapped up in his shirt. "And it looks like this is what did it, if I were to bet. So it looks like we'll have to handle this relic with care."

My heart's still pounding against my ribs, and no matter how normal Elias is now, I can't seem to calm it down.

His gaze finds me, and he frowns. "I'm sorry if I scared you," he says, voice low. "I hope you know I would never hurt you…"

Intentionally, maybe. But under the spine's influence, I wouldn't say that for sure.

Dorian gives him a sympathetic pat on the shoulder. "I think that's enough excitement for one day, don't you think?" Gently, he takes my satchel from around my shoulder and places the relic and his sweater inside. "I hope you don't mind."

Without waiting for me to reply, he throws it over his head and winks at me. But I don't care. I'd rather not have any more incidents.

In stiff silence, we gather ourselves and head for the exit, making sure to hurry over the trick floor and take our time leaping across the crater in the middle of the stairs. When we finally come upon the stairs leading out, Tavis's shadowy figure darkens the doorway.

"Did you find it?" he calls down to us.

Elias is the first to step out, and when Tavis sees his bloodied and scratched-up face, he winces.

"Well, fuck…"

Dorian yells up from behind me, "You can say we found it and much more."

Boy, was that an understatement.

Once we're all on solid ground again, we empty our pockets and pass over the handfuls of Night Queen Blossoms to Tavis. His eyes widen in disbelief.

"Hopefully that's enough for you and your pack," Elias tells him.

Grinning broadly, he nods. "It is. Thank you," he

says. "Were you able to find the other object you came for?"

Elias's expression hardens, and he clenches his teeth. "Yes."

Tavis doesn't seem to notice; he's too focused on the flowers in his hands. He's almost giddy with excitement. "I don't think you realize what this means for us. We owe you a great deal. You've saved us all."

His gratitude is welcome, especially after everything we went through to get the damn things, but I can't help the worry still spinning through me. We may have another piece of Azrael's harp, but at what cost? What does this mean for Cain? The spine was supposed to be Banner's payment.

Collecting all the relics is my path to securing my freedom, to getting out of the demons' contract. It'll ensure Elias and Dorian can return to Hell.

But then, that would mean we would lose Cain... forever.

DORIAN

I don't know how Cain does it. How he deals with all this stress and responsibility all the time. It's no wonder he's always so uptight. I've had a headache brewing since Cold's Keep, and it's only getting worse.

I'm not made for this shit.

It's too much for me.

I can't stand it.

Once we snap Cain out of it, I swear, I'll never bust his balls about having a stick up his ass again.

Okay, maybe that's an exaggeration. I do enjoy seeing the steam come out his ears, but still.

Now I have Elias's brooding to deal with and Aria's silent and stubborn thinking. Yes, I know we had a rough go of it in Scotland with the Black Castle. We definitely didn't expect to find a relic or to be faced with the fact that we were meant to give it up to the necromancer to save Cain's life, but life's funny that way. Always throwing challenges at you to see how much you squirm.

Cain is better equipped to handle this stuff than me. And that's why I've already decided what we're going to do with the spine.

Give it to Banner.

I don't know if Elias is on board with this plan, but I have a pretty good feeling he is. We both owe Cain too much to give up on him that fast.

So, as we all sit on the jet back to the states, each of us reserved to our own thoughts, I decide now is the best time to lay everything on the line. That way we all know where we stand.

I glance at Aria's satchel that I've tossed on the opposite seat and then at my new, very wrinkled, collared shirt. Since the spine is currently wrapped in my sweater in the bag, I was forced to make a quick swap for the first thing I could find in my luggage.

Clearing my throat, I wait for Aria and Elias to look over. "I think we all have something on our minds, so it looks like I'm the one with the big enough cojones to say it out loud." I draw in a breath. "We have another relic. The spine. And I think we all know what we have to do with it."

Elias crosses his arms and sinks lower in his chair. Aria scoots to the edge of hers, nervously chewing on her bottom lip.

"We're going to give it to the necro and save Cain, of course," I say.

Aria lets go of the breath she's holding. "Oh, thank God."

"God has nothing to do with it, sweetheart." I laugh. "It's common sense, really."

Aria turns to Elias, who still hasn't said a word.

"What say you, hellhound?" I ask him. "You have an opinion on this?"

His chin lifts, his expression still heavy with anger and regret. "There's nothing left for me back in Hell," he mumbles before looking at Aria, and it doesn't take a rocket scientist to know what he's referring to. Serena. "Cain's life is more important. I say we give up the spine. It's only trouble, anyway."

"I wasn't too keen on the place either," I reply and glance at Aria. "Besides, Earth's growing on me."

A blush touches her cheeks, and she smiles.

"Then we're all in agreement?" I ask the room. They nod their answer. "No matter what, we save Cain first. Hell can wait."

CHAPTER FIFTEEN
ELIAS

"Thank fuck we're almost home. I never want to see another castle for as long as I live," I state, emerging from the airport with bags in hand and staring up at a familiar night sky.

Aria steps up alongside me, cradling Cassiel in her arms, while Dorian drags the rest of the bags, mostly filled with Scottish shortbread cookies for her. I tried them on the flight back home and they weren't anything to rave about, but if my little rabbit likes them, then she'll have a pantry's worth.

"I think I slept most of the trip," she says while yawning.

"No, you didn't sleep the whole way," Dorian corrects her. "You stirred the whole trip and put your legs all over me." He is already storming ahead of us toward the small parking station for those who fly in on private jets. "Let's go and get this shit over with already," he calls to us over his shoulder.

Aria dashes after Dorian, and I march after them, not in the mood to deal with a necromancer after a ten-hour flight. But I also want to heal Cain and get the hell out of dodge, then return home.

By the time we are on the road, everyone falls quiet, and it's only the purring motor and tires racing along the asphalt that sounds, and I feel uncomfortable. I hate being in damn cars, especially a tiny Ferrari.

"Why are you fidgeting so much?" Dorian asks.

"Hate this fucking car. It's a tin can with us squished in here like sardines."

Dorian barks a laugh. "The only person feeling that way is you, bruh. Just sit back and chill."

He leans forward and jabs a finger on the radio button. "Staying Alive" by the Bee Gees plays. Dorian and I groan in unison as he beats me to reach for the button to change the station.

"Leave it," Aria calls from in the back seat where she's lounging with Cassiel, humming to the song.

I exchange looks with Dorian, who shrugs and focuses back on the driving, his fingers already tapping the steering wheel to the beat. And suddenly we're flying down the highway. I grip the door handle, my teeth clenched so tight I'm going to snap them.

"Slow the fuck down," I bellow over the music.

"Whatever, grandpa," he responds.

All I can think is how easy it would be right now to slam my fist into the side of his head, but I don't want to hurt Aria when lead foot here ends up slamming into a tree or something.

Huffing, I tug at the seatbelt strangling me and turn my attention to the forest we fly past.

The song does nothing to soothe me; the words are way too close to home. We're constantly trying to stay alive, it seems. I realize in that moment that the danger escalated around the time Aria joined us, and that makes me fucking adore her even more. As a demon, I'm a damn magnet for trouble, but to see my girl have the same magnetic attraction to all things dark warms my blood.

Unsure how long we've been driving with a madman at the wheel, I grip onto the door and let myself drown in the awful music. It's only when we slow down to a cruising pace that I perk up. We pass the Norwich town sign.

"We're close." Aria voices my exact thought, and the eagerness in her voice to finish this has me twisting my head to glance back at her. She's staring out the window, almost with awe at the quaint town, while Cassiel, who's draped over her lap, stares at me like he's staked his claim.

Joke's on you, cat.

The rest of the trip doesn't take long, and it's only when we turn down a narrow dirt road amid massive pines that I start noticing that nothing looks familiar. "This isn't where we traveled last time?"

We're jostling in our seats like popping corn, the rough land slaughter to the car's suspension, and even our high beams are jumping all over the woods. I hold onto the door with a death grip. "I-I d-don't think this is a road."

Cassiel half-meows, half-growls from the back.

"Ramos texted me with a shortcut he found to the bridge," Dorian yells over the music and crunching soil under our wheels. "That way we don't have to carry Cain through the woods for miles."

"W-well, I can't argue with that."

"Cain's already here?" Aria gasps with excitement from the back seat.

Before Dorian answers, his headlights splash across our black Town Car, parked near a clearing in the woods up ahead. Ramos is standing outside the car, staring our way, dressed in black pants and a matching shirt like he's trying to dull the stark whiteness of his hair and skin.

We stop, and Aria leaps out of the car, Cassiel on her heels before Dorian even switches off the engine. She darts to the Town Car as Ramos opens the back door to where Cain must be.

I get out and stretch my back, my spine cracking from being cramped up, while Dorian heads to the trunk and grabs the wrapped-up relic. The moment we discovered we had retrieved a relic that we needed to open the portal to Hell for us, there was no doubt in any of our minds that we'd use it to save Cain. But still… we are about to give away an object we'd sought after for decades.

I breathe heavily, having no real intention of

leaving it here for long. First, heal Cain. Second, find a way to take it back. One step at a time.

I join Ramos, who says, "You took your time getting here. Been here for over an hour."

"Dorian had no idea where he was going." I lie on purpose, sensing Dorian coming up behind me.

He glares at me, then turns to Aria as she twists to face us. Cain is lying inside on the back seat, all cradled with pillows and blankets, his legs bent to fit in. My stomach tightens to see him this way. He's always been the strong one who never fell down, who stood by all of our sides.

It fucking stings, because I can't lose him… we can't lose him. He's kept us together. As annoying as he can be, he's everything. Fuck.

"He looks bad—really bad—like he's almost dead." Her cheeks pale, and I hear the panic in her voice. "Is he going to be okay?" She keeps looking back into the car and then at us, her arms wrapping around her middle.

"I had to move him from the stasis, so he'll be deteriorating quicker now," Ramos explains.

My chest tightens. He's a thorn in my side most days, but he's my family, the brother I never had, and I sure as fuck can't lose him.

"We need to hurry," I say.

"Then let's do this. Who's carrying him?" Dorian asks, looking at me.

"I'll do it," Ramos states before I can respond, standing tall like this is a burden he feels responsible to carry. And I can't take that away from him. "He's my master, and this is my task."

No one says a word, but we all watch how skillfully Ramos pulls Cain out of the car, feet first, then leans in and retreats swiftly with Cain leaning over his shoulder. The dhampir doesn't struggle with the chore. I shut the door behind him.

"It's this way," Aria murmurs. "The magic is heavy tonight."

I nod, mostly to myself. She's right—the air feels thick tonight with magic, with tension, with trepidation.

Dorian and Aria take the lead, with Cassiel in her arms. While I'd prefer she leave the furball behind, that's not an argument I want to have now. Not when the priority is healing Cain, and fast. I fall back, staying close to Ramos in case he needs assistance.

My skin dances with the hum of magic. It's like a drizzle of rain across my flesh, a reminder that what we're dealing with here is dangerous as fuck.

We move quickly now through the woods, and there is barely a pause in Aria's step when she reaches the invisible bridge. Like the first time, once we cross and the town comes into view, the place is empty, but there's no wasting time as we hurry down the street.

Anyone looking at us might find us an odd bunch, but something tells me this town is used to a lot of oddities. Then again, with seeing no one, most houses with no lights, I wonder if anyone even lives here. Well, except for the necromancer.

The front gates of the cemetery sit open like we're expected. I dart forward and push them wider, making it easier for Ramos to pass through with Cain, and then we're practically running through the graveyard to the crypts in the back.

Urgency bites my insides. The more I stare at Cain's limp body, at the way his arms dangle across Ramos's back like he's nothing but a sack of rice, the more my heart thunders in my chest with worry that we've wasted the last days he had.

Without a doubt, when I walk out of this cemetery, it will be either with Cain by my side, or I'll have just buried the necro's broken body in a fresh grave.

ARIA

My toe twitches like crazy as we enter Banner's crypt, Cassiel held tight under my arm so he doesn't try eating one of those dead rodents. My skin crawls. I hate being back here again, inhaling the heavy stench of earth, swerving around dead rats. But they're not really dead—we saw that last time. I want to scream every time I accidentally step on one, and I cringe at the sound of breaking bones. Can they feel it when they reanimate back alive?

Dorian has taken the lead, and it isn't long before we all cram into Banner's room that smells stuffy and for some reason like talcum powder. Elias shuts the door behind us.

"Quicky, place him here," Banner instructs, his hand flapping over the table, while Dorian, Elias, and Ramos gently maneuver Cain's body onto what looks like an operating table, being careful not to touch the vials of blood dangling above.

I'm patting Cassiel, who is surprisingly quiet and curled in my arms.

Banner claps, almost too excited, looking ridiculous as he smiles widely. Like before, he's wearing thick-framed glasses, his hair wild. He's in his nerdy personality, but he's dressed in tailored pants and a white button-up shirt like he's about to go out on the town. Except the town was dead out there when we passed through.

Maybe he has a date? I almost laugh at that. Would anyone want to date a necromancer?

Says the girl infatuated with three demons.

I'm chewing on my inner cheek, my eyes glued to Cain laying on his back, his eyes closed. My stomach hurts with worry. It takes everything inside me to not rush over to his side, hold his hand, and whisper in his ear how much I missed him.

"I'm guessing this means the trip was a success?" Banner asks, sticking his chest out. His eyes flick between all of us before landing on the parcel wrapped up in Dorian's hand.

That's when something glinting around Banner's throat catches my attention. I squint for a closer look at the golden chain, following it down to the golden wing pendant over his chest.

Fire ignites in the pit of my chest.

Is he kidding me right now? I lower Cassiel to the floor because I don't trust myself right now not to throw him, claws and all, to attack Banner.

"That's my necklace," I hiss, grabbing everyone's attention. Fury licks across my nape.

I forget everything but the anger rising through me like waves. The one thing I have from Cain... To see this grave-digging, rat loving, asshole wearing what belongs to me burns me up alive.

He glances down and fingers the pendant, flipping it across his chest.

My heart hammers, my breaths sawing in and out past my lips. "Give it back!"

He lowers his arms by his side, stiffening. "Nah, I think I'll keep it."

I take a step forward. "You fucking—"

"What she means to say," Dorian interrupts me, his strong hand around my waist drawing me against him, "is that we want to get this over with as fast as possible. We're on a tight deadline here. Then we can exchange the relic for the necklace."

I'm glaring at Banner, who hasn't taken his eyes off me, the corners of his mouth twitching into a cruel smirk. He enjoys seeing me suffer... Why else would he wear what belongs to me? The fury bubbling inside me builds until my whole body trembles. I try with every ounce of strength to bite my tongue, to stop myself from crawling right over Cain and ripping it off his puny neck.

"Hand over the object," Banner commands, jutting his arm toward Dorian, his palm upward, fingers curling back and forth with urgency.

"That's not part of the deal," Elias barks. "We got what you wanted. It's right here. Now heal Cain." A growl hangs at the end of his words, tension billowing in the room.

"I don't have to do anything for you. Give me my object or your friend dies."

"Master," Ramos pleas, turning to Dorian, imploring him with huge eyes. He wants us to just do as the necromancer demands.

Ramos is right, as much as I hate admitting it. Banner holds the upper hand over us. I never knew I could hate a stranger as much as I do him.

"Heal him," Dorian demands, energy sparking over my skin as his power expands. Only, Banner looks unfazed.

"You're wasting my time with your meager parlor tricks," Banner snaps, his voice echoing off the walls around us. "We had a deal, so hand it over or get the fuck out and take your dead friend with you."

Silence permeates the room. There is no way Banner is going to back down. While I promise myself I won't leave until I claw my necklace from around his neck, I want Cain healed.

"Dorian, just do it," I say, my hands fisting. I

swallow past my dry throat and can barely breathe. "Cain comes first."

"Good girl," Banner patronizes me. I loathe the way he's leering at me, and images of being alone with him cover me in goosebumps.

A gravelly growl steals my thoughts and draws them to Elias, who's seething.

Dorian steps past me and sets the spine, still wrapped up, on the table next to Cain's legs. My toe hasn't stopped buzzing in its presence, twitching inside my shoe.

I can only imagine how hard it must be for Dorian and Elias to give up one of the keys to getting home.

With shaky hands, Banner tenderly unwraps the relic. The moment he reveals the white, curled spine, the faint music plays in my mind again, just as it had back in the Black Castle. My toe jumps about in my shoe like crazy. Of all the relics I've seen to date, this one has to be the creepiest, resembling a real spine way too much for my liking.

"Don't touch it with your bare hands," Dorian warns sharply, throwing out his arm to stop his grubby fingers from making contact.

Banner licks his lips excitedly. "So you found out first-hand the power it carries, did you? Who was it? Who touched it?"

No one answers, and he scoffs. "You are no fun." He flips his hand at us, like suddenly we are the boring ones not bringing him entertainment. I'm still livid that he is wearing my necklace, and I glare at him the whole time.

Not that he notices.

He hurriedly wraps the spine relic back up, grabs it, and carries it to the set of drawers against the back wall. There he pulls open the second drawer and slips it inside. We are all watching him, and when he turns to us, his expression is no longer the cheery, nerdy man, but he appears to have almost morphed back to the man we'd met in the graveyard on our first day. He stands tall, his shoulders seeming broader, and he even takes his glasses off, then pats his wild hair down. The man before us is terrifying.

With a click of his tongue, he turns his attention to Cain, while shadows seem to gather around the necromancer. I blink, unsure if I'm seeing correctly. Inside me, Sayah is doing somersaults, sensing all the dark magic around us. And maybe the danger.

His lips are moving, but no words come out, and I realize he's started his mojo to heal Cain. Okay, that was sudden, but I'm not complaining.

I stay completely still. So do Dorian, Elias, and Ramos. We're mesmerized to see this happen.

Sure, Cain isn't dead, but he's so close to death's door, it mightn't be much different. Nerves wriggle up my spine, and as if sensing my unease, Dorian places a hand against my lower back while Elias, on my other side, takes my hand into his, our fingers intertwined.

Banner swiftly bends forward, rummaging with

something under the table we can't see, then emerges gripping a long-ass syringe and a small metal cage with a rat inside.

A gasp escapes my lips, but like the rest of us, I don't say anything else. Elias's hand squeezes mine slightly, a comforting gesture, yet my heart doesn't stop beating.

Banner begins chanting a tune with incomprehensible lyrics, something slow and almost painful to listen to, something sorrowful. Maybe he's singing for death to stay away.

With the rat in the cage set between Cain's legs, Banner pulls up Cain's sleeve, taps his inner elbow, then unceremoniously jabs the needle into his arm.

I cringe at how painful it looks.

He draws the plunger at the base of the syringe backward, the barrel quickly filling with Cain's black blood. Once full, he yanks the needle out, then reaches for the cage. He flips open the door on top, then sticks his hand in and lifts out a rat that looks already half dead. It doesn't even make a sound, hanging limply from his hand.

Banner never once stops his song, not even when he jabs the needle into the animal and plunges Cain's blood into him.

I'm holding still, struggling to breathe, my thoughts running with panic and hundreds of questions, mostly revolving around this rat having Cain's blood. Could it be used against him in the future?

Banner dumps the rat back in the cage, locks it

up, then leaves it there at the end of the table. Quickly he returns the syringe under the table, and when he rises back up this time, he exhales loudly, the song on his lips diminishing.

A chill crawls up my arms, my breath misty and floating in front of my face suddenly, like we've been plunged into icy waters. I curl up against Dorian's side, while Elias closes in, pinning me between them as my teeth chatter.

"Arise, arise, I charge and command thee." Banner raises his arms into the air and repeats the words, and with it each time comes an unbearable coldness. Ramos doesn't notice, but then again, he is a dhampir, so wouldn't feel the chill.

The dark mist has returned from behind Banner, sliding through the air like tentacles, each reaching outward for Cain.

I stiffen, my nails digging into the palm of my free hand. A growl erupts around us, something deathly dark and terrifying. I swing my gaze left and right, all around us, but all I see is more of the mist filling every crevice and space in the room. It seems to be closing in around us.

Banner unleashes a screeching sound that has me jumping in my skin.

I jerk my attention to him as he lays his open palms onto Cain's chest. Dark serpent-like limbs made of mist spear right into Cain's body, over and over. Then they swoop back out of him from under the table, each then rushing toward the caged rat, doing exactly the same to the critter. Though the thing just sits there, its nose twitching.

I don't know how long this goes on for, but it feels like it's hours, when it's most likely only a few minutes.

Fog rises around us now, thicker, heavier, stealing from us our vision. I wrench my head higher to see above the mist, not wanting to lose sight of what Banner is doing. But it's futile, as it comes at us fast, enveloping everything in sight.

I cling to my men while a sensation of drowning overwhelms me. My vision is stolen, and I blink against the dark mist, and in that moment we could be anywhere. The only thing keeping us grounded is Banner's rising voice.

"Arise, arise, I charge and command thee."

The hairs on my arms rise, and I can't help but take a step forward to see what's going on. It's a cruel thing to conceal Cain from us.

My heart thunders as I search through the fog for movement when Banner stops chanting.

Silence.

It's dead quiet, and I feel the rush of air against my face, plunging through my hair, icy to the touch.

I tremble as a shudder races through my stomach. An unexpected gasp of breath slips through the room, and with it, the fog diminishes before our eyes.

The first thing I see is the damn rat laying in the cage on its side, tongue sticking out of its mouth. It's dead. Frantically, I push forward, scanning the table. My gaze rushes up Cain's body.

He abruptly jerks upward to sit up on the table, knocking into the dangling vials of blood. His eyes are wide open, bloodshot, a deathly bellow on his lips.

I flinch, my insides tight as an elastic band, and it feels like I'm going to burst from the tension gripping me.

Next thing, he collapses back down on the table, his back and head thumping the hard surface.

"Ouch," I mumble under my breath and then ask, "did it work?"

The rat is dead… so it has to have worked. I can't take my eyes off Cain, at the color that has come back into his cheeks, the steady rise and fall of his chest.

I want to cry, to scream with glee, yet I'm caught on the fringe of having a full-blown panic attack that he may not be alive. I want to desperately shake him awake, to make sure I haven't lost him.

Dorian is at Cain's side, Elias at mine, while Ramos is staring in disbelief.

"Well, that's it," Banner assures me, his remark flippant.

"Then why isn't he awake?" I snap back, so sick and tired of this guy. He turns his back to me as he heads across the room.

"Careful, you damn shaggy cat!" Banner suddenly screeches, lunging toward the bookshelf against the back wall.

That's when I notice Cassiel perched up on the top bookshelf, precariously balancing on the thin ledge in front of a collection of objects. It all happens so fast. Cassiel jerks to the attacking necromancer, panics, the back of his neck fuzzed up. He darts across the shelf to leap off. His back leg kicks into the hurricane-shaped vase filled with what looks like soil. The same one I'd seen on my last visit here.

Cassiel leaps away.

The vase tumbles and hits the ground, crashing loudly, glass and soil thrown in every direction.

Banner bellows like a beast, like somehow this is the worst thing in the world.

Electricity snaps across the room like tiny white threads of web, striking each of us, throwing us back and against the wall.

I cry out, slamming into a chair that breaks under me from the impact. Dorian is groaning, Ramos is sprawled on the floor, and Elias is already climbing up.

In front of us, a plume of electrifying energy billows upward from where the vase crashed, rising like a mushroom cloud. It reminds me of images of the atomic bomb going off, and a sharp whine slips from me.

This is bad. Really, really bad.

"Fuck!" I shove to my feet to reach Cassiel, terrified Banner is going to hurt him, while Elias rounds the table on the other end to find him. The electric storm takes up half the room, messed-up white threads twisting and threading together like a tangled spiderweb. Energy sparks each time two of the lines rub against each other.

"Cassiel," I call out while Ramos and Dorian rush to get Cain out of danger.

Cassiel bursts out of the storm cloud, meowing loudly. He's leaping and bounding over the shelves and cupboards, unable to get away fast enough, his fur explosive across his back. Aside from him freaking out, he looks unharmed.

Suddenly, Cassiel lunges for the table in the middle of the room, and Elias snatches him midflight.

"We need to get out of here," I choke out. Except my attention hooks on long, talon-tipped fingers emerging from the chaotic, dark miasma. I stare at them with horror, unable to move. I draw in sharp, shallow breaths.

A figure emerges from within, wearing an expression of death. He stands tall, broad shoulders, his torn clothes revealing leathery, dark flesh. Snarling, he lifts his snouted head back, then a roar bursts from his throat. The ear-piercing sound ricochets around us. I'm reminded of something that resembles a cross between the Hulk and a swamp creature.

A tremor shakes my chest with my strangled whimper. What the hell has Cassiel released from the vase?

The thing standing in front of us jerks his head down toward me, staring right into me with jaundiced yellow eyes. I'm paralyzed with terror, trapped under his gaze, and a familiarity washes over me. There are screams behind me, someone calling my name, but I'm frozen in shock.

I swallow hard because I'd been wrong. So fucking wrong.

This thing standing before us is no unleashed beast.

It's Banner.

What the fuck has he turned into?

CHAPTER SIXTEEN
CAIN

*C*olors flash before my eyes. Bursts of blue, red, yellow, and green.

Slowly, they move and take shape, becoming forms I recognize. The first thing I see is Aria. She's kneeling in the center of a pentagram laid out in soil, surrounded by candles. As always, she's a vision, wearing an exquisite ball gown made of lace and tulle. Her hair is twisted into a braided bun, and when her chin lifts to look at me, her painted red lips split into a brilliant smile.

My heart beats fiercely at the sight of her. She's the most beautiful woman I've ever seen in all my existence.

Dark eyes pinned on me, she rises to her feet, just as another burst of color flashes before my eyes. Then, like magic, the dress she was wearing is gone. She now stands before me completely naked.

A tingle of excitement zips right down to my

groin. I know what this is. I know what's happening here; I've witnessed this before, had participated in it with Elias and Serena. The binding ritual.

But this time, there is only me and Aria.

We are about to be bound together for all of eternity.

To my own surprise, I'm not worried like I expected to be. There's no doubt or overthinking. Just happiness. Anticipation. Especially for what comes next.

It's the part Dorian and I skipped but Elias had taken part in. The sex.

Just the thought of taking Aria lights an inferno in me.

When I glance at Aria again, blood trails down her breasts. Not her blood, though.

Lifting my hands, I find my palms cut, more of the stuff pooling.

Aria smears the blood across her chest, down her stomach, and between the apex of her thighs. I'm captivated. Her movements are sensual, her gaze heated with lust, and I'm transfixed, unable to look away. Then she reaches out, takes my hands in hers, and guides them over her body. Her skin is slick from the blood, soft, but oh so warm. She never breaks eye contact, and there's something animalistic in her gaze that awakens my own demon.

My blood blackens, mixing with the red as we both rub her breasts, squeezing, kneading, pinching her nipples. Touching her like this, covering her in my very essence, is almost as intimate as sex itself. It makes my cock hard to the point of pain, and we haven't even gotten to the really good part yet.

With her hands still over mine, she leads me to my erection and wraps my fingers around my shaft. I hiss with an excruciating desire to release. And it's also when I realize I'm naked too, my clothes having evaporated at some point without my knowledge. But I don't give a shit. All I can focus on is the delicious pressure of our hands as she starts to move them up and down, my body humming with the growing need to plunge into her.

Unable to stand it anymore, I grab the back of her head and crush my mouth against hers. My tongue dives past her lips, desperate to taste her, and she grips my chin roughly, kissing me just as aggressively while speeding up our strokes down below. Her moans drive me insane.

I growl into her mouth as the pleasure mounts, but I don't want this to end yet. Not like this.

I pull away. But as my eyes refocus, the scene around us has changed again. The pentagram, the candles, the dirt—it's all gone. Instead, we stand at the front of a grand room, hundreds of onlookers watching us with lustful eyes. They're all dressed for an expensive costume party, in medieval gowns and tailored suits of either black or red. Above us, a massive candle chandelier burns dimly, casting shadowed masks across every face. I recognize a few of the people in the crowd—first Dorian and Elias toward the front, and then Nix, Maverick, Torryn, and my other brothers.

In the back corner, I spot my father. Lucifer himself, leaning against a column in his famous black suit, with his crown of bones and teeth upon his head. Residual anger stirs in my gut at the sight of him, but when he catches me staring, he lifts his chin, as if approving of what he's witnessing.

Confused, my gaze drops, and Aria is on her knees again, tongue darting out to tease the tip of my cock. We're both still naked and covered in blood, and I realize what this party is really about. It's to witness our union.

There's a thrill that comes with being watched. It only heightens the desire spinning through me.

Aria's mouth closes in around my dick, and I can't peel my eyes off her now. Her red lips are wrapped around me, drawing me deeper and deeper, then pulling me out, worshipping me with her tongue. My fingers rake through her hair, which is now loose in thick curls around her shoulders, and use my grip to hold her in place.

When she takes me in all the way, I can feel the curve of her throat, and my mind reels with pleasure. At the same time, her fingers gently squeeze my balls, massaging, and when she pulls back again, her teeth rake across my shaft. She may not know it, but it's the kind of pleasure and pain I crave.

I moan, shivering all over.

Another flash of colorful light bursts, momentarily blinding me, but when my eyes adjust again, I'm peering up at a large gold throne with my Aria sitting in my father's place, as ruler of all of Hell, wearing the beautiful black gown I'd seen her in before. Still covered in my blood. But now, the crown of bone and teeth is upon her head.

My heart pounds in my chest at the sight of her being in charge of the underworld, both ecstatic and scared for her.

As she smiles down at me with admiration, her pupils grow, the blackness swallowing the irises and whites entirely.

Then comes the screams.

DORIAN

"Ramos, get Cain out of here," I bellow above the roaring screech behind me. I guide Cain's limp body against Ramos's to carry him the hell out of here. I have no doubt that it's Banner we're dealing with in that monstrous form. His earthy, deathly scent hasn't changed, and really, neither has his 'Dr. Jekyll and Mr. Hyde' disorder. Except, he's surprised us with a third persona. Whatever the fuck Cassiel knocked over in that glass jar has released magic. It still pricks along my arms.

"But is he healed?" Ramos asks, worry threading his words, and as if his question prompts Cain to wake up, a groan rolls from my old friend's throat.

Relief coats me despite all the chaos around us. "Sounds awake enough for me," I say, helping lift Cain onto his shoulder.

A thunderous bang sounds, shaking the ground. I snap around to find Elias sliding down from the entrance door he's just slammed into. The beast leaps after him.

"Oh fuck, change of plan. Keep Cain in the corner, protect him with your life," I order and swing to find Aria against the far wall, embracing a startled Cassiel.

I hate seeing the fear in her eyes, hate the way it wraps around my heart, squeezing until I can't breathe.

I whip around, my body buzzing with my demon side pushing forward. I embrace the darkness, let it smother me.

Banner in beast form lands on top of Elias, the necromancer growling, teeth bared. I don't wait a second. I lunge into the battle, ready to tear flesh and spill blood.

Smacking right into Banner's back, I drive him off Elias, both of us rolling to the ground. His eyes widen from the shock, and I laugh in his face, seizing his neck, squeezing. I drive a fist into his gut as Elias leaps onto him, slamming fist after fist into his face. Blood spurts in every direction. I watch, curious, enjoying every second as Banner belches a painful sound.

A sudden chill slides over my skin and Elias jerks back, meeting my gaze. He feels the change in the air.

Banner stiffens beneath us, falling quiet, blood spilling from the corner of his mouth. He's pinned against the floor yet grins like somehow he's got the upper hand on us.

Just as fast as we pause, tendrils of smoke pour out from his mouth, from his nose, like serpents. They spear toward us, striking everything and anywhere. My cheek, my neck, my chest, my thighs. I fling my arms at them, my touch rushing right through them, only to have the severed misty limb re-emerge.

"Fuck!" I stumble backward, as does Elias, the spots the attack hit stinging fast and brutal. The sharp pain lingers, but there is no break of skin. It's a pure magical strike, meant to hurt, to scare us off.

And it's fucking working.

Up on my feet, I recoil out of reach just enough to catch my breath and gather my wits. What the hell are we dealing with?

"Death touch," Elias mutters as if he reads my thoughts, both of us facing off against Banner, who suddenly appears larger than before. A big fucking brute, his shirt hanging off him in shreds, his skin dark and leathery like so many demons I've seen in Hell. What pact has he made to hold such power?

He looks like a disturbing sonofabitch with his mouth gaping open and black things spilling out of his mouth and nostrils.

A haunting question slips over my mind... If Banner is harnessing the power of death, how can we kill him? How do we kill something that teeters on the edge of life and the afterlife?

My boots crunch on the spilled earth from the broken jar, sidestepping him as he turns toward Aria, who is now near Ramos. Cain is standing on his own two feet, looking dazed, letting the wall hold him, but *shit yeah*, he's back.

"We do this." I throw myself after Banner, throwing over my shoulder, "We restrain him if all else fails and get everyone out of here."

Elias is stripping before I finish my words, the sparks of energy from his transformation racing up my arms. His body contorts, and he falls to his knees, transforming, the agony clear. I never envied his ability to shift.

I crash into Banner, my impact forcing him sideways. He collides into the table, his head knocking into the hanging vials of blood. I hate those damn things, and I snatch one, ripping it from the rope and smashing it into the side of Banner's head.

"You fucking asswipe," I growl, reaching for another, figuring the rope will be great for tying him the hell up.

He swings around so fast, blurs are all I see in front of my face. His death limbs strike, punching me over and over.

I yell, the agony slicing through me.

Elias comes out of nowhere, slamming him from behind, and we're on the ground once more in a tangle of excruciating pain from his damn attack.

"Back the fuck down!" I shout in his face, but my voice, my power, has zero impact on him.

We are so fucked.

ARIA

I flinch as the guys and Banner hit the ground fast, my heart threatening to break past my ribcage. Cassiel remains in my arms, the poor thing shaking.

"The soil," Cain gasps, the word breathy. He's recovered and I should be cheering, except I'm petrified of what Banner has become, of what he'll do to us.

"W-What?" I drag my gaze from the battle to Cain, who's breathing heavily, Ramos still helping him stay upright.

Cain points to the ground where the spilled earth covers the floor, along with shards of glass. "Earth holds magic. Throw it on him," he gasps, sucking in shallow breaths.

"You need to rest," Ramos instructs him.

I set Cassiel down, churning over his words. I don't understand how that will help, but I'll try anything.

My feet seem to move on their own, around the table, and I freeze at seeing Elias and Dorian embroiled in a fight on the ground. They move so fast, so terrifyingly so, all I see are arms, legs, and a black mist.

Soil. Right.

My pulse is on fire and every inch of me shivers, but I know we don't have time. Practically leaping over them, I rush to the back of the room where there are more shelves with all sorts of artifacts. Soil is all over the floor, scattered thinly, sprayed over everything. And of course there is no broom in here.

So I do the next best thing. Frantically, I scoop as much dirt as possible, shards of glass included, and stand up, suddenly feeling lost on what I'm meant to do.

Throw it on Banner.

God, is this right?

He's still caught up in the fight, Elias in wolf form suddenly snatching him by the arm and flinging him into a set of shelves, everything from it tumbling down and crashing down on his head.

Panic flares inside me, spreading through me so fast. But I don't let it get to me. I rush forward, and just as those smokey snakes strike up for me, I toss the pile of dirt I've collected right into Banner's face.

Recoiling, I hold my breath, waiting to see what happens. Banner screams almost instantly, and the beast before us seems to melt away like it had been a mask this whole time. Yeah, a mask for his entire body.

I cringe and almost gag at how gross it looks to watch skin peel away.

"More soil," Ramos yells out, and I jerk my head up to see Cain telling him what to say. "Don't stop until he's gone."

"Okay." So many things are going through my mind, so many emotions, but I hit the floor and rapidly scoop up more. Then I rush over and dump it on Banner, who is shuddering, attempting to get to his feet.

Dorian and Elias join in and help me. No time to waste.

Banner screams, grasping the pieces of his face and neck as they continue to peel from his bones. As if it's acid. The more dirt we fling at him, the faster it does its job. The putrid odor of rotting flesh assaults my nose.

I am already reaching for another pile of loose earth when a hand taps my back. A small cry rushes past my throat and I spin around, coming face to face with Dorian. I'm so tense, so high strung, that I feel like I might burst apart.

"It's done, he's gone," he assures me, while I keep staring at the purple bruises across his face and neck, the cut below his hairline near his temple. Elias isn't faring any better, but they'll heal fast. I've seen them do it.

I glance past Dorian and over to Banner, who's back to his normal, nerdy self, slumped on the ground. His skin is pale blue, like he's been dead for a lot longer than a few seconds, and his body is stiff, like rigor mortis has set in… which can't be right. It doesn't happen so quickly.

"Whatever he's been doing," Dorian explains, "it seems like he sold part of his humanity to possess such power. So death comes for him quickly now."

I lower my head, no longer wanting to look at his dead body or how he's decaying right before my eyes. I should be celebrating that he's defeated, that somehow a bunch of soil was his undoing. But I just want to leave this room… His tomb.

Except he still has my necklace. I push past Dorian and hold my breath as I lean down and reach for the golden pendant. Barely able to stand looking at Banner this close, I quickly tuck my hands behind his neck and unlatch the chain. My skin crawls at touching his cold skin, every inch of me demanding I scream. All I picture is him coming to life and grabbing my arm.

"I want to leave," I say hastily, retreating back across the room, tucking the necklace into my pocket. "No more cemeteries for me."

"Couldn't agree more." Dorian retrieves the relic from the drawer where Banner had hidden it. Of course he won't forget that… It's another piece to help get them home. I push aside the avalanche of emotions that roll over me each time I think about the relics and where they will eventually lead.

Elias is back in his human form, naked and spectacular, but he's already pulling his clothes on. Cain, with Ramos's help, is moving toward the door.

Cassiel rubs himself against my feet, vibrating with his purr. I lift him into my arms, and he feels heavy against me. Or maybe my muscles are so worn out that I can barely stand on my own two feet.

As everyone begins to leave, I stare back into the room on my way out, my eyes finding Banner. If what Dorian said about Banner is correct, then there is nothing to mourn. When he chose this path, he knew fate would eventually catch up with him.

I turn and hurry outside.

My muscles quiver by the time we emerge from the crypt and step into the cool night's embrace. I breathe easy, my shoulders sagging as Cassiel snuggles up against my chest. "It's finally over," I whisper to him.

"Is it just me or does Cassiel look… even bigger," Elias says to me, staring down at my little cat as I lift my gaze to him.

"He's probably still fuzzed up from being terrified in there. Plus, you know he's a growing boy." I kiss his head again.

He eyes us both, looking like he might say something, but I don't care tonight about his jealousy of Cassiel. I'm just glad that Cain is healed and we all survived.

CHAPTER SEVENTEEN
ARIA

The car hums beneath me, but then again, I am in the Town Car with Ramos at the wheel, who unlike Dorian, doesn't drive like a madman. Cain sits alongside me in the back seat, still looking sickly pale, which is a huge improvement compared to how he looked on death's door back in the crypt. My hand is on his and I squeeze it, my heart beating faster than it should. My touch gains me a soft smile from him.

In that same moment, Dorian's Ferrari bullets past us, and I can almost hear Elias groaning in protest. He went with Dorian, which I bet he regrets now.

Cain makes a mocking sound in his throat at seeing Dorian fly by us.

"You know what's funny," I say. "Elias insisted on taking Cassiel with them so he could use him as an excuse for Dorian to slow down his driving."

"Doesn't seem to be working." Cain groans, then clears his throat.

"As long as Cassiel isn't hurt, they can bicker all they want." Though I also know they'd do anything to protect him, like how Elias saved him in the crypt. It warms my heart to see him caring for my little cat. Which reminds me of how we defeated Banner.

"Cain, how did you know the soil would be Banner's kryptonite?"

He shuffles to get more comfortable in the seat, while shadows gather under his eyes that have everything to do with his body still recovering. "Soil is a powerful element that holds onto magic, especially death magic. When I saw what impact the spilled earth had on the necromancer, it made sense that whatever spell he'd used to empower himself was in the soil. You know that many necromancers make deals with demons. Their soul for unimaginable power, but there is always a weakness, and for Banner it was he had to keep his power close to him. Unleash it, and his ability is shattered."

"I had no idea." The more he tells me, the more I want to read up on all the different supernaturals and their abilities. To better understand the world around me.

"But I don't care about him anymore. Just us." He's wearing a serious expression, and my heart beats quicker. "I failed you, Aria. I vowed to keep you safe, not the other way around, because you are meant for such great things."

"Hey, who said I can't be the hero sometimes? And I did have some help from Dorian, Elias, and even Cassiel over in Scotland."

His brows rise. "Scotland?"

"Oh, Cain, you will not believe what we went through." I twist to face him, adjusting my seatbelt, and dive into telling him about our adventure, my voice a lot more excited than I had expected. From the Scottish shifter pack, the curse, my Harry Potter tourist binge, the secret room, the Black Castle, and most importantly that we found another relic.

I realize I've been talking for a long time once I stop and my throat is parched.

"Aria," he murmurs, softness capturing his expression as he gets me a bottle of water from the side pocket of the door. "You did all that for me?"

"We all did. You'd do the same for us."

I accept the water and start drinking, then twist the lid back on and dump the bottle on the seat next to me. Memories crowd in my mind of all the times we faced danger and uncertainty, the ache of losing Cain driving me to never stop.

"I would lay my life down for you." He reaches over and cups the side of my face, his palm large and warming.

His words take me by surprise. I mean, I put myself in danger for him too, yet the way he says it is so heartfelt, so sincere that it takes me off guard.

"I've missed seeing your smile," I say. "I never want to lose you again. We came too close."

He tilts his head to the side, studying me. "You care that much?"

I huff as if he hadn't just asked me that question. "Of course. Isn't it obvious?" A blush runs up my neck, heating me at how easily I admitted that out loud to him.

The corner of his mouth curls upward in an adorable, lopsided smile that looks utterly gorgeous on him. The way he stares at me destroys any walls I hold up between us, and I forget everything else. Maybe it's the whole 'Cain's not going to die' vibe, but I can't remember a time I've been happier to be in his presence.

He blinks slowly. Clearly his body is still recovering, soI lean gently against his touch.

"How are you feeling?" I ask.

"Aside from the need to sleep for a week straight, I feel incredible. No more pain." He lowers his hand from my face and his solid arm scoops around my waist, drawing me closer to him.

I stare back up at him, at his smile, and my body quivers, my cheeks flushing with heat from the way I can't stop myself from staring at his lips. How much I missed them on me, his attentiveness. When did I let myself become so smitten with Cain? He's like a drug I can't seem to get enough of. I'm addicted to him, plain and simple. I finally have him here with me, yet I'll always want more of him.

He leans in and kisses my lips, powerful and short. I cling to him, letting myself be in the moment, to let it sink in that Cain is safe, that we succeeded, that for once we don't have danger on our heels. He breaks away, and I nestle my head on his chest, content.

"I never want you to endanger yourself for me again," he whispers softly, kissing the top of my head.

My mouth parts with a response, but his fingers brush over my lips, stealing my words. "I'm not negotiating this with you. Thank you for everything, but I should have been the one to keep you safe, not the one falling. I am the person who will make this world safe for you." His voice cracks, and he holds me tighter against him.

As much as I want to protest, I decide to just stay in his arms, to let him feel a level of contentment. He feels guilty? God, I know that feeling all too well, so I just stay by his side so he knows I'm there for him. Cain has always been the strong one, taking charge, so to hear him struggling with the insecurity of guilt is new. And I can't help but adore him even more for it.

As his breaths deepen, I stay wrapped in his arms, knowing he's drifted off to sleep. I try to consider his words, knowing without doubt he spoke from a place of fear from how close to death he came. When the time comes, I will need to find a way to explain to him that it's alright if he sometimes stumbles. That's why we have each other.

For the rest of the trip, Cain slips in and out of sleep, but he never once releases me from his hold. I kiss his arm around me, then notice that despite the night outside, the streetlights and woods look familiar. I stiffen and stare out the front of the car as we drive through the front gates of our mansion.

"We're home," I whisper.

Home. The world lingers on my mind. When did I start thinking of the demons' mansion as my home?

I'm too exhausted to think beyond that, especially when I remind myself that I don't really have another home to go to, not after losing Murray. Sure, I have Joseline, but she's already got a roommate. I have nothing, no one... is that why I cling to these three demons? Because they offer me what I don't have?

Gravel crunches under our tires as we cruise up to the front door of the house, and I am just eager to climb into bed and sleep. Cain wakes up, turning his attention to the yard.

"It feels great to be back," he murmurs.

The cool night air greets us as we climb out of the Town Car, and I yawn, stretching my back. My whole body hurts, from my ears, for some reason, down to my toes. Ramos is quick to help Cain into the house when the Ferrari roars down the driveway.

How the heck did we beat them back here? Knowing Dorian, I would not be surprised if they took the scenic route.

They pull up near the Town Car, and the passenger door swings open instantly. Elias bursts out, sporting a huge tear across the front of his shirt.

"What the hell?" I mutter.

He eyes me like somehow I've done something horrible. "We have a small... no, a big problem."

Coldness washes over me, and the same dread returns. "What now?"

He leans back into the car and pulls forward his seat just as Dorian emerges from the driver's side. He greets me with the same judging look, as though whatever happened, they are blaming me.

"What's going on?" I ask.

A huge, striped, gray blur lunges out of the vehicle. It takes me moments to work out what I'm staring at.

I blink, frozen on the spot, convinced I must be seeing things. A full-sized lynx, easily reaching my hips, pounces around the front yard, sniffing a nearby tree.

"Cassiel?"

His head props up and he swings around, coming right in my direction.

"He's your problem now," Elias practically roars, and that's when I notice the tears on the back of his shirt too. He marches inside, right past Cain, who is watching, as stunned as me, from the doorway.

"What the hell did you do to Cassiel?" I ask, hoping Dorian will be more forthcoming.

"Gorgeous, this wasn't us, but I'm guessing whatever he spilled in Banner's crypt has somehow sped up his growth. Except he still seems to think he's a kitten. He's torn up the back seat of my Ferrari!" He cuts Cassiel a glare as the feline rubs up against me, almost pushing me over from his sheer size and strength.

"Oh, Cassiel." I glance down and rub the thick fur across his head and ears. It's so soft and lush. "My boy, look what happened to you." He keeps pushing his head against my leg, and I crouch down in front of him. His head is the same size as mine, but I don't for a minute feel intimidated. He's my baby cat, and I hug him. "I still adore you, no matter your size. We may just need to work on your scratching."

My mind chokes on trying to understand if the magic soil affected Cassiel too, but my brain hurts from exhaustion, so I decide that's a job for tomorrow. I get to my feet. "Let's go to bed."

Cassiel groans and stares up at me, and I know that expression in his eyes.

"Okay, fine. Midnight snack, then sleep."

As if he understands me, he lunges toward the house and vanishes inside.

"He's going to be a huge handful," Dorian says to me as I step into the mansion. "Are you sure about keeping him?"

I gasp out loud. "Just means there's more of him to love. He is part of our family. No matter what, he's staying with us."

I crash onto the couch in the parlor in front of the crackling fireplace while Cassiel stretches out on the floor, warming himself. Elias is on the loveseat, legs stretched out, while Cain sits at the end of my couch. Dorian is the only one missing, so I guess he's sleeping in even later than me.

Cain looks more alive than yesterday, his eyes no longer bloodshot, his skin awash with color. I secretly thank Banner for helping us with Cain, even if things didn't quite turn out well for him. But when it came to him or us, we weren't going to let him take us down.

"I can't believe I slept until three p.m.," I say and lift my legs up on the couch. Cain takes them into his lap, rubbing my toes, grinning at me like his mind swims with other intentions. The kind that awakens sparks of desire through my body.

Okay, I may have just found my perfect heaven.

"Waking up this late is a first for me," I say, sinking further into the couch under Cain's tender foot rub.

"You're not the only one," Dorian answers, strolling into the room midway through pulling a black henley shirt down his chiseled chest. "I'm starving," Dorian adds. "And our cook is off for the day."

"I can make pancakes," I suggest.

"So no one is going to mention the big fat gray

furball in the room?" Elias states, ignoring the plea for food.

"Hey, he's not fat, just big boned," I say, looking down to Cassiel, who lifts his head like he understood the insult.

"Don't listen to the bad demon. You aren't fat," I coo, which has him flicking his head back down in front of the fire.

Cain says, "The necro's soil may have been responsible for the cat's growth. Although it'd be unlikely it'd be just that. Otherwise the rest of us would have been impacted too."

My thoughts fly instantly to the Storm markets, to the incident involving Cassiel. "Before we went to Banner's, I was at the Storm markets with Cassiel and he knocked over some green goo that covered him. I have no idea what that potion was, but maybe it's a combination of that and the soil?"

"You took him to the markets?" Cain asks, which is completely the wrong question to ask, seeing as I might have just worked out the reason Cassiel has grown so big.

"It's set then. Cassiel is a klutz, and nothing is safe around him," Elias throws in just to be an ass.

"It makes sense to me," Dorian mutters. "It's the only thing that explains the sudden change."

"We should definitely watch him to make sure there aren't other side effects," Cain says.

I chew on my lower lip at the implication that

anything else could happen to my Cassiel. "I think he'll be okay," I say, more to reassure myself, I think.

"Well, I'm starving," Dorian reminds us. "I'm in the mood for Chinese and some of those big egg rolls."

Just hearing him talking about food coaxes a groan from my stomach, getting everyone looking my way.

"Are you volunteering to get takeout since it'll be mostly you doing all the eating?" Dorian asks Elias. "They won't deliver out here in the woods."

Elias groans. "Fine, I'll go."

"I'll join you," I pipe in, figuring I can order what I like once we get there. "After dinner, who feels like a movie night? I want a night to completely chill and just watch something funny. I think I'm done with horror."

For the first time in too long, it seems like I'm moving forward with life, and dare I say, I even feel a bit of normalcy. Maybe it's just me craving for my life to be boring for a while.

Elias gets to his feet, rousing Cassiel to lift his head and stare at him. Both of them have a staring match before my lynx flops his head back down on the rug he's claimed. "I'll go arrange the Town Car."

"Don't be long," Cain adds, never taking his eyes from me. There is something mesmerizing to see such a gorgeous man want me by his side. Maybe the whole near-death experience has changed him a bit.

He's been more quiet than normal, but I'm sure that's just him still healing.

"We'll be back soon enough." I scramble off the couch and hurry out into the hallway where I put on my shoes and move to stand outside to wait for the car.

In no time, we're in the Town Car, Elias in the back with me, and we're in town in practically no time. He's sitting so close to me, our hips joined, which of course means he slides an arm around my back and holds me even closer.

"How are you holding up?" Elias asks, his voice soft, his fingers stroking across the side of my ribs so gently it borders on being ticklish.

"I'm ridiculously happy we aren't running for our lives anymore. Is that an emotion?" I half laugh.

He chuckles, and his warmth brushes against my body. "I'm relieved just as much, little rabbit. I think the worst has passed now."

"I hope you're right." I'm not sure how much more my heart can take.

Holmes is in the driver's seat and twists his head to face us. "This is the closest I can get you to the restaurant."

It's only then that I realize we're already parked on the curb.

"It's perfect," I say. Elias is already getting out, and I'm right behind him. "Do you want us to get you anything?"

The older man's face warms. "No thank you,

Miss. But I appreciate the thought." I shut the door and say, "We won't be long."

The streets are busy. Elias takes my hand in his and guides me through the throng of people on the sidewalk. I'm not blind to the attention he garners from numerous females. How can I blame them? If I saw a god like Elias in my path, I'd probably trip over my own feet. He is anything but ordinary, being tall and broad, and that rugged look on his face framed by wild hair would be any woman's weakness. Except he's mine, and I press myself closer to his side, beaming to see how oblivious he is to the attention.

We step past a couple who have stopped directly in front of us to have a long-winded conversation. Elias groans under his breath. "Why are there so many humans around?"

The couple looks our way strangely, and I quickly rush Elias down the sidewalk to the restaurant before he can say anything else.

My gaze suddenly falls on flowing, mousey-blonde hair and a face I know all too well. It's Joseline stepping out of a clothing store several feet away. She's laughing and holding onto the arm of a guy with super dark hair, cut short. He's got piercings on his lower lip, nose, eyebrow, ears, and I'm pretty sure a few other places I'd rather not find out. There are two other women with them, all laughing, carrying bags of purchases.

I don't recognize any of her friends, which can only mean one of them is her new witchy roommate.

Joseline looks so happy and stunning in a short black skirt that flutters around her thighs. Her top is made with strips of pearl silk running down from her shoulders, seeming to barely cover her breasts, cinched in at her waist and tucked into her skirt. She's in black high heels, too.

Sure, she's always raged on my fashion sense—or lack thereof—but I've never seen her in anything *this* revealing. And expensive-looking. She doesn't look like the friend I used to share a room with.

"You okay?" Elias asks as I pause, then he follows my line of sight. "Hey, isn't that your girlfriend?"

I nod and call out to her as I hurry closer. "Joseline."

Elias remains by my side. The four of them stop in their tracks and turn to face us, their gazes tracking us up and down.

Joseline blinks at me with a blank expression, like she's deciding if she wants to acknowledge knowing me or not.

"Oh, hey Aria," she finally says and stares up at Elias. "You've got your escort with you for your weekly outing, hey?"

I stiffen, her words like blades.

"Who's this, Josy?" the guy still holding onto her arm asks.

"Josy?" I ask, my gaze flipping to the two girls studying me, who are just as dolled up with perfect hair, glossy lipstick, and tiny dresses and heels. Suddenly I feel completely out of place in my old jeans and wrinkled graphic tee. I cringe hard. I'm burning this shirt when I get back to the mansion.

Joseline shrugs and answers defiantly, "Yeah, it's the new me. Anyway, what are you doing here?"

"We're here to order Chinese and egg rolls," Elias answers, deciding to butt in now, of all times. One of the girls giggles, and I decide I really dislike Joseline's new friends.

"Maybe we can catch up sometime soon," I say, reaching out for my friend's hand, taking it in mine, trying to get her to look at me and not her new friends.

She twists toward me, and there's a new depth behind her eyes, something almost dark.

"Maybe." She almost whispers the word before the guy with dark eye makeup and three rings in his eyebrow draws her against him.

"Shall we head off? The girls are getting restless." He looks behind him at the two women, who seem to be too busy eyeing Elias to hear the goth guy.

"Yep, I'm ready." Joseline practically bounces on her toes, her earlier expression stolen by the forced smile she wears. "See you later, Aria."

They turn and saunter right past us, my gut clenching.

"Bye, Joseline," Elias calls out loudly, then he leans in closer. "Has she always hung out with witches and a warlock?"

I gape up at him. "Wait? He was a warlock? You could sense what they were?"

He nods and starts walking toward the Chinese restaurant at the end of the block, and I hurry to catch up to him. "I could smell the magic on them. It reminds me of burned toast."

I take more steps forward and glance back to Joseline, who's laughing with her new friends. All I can think about is the last time I visited her apartment and the dark magic in her bedroom. The same items she insisted belonged to her roommate. Now, after seeing the strange expression on her face, worry curls in my chest that Joseline may be in a lot more trouble than I originally realized.

CHAPTER EIGHTEEN
ARIA

*L*ater that night, I struggle to sleep, unable to stop thinking about Joseline. What has she gotten herself into? I don't know much about witches and warlocks, except that they stick to themselves and that there are different kinds based on where they draw their power from.

I pad on bare feet out of the kitchen after enjoying a snack of leftover Chinese, and now I'm heading back upstairs, toying with the idea of paying one of the demons a visit. I doubt Dorian is asleep.

A flash of white catches the corner of my eye. Heart skipping, I turn sharply toward a window to see thick snowflakes falling from the inky night sky.

That must be what I saw. The snow.

I keep walking down the hallway toward my room, passing more tall windows with treetops already dusted white in the distance.

Just before reaching my door, something moves

across the last window, halting me in place. Okay, definitely not just the snow.

As I creep closer to the glass, a blur of white bursts from below, making me stumble backward until I hit the wall. The picture frames sway.

Stunned by what's before me, I blink. A man hovering mid-air with large, silver feathered wings. He smiles, his entire boyish face lighting up. Snow sparkles in his white hair, adding to his overall ethereal look, and I recognize him right away.

The angel. My stomach tightens at seeing him again.

There's now no doubt in my mind that's what he is. He's even got the wings to prove it. Enormous, beautiful, feathery wings that span out so wide, they take my breath away.

He points to the lock on the window, wanting me to open it. I hesitate.

Should I? I still don't know much about him, but angels are supposed to be a trustworthy lot, aren't they? All virtues and goodness? The exact opposite of demons? I just don't understand what this one wants with me. It can't only be to help me with Sayah, like he's claimed before. There has to be something else.

Cautiously, I walk over and undo the window latch. He pulls it open, and instantly, the frigid winter air rushes inside, chilling me to the bone. He perches on the ledge like an oversized, perfectly balanced bird and regards me with a friendly but curious look. Now that he's closer, I can see his wings seem to be missing some of their feathers. There are bald patches in places, red marks as if they've been ripped out. Has he been in a battle recently? It sure looked like his wings have taken some hits.

"Hello again," he says, pulling my attention back to him.

I don't respond. I wait for him to come inside, but he doesn't. He stays at the window and glances up and down the hall.

"Are we... alone?" he asks.

Trepidation prickles up my spine. "Not really. The demons are home, somewhere in the house."

"But not here, here." He grins, showing perfectly white, straight teeth. "It's just you and me?"

His words cause a flutter of excited nerves in the pit of my belly, and I don't know why. He doesn't say them in any peculiar way, but the idea of being alone with him stirs up something within me. My strange, unnatural draw toward danger or just plain ol' curiosity—who knows.

But I'm also not dumb enough to tell him I'm completely alone. I could always scream for one of the demons if I really need to. They were just nearby, after all. Still in earshot if need be. And I don't know what this angel's true intentions are. I have to be careful.

"I'm never alone," I tell him, lifting my chin. Which is also true.

"Ah, yes. Your shadow," he says. "I suppose that is

right, then. Speaking of, how have things been going with it?"

"After our little encounter last time and how I nearly passed out, not much better."

He chuckles, which only irritates me.

"You said you were going to help me control it," I say. "But it was worse."

"That's because you've been underestimating the darkness that's inside you, Aria. You've only touched the tip of the iceberg."

Had I ever told him my name? I can't remember. Even still, his ominous words make me shiver.

"I am partly to blame as well," he goes on. "I, too, underestimated the extent of your gifts. You are quite a marvel. Nothing like I've ever seen before."

Join the club, buddy. We're making t-shirts that say 'What the fuck is Aria?' at this point.

"But I think I've figured out how to help you. *Really* help you this time," he says.

"Oh? And how is that?"

"You just need to wear this." He twists something around his finger, pulls it off, and holds it out to me. It's a ring with a thick silver band and large emerald stone. Intricate designs are etched into the sides. Thorny vines, I think, but it's hard to tell without getting closer.

Familiarity flickers in my mind. I've seen a ring like this before… But where?

"It'll help you," he insists. "You just need to wear it."

As if knowing what's happening, Sayah jumps around inside me, zigzagging side to side. Of course she doesn't like the ring. If it really can control her, she'd be afraid of it, right?

But still… my pulse gallops with uncertainty. Sayah's anxiousness has become like my own. Only another sign that she's growing too powerful. She's influencing me more and more.

"It'll help you control the creature," the angel repeats with a bit more urgency this time. He pushes the ring out farther. "Here."

I glance between it and him, debating what to do. Sayah continues to spin inside me, her movements making me more and more nauseous by the second. She wants to come out, to run, but I'm holding her back with every ounce of strength I have, which only adds to the sickly feelings seizing me. Heat crawls up my neck, and I'm trembling. If I fight her any longer, I'll either lose my dinner or pass out again.

"Take it!" the angel demands.

I snatch it from him and quickly slide it on my finger. Immediately, relief washes over me. Like a wave of crisp, cool ocean water cooling me on a muggy day. Just like that, Sayah's overwhelming presence is gone. *Gone.* I don't even feel her hiding in the background. I don't feel her at all.

Shocked and still a bit confused, I laugh. I'm almost giddy; I'm lighter. I've never felt like this. Never felt this… free.

How is this even possible?

I lift my hand to look at the ring. Even though the angel's hands are visibly bigger than mine, it fits snugly around my finger, and the emerald sparkles despite the lack of light in the hall. All this time fighting Sayah, resisting her, and almost losing myself completely to her—all of it could have been stopped by a piece of jewelry?

I laugh again, but this time at the absurdity of it.

"How does that feel now?" he asks, studying me with a pleased smile.

"So much better," I sigh. I study it and how it glints beneath the moonlight. "Thank you."

He nods. "You're very welcome. I'm glad we were able to get that sorted out." He turns on the sill and prepares to leap off.

"Wait!" I shout.

He stops and peers over his shoulder. "Yes?"

"You're just going to leave?"

Slowly, he spins back around. "Well, I came to help you, and since I did, there's no other reason for me to be here."

"Yeah, but what I don't understand is *why?*" I reply. "*Why* have you been trying to help me?"

He lifts a shoulder in a half-shrug. "It's what I do."

"Because of what you are?" I ask. "An angel?"

His smile widens. "You could say that."

"You know, I don't even know your name."

"Is that important to you? Knowing my name?"

"You know mine," I retort. "It's only fair."

He rubs his jaw, debating. After a long moment of stiff silence, he says, "Maverick."

Maverick, huh? Okay then.

My lips tug up at the corner. "Now, was that so hard?"

He throws his head back as he laughs. "No, I guess not."

Glancing up and down the hall once more, he holds out his hand as if offering it for me to take. It reminds me of the last time we met, when we'd touched and there was that strange zap of electricity before I was drowning in Sayah's darkness.

I step back, unsure. "What?"

"Come with me," he says and wiggles his fingers as an invitation. "I want to show you something."

"Uh…" I look at his outstretched hand. "Go… with you?"

He nods.

My gaze switches to the window and the snow falling harder outside. "In this weather?"

Again, he nods. "You look warm enough."

Since I'm just in a tank and shorts for pajamas, I'm sure he must be joking.

"Come on. We'll be quick. I'm sure you'll like it."

Do I trust him? I'm not entirely sure at the moment.

But he did give me the ring… And so far, it's working. I feel liberated. And he hasn't even asked for anything in return.

Nothing.

Maybe I can trust him. He is an angel after all, right?

When I look up at him, his brilliant smile is back. It's one that's hard to resist.

"One second," I say and quickly turn back into my room to grab a coat, gloves, and boots. I meet him again in the hall two minutes later. "Okay, now I'm ready."

His hand is still out, waiting for me to take. Carefully, I move closer and slip my hand in his. Like last time, there's another weird zap of energy between us, but no fearful emotions follow. Instead, I'm flooded with excitement and anticipation. It's like how I always imagined Christmas Day would feel like, if I hadn't been in foster care and had actually gotten visits from Santa and presents.

Maverick tugs me up onto the windowsill with him. The wind rustles through my hair, tossing it up and over my face, but he wraps his arms around me, and before I know it, we're leaping out the window.

Part of me wants to scream, but with this odd flood of adrenaline rocketing through me, I can't. When his wings catch the air and beat to give us more altitude, I peer down at the blanket of snow covering the mansion's yard. It grows farther and farther away as we climb higher, even surpassing the treetops.

I should be terrified. I really should.

The memories of Sir Surchion as a dragon clutching me in his claws as we flew away from the city rush to the surface, but again, I can't seem to hold on to the fear. It's unreachable to me.

I find myself laughing instead, loving the way the cold nips at my ears, nose, and cheeks as Maverick propels us forward. The wind whistles past my ears, reminding me of birds chirping. I'm even liking the feel of Maverick's strong arms holding me tightly against him. There's a real possibility that he might drop me, and if the speed we're flying at doesn't kill me, the drop from this height sure will. But, as bizarre as it is to say, I feel safe.

He flies us over a lake that's mostly frozen over, and our blurry reflection follows us as we rush across.

When I glance up at Maverick, he's watching me with an amused smirk, his dark eyes smoldering against the paleness of his skin and hair.

"Where are you taking me?" I yell up at him over the loud whooshing of the wind.

"Almost there," he replies, intentionally ignoring my question. Ahead of us, a snowy mountain range rises from the haze. Holding me tighter, we rush toward it.

The closer we get, the warmer the air becomes. A thick fog settles over the snow-covered earth, and the sounds of hissing and bubbling become louder as we move deeper into the warm mist. My hair dampens, but I'm no longer cold. I'm sweating with all this heat.

Maverick slows, lowering us both to the ground.

When we land, I realize we're still holding hands, and I quickly pull mine away. The overwhelming sensation of giddiness fades away.

"Where are we?" I ask him as he walks away from me a few steps and disappears into the vapor. I try to follow him, but it's hard to see anything more than two feet in front of me.

"Hot springs." His voice drifts from my right, and I twist that way. The dark outline of his body fades as he moves again. Next time, his voice comes from behind me. "Quite incredible, isn't it?"

I spin around.

"Yeah…" A blast of warm air hisses past me from my left, making me jump.

This is starting to feel a lot like a fun house type situation.

I squint, trying to find Maverick again, but all I see is whiteness. I need to keep him talking.

"I never knew Vermont even had hot springs," I say and wait for his response so I can track him down.

Only silence answers.

"Maverick?" I walk blindly, searching for any sign of him. He wouldn't leave me here, alone, would he? "Maverick? Where are you?"

A warning tickles the back of my neck. Whipping around, I collide with something solid, hard enough to steal the breath from my lungs. Hands clamp around my upper arms, and when I look up, my face is inches away from his, his mouth hovering close to mine. Too close.

His white hair is slicked back, and more wetness shimmers across his skin. God, he's good looking.

His hypnotizing dark eyes sweep over me, his lips parting, and my heart jumps into my throat.

Oh no... He's going to kiss me.

But I don't move. My feet are planted in the snow, and his grip on my arms is strong enough to bruise.

Right before our mouths touch, he pauses. His breath fans over my cheek, and I can hear my heartbeat thudding against my eardrums. It's hard for me to think straight; I can barely process what is happening.

"You're a magnificent creature," he murmurs, almost too softly for me to hear. "I've never met anyone like you."

I don't know what to say, so I keep quiet. I can't concentrate on anything but his eyes, his closeness, and the tingling radiating up and down my arms from his touch. It's all I can focus on.

"I'm starting to understand why they kept you…"

His words strike a match in me, drawing me in like a moth to flame. *They.* Meaning the demons. *My* demons.

Cain. Elias. Dorian.

As if shaken awake from a dream, I blink, press my hands against his chest, and push him back a few more steps. His hands drop from me, and the more distance I put between us, the better I feel.

"I... think I should go back," I say. Suddenly, this doesn't feel right.

He frowns but nods once. "If you insist."

I hug myself, suddenly feeling the chill underneath all the stifling heat. "I do."

A shadow passes over his face. Annoyed, his gaze darkens on me, and he reaches out a hand for me to take. "Very well."

ELIAS

Sitting on the couch in the parlor, I close my eyes and listen to Dorian drone on and on as he continues to read his book out loud.

"Love, which absolves no one beloved from loving," he says in a dramatic way, like he's part of a Shakespearean play, "seized me so strongly with his charm that, as you see, it has not left me yet. Love brought us to one death."

He draws in a deep breath, about to go on, but I use the opportunity to cut him off. "Do you really need to read it aloud like that? And so... dramatic?"

Dorian cocks an eyebrow at me. "As I told you before, you could use a bit of culture," he replies. "Figured I'd help you out."

"No thank you. I'm good."

He snaps the book shut. "Fine. Although Dante had some things right about Hell, didn't he? Seven levels. Fire and brimstone." He sighs. "There are some things I'm going to miss."

"Miss? Why? We have the spine. We still can find the other pieces and open the gate to get home."

Dorian places the book down in between him and the chair's arm. "Yeah, but I'm not sure I want to go back anymore."

His words take me aback. "What do you mean? You *don't* want to go back?"

He presses a finger to his temple and squeezes his eyes shut, as if talking about this topic pains him. We'd always been on the same page, had the same goals. It's always been about finding the relics and getting back to Hell, finishing what we started. How long ago had he changed his mind?

Though in truth, similar thoughts have crossed my mind… not that I'd admit it to him, as I'm still uncertain.

So was he planning on ever telling us?

"I don't know," he groans. "I'm not sure what I want anymore."

That shocks me even more. Dorian's always been the certain one. He has a one-track mind, and even though that track usually leads to sex, he would have a goal and not stop until he achieved it. So to see him struggling like this is strange.

"It's Aria, isn't it?" I ask.

His chin lifts. "What makes you say that?"

"It's the only thing that fucking makes sense. Ever

since she popped into our lives, we've been questioning things we normally wouldn't."

"You're right," he says. "Things are different now. Denying it would be pointless."

"Does Cain know?" I ask.

"No," he replies sharply. "And I'd like to keep it that way."

I stare at him.

"He's gone through enough these last couple of days. Now's not the time," he explains.

That may be true, but he will need to know eventually.

Dorian must see my thoughts through my look because he follows up with, "I'll tell him. Soon. But not now. Soon."

"I don't—" My argument dies on my tongue as a zap of foreboding shoots over my skin, raising hairs. Sensing extreme danger, my hound shoves forward. I jump to my feet, and my gaze snaps up to the ceiling.

Whatever it is, it's upstairs.

"What?" Dorian scrambles out of his seat, looking up now, too. "What now?"

Our gazes lock, and in that instant, dread seizes my chest.

"Aria," we say in unison. Then we rush out of the room and up the stairs.

I leap ahead of Dorian, taking four steps at a time. I reach the third floor in record time and skid into the hallway just as Aria steps down from the open window and shakes off the snow clinging to her shoulders.

Her hair and coat are soaking wet, and she's visibly shivering.

I trudge over to her, and when she spots me, her eyes go wide as if I just caught her red-handed doing something she shouldn't be.

"Uh... Elias. I—"

I look out the window and see only snow and the darkness of night. What the fuck was she doing? Was she about to jump?

Grabbing the latch, I slam the glass shut and lock it before whirling on her. "Explain."

"What did I miss?" Dorian appears at my side. When he sees Aria's wet and disheveled ensemble, he glances at me for an answer. Only I don't have one to give him.

"I... I..." she stammers, trying to piece together a lie to tell us.

I clench my jaw, anger stirring. "Were you trying to escape?"

"What? No!"

"You said you wouldn't run off again!"

"I wouldn't—I didn't!"

"Elias." Dorian steps in, trying to defuse the situation, but my temperature is rising with my rage. She promised, after all. Or was that all a ruse until she found the right moment? Wait until we get comfortable and...

"Maybe we should let the poor girl explain herself

first before we jump all over her," Dorian goes on. "There could be more to it than…" His voice trails off when his gaze lands on something on her hand.

Suddenly, his expression hardens, and he snatches her wrist and yanks it up for us to get a better look at.

A silver ring with a large emerald stone sits on her finger. The thorned vines around the band are what gives it away.

The symbol of one of the seven deadly sins. The ring of Greed.

Maverick.

Fuck.

Fear is all over Dorian's face, too. The bastard got to her.

"How did you get this?" Dorian shouts. The nice guy act is gone now.

Aria winces, not expecting the harsh reaction. "What? The ring?"

Dorian tries to tug it off her, twisting and pulling, but the thing won't budge. She cries out in pain and rips her hand away. "Stop! That hurts!"

"You need to take it off. Now," Dorian commands. "Right now."

She cradles her hand to her chest. "Why? I don't understand."

"Aria, listen to me," Dorian tries again, a bit more gently this time. But I can see the frustration knitting his brows. "You need to take that ring off. It's dangerous. It's—"

"It's the only thing helping me control Sayah," she confesses, which surprises me. "I haven't felt like this in… Well, in my entire life."

Dorian and I exchange worried looks. There's no way Maverick gave her his ring just to help her with Sayah. No. There's something more to it. There always is.

Do we tell Cain? We have to. He'd know a way to remove it safely.

"Who gave it to you?" I ask her.

She hesitates, her gaze jumping between us. Unsure if she should answer truthfully.

"Dammit Aria!" I growl in warning. "Tell us!"

"An angel gave it to me," she blurts out.

An angel?

I don't know whether to howl with laughter or curse at that. Maverick, an angel? That slimeball is the furthest thing to. He must've put on the holy facade to charm his way into Aria's good graces and get her to trust him. And I'm sure his power of emotional influence had some play in it, too.

That bastard!

Dorian must be thinking the same thing, because he snorts a laugh.

Aria doesn't seem amused. She puts her hands on her hips and glares at us. "An angel. Is that so hard to believe?" She points to me. "You told me yourself they existed. And this one's been helping me control Sayah. Then he gave me this ring, and it worked. It actually worked. I don't feel her anymore. I don't—"

"Aria," Dorian begins, "you don't understand. That person was no angel, and that ring is no miracle cure. It needs to come off."

He reaches for her hand again, but she steps back. "I don't expect you to get it," she snaps. "I've never felt so relieved. It's like the darkness has been lifted from me. This is all I've ever wanted. Don't you understand?"

Dorian's mouth tugs down into a deep frown. "Aria…"

"No!" She takes another step back toward her bedroom. "I never thought something like this was even possible. I'm free. I'm finally free of her."

Then she whirls on her heel, storms into her room, and slams the door shut.

Annoyance growing, I lunge for it, ready to rip the door off its hinges, pin her down, and rip the ring off her finger myself, but Dorian's hand shoots out to stop me. He shakes his head.

"We don't know what it's really capable of," I bite out. "It needs to come off."

"I know. I know. But we can't just cut off her finger."

"And why the fuck not?"

He gives me a deadpan look.

"Whatever Maverick has planned, it worked. We need to tell Cain and figure out what we're going to do about it next."

I throw one more glance at Aria's door. As much as I hate it, I relent and nod. When it comes to the original sins and Maverick, Cain knows more than either of us. It'll be better to tell him what's happened and take it from there.

Dorian sighs. "So much for not bringing more problems to his door."

CHAPTER NINETEEN

ARIA

*A*fter stewing all night over the demons trying to manhandle me and wrestle the ring off my finger, I walk to Cain's office early the next morning to tell him about the angel and why this ring is so important to me. My hope is that he'll understand, unlike Dorian and Elias, since he too lives with an oppressive darkness inside him. We share that part of ourselves. Or at least I like to think so, anyway.

It's how I'm going to get him to understand—plead with his sensibilities. *If* the prince of Hell has such things.

When I enter his office at the corner of the library, I find him standing in front of the room's only window, staring outside. He's dressed casually today. Jeans and a loose-fitting white tee, feet bare, his hair messy and without product in it... He looks almost *human*, as bizarre as that is to say. I've never seen him like this before.

But I like it.

The morning sun drenches him, giving him a soft glow, yet there's still a great deal of rigidness to his broad shoulders, worry from the things he can't fully shake.

I glance down to the emerald ring on my finger. Maybe this isn't the best time to talk to him about it. Maybe I should just…

"Morning, Aria," Cain says as he turns to face me and leans his back to the windowsill. Despite the softness in his voice, a hardness lingers in his eyes. His attention drops to my left hand, and when he spots the ring, his nostrils flare.

Looks like Elias and Dorian beat me to explaining things to him. Dammit. I should have seen that one coming.

Their overreaction still burns through my veins. They didn't even want to hear me out. They don't understand how free this ring makes me feel, and I doubt they ever will. It's like being held underwater for years, only allowed the tiniest gasps of air right before fully drowning, to then suddenly be rushed to the surface and yanked from the icy depths once and for all. I'm no longer suffocating in Sayah's overwhelming presence. I can finally just be *me.*

Taking a long breath, I step deeper into the room.

"I don't want to argue," I begin, which is the truth. "After everything, I just want some peace and calm. I don't want to go back to our vicious cycle of fighting each other and then… not. You've been through a lot these past couple of weeks, and—"

"You have, too," he says.

"Well, yeah. I guess we all have, but…"

"I don't want to argue either," he goes on gently.

I blink. Okay, then… I definitely didn't expect him to agree with me right away.

He takes three steps forward, closing the distance between us, and brushes his fingers across my brow to push loose strands of hair off my face.

"I heard you, you know. While I was hovering between life and death. I heard your voice. I saw your face. You were the only thing keeping me on this plane… The promise of seeing you again."

Rubbing my lips together nervously, heat touches my cheeks. "You… heard me?"

Well, that's embarrassing.

He nods, and his fingers trail down my neck in the softest of touches until he reaches the gold pendant between my breasts. Lifting it, he smiles. "And I'm glad you decided to stay."

"I'm glad you decided to hold up your end of the bargain."

He laughs, the sound soft and so beautiful.

When he steps away, my gaze lands on the ring around his finger. A gold band with a single dark crimson stone and winged carvings on the sides.

Now I remember where I've seen something like Maverick's ring before. It was on Cain's hand.

But they're just rings, and lots of men wear them. That's really the only similarity to them. Nothing else between them matches.

Still… my curiosity gets the better of me. "Cain?"

"Hm?" He moves back to the window and stares out on the freshly fallen snow. Everything outside is a brilliant white, and the morning light reflects off of it, throwing even more brightness into the room.

"Your ring… Where did you get it?" I ask him.

Gaze still cast outside, the muscles in his jaw clench. A part of me wishes I hadn't asked the question after all. It's clearly a sore topic for him.

"My father," he says.

Ah. Now I understand what the rigidness is all about. Cain and Lucifer don't exactly have the ideal father-son relationship.

"If you two don't exactly get along,"—and I knew that was an extreme understatement—"then why do you still have it? Why not chuck it into the trash? Or better yet, a fire?"

He starts to turn the thing around his finger, lost in thought. "That's a good question," he muses. "One I don't really have an answer for."

"Because?"

"Because I'm not quite sure why."

My guess is that it has something to do with wanting that last connection to home, as fucked up as it may be. It was like with me and Murray when he died. Sure, the guy had his flaws, but his place was the closest thing I had to an actual home in... well, in forever.

"Elias and Dorian told me you were given a ring last night as well?" he prompts.

Talk about a segue.

"Yeah."

"By an... *angel*?"

I sigh. "Don't tell me you're doubting me, too."

He turns. "Do I think you were visited by an angel last night, Aria? No. I don't."

Annoyance prickles across my skin.

"Do I think you were tricked into putting on that ring?" he continues. "Yes, I do."

Even though his tone is strangely calm, I can still feel us edging closer to the argument I really didn't want to have.

Of course he would side with Elias and Dorian. Demons sticking together with their kind, or some shit.

"I'm not taking it off," I snap. "I'm *finally* rid of Sayah. She's gone. I've never felt better than I do right now, and I don't know how, but it's all because of this little piece of jewelry. If that's all it takes, then I'll never take it off."

"I'm not asking you to," he says, which takes me aback. "But I am telling you that there are things going on here that you don't know about. That you wouldn't understand."

"Well that's incredibly cryptic."

What does he even mean by that? *Things I wouldn't*

understand. How could he possibly know that for sure?

"Why don't you tell me about what's going on so I'm not out of the loop? Then I can judge that for myself."

He glances away, giving me my answer.

I guess some things never change, near-death experience or not.

I hate the idea of the demons keeping secrets from me. Sure, I'd kept stuff from them in the past, but I'd come clean on all of them. Why did they feel like it was okay to still keep me in the dark?

"There will be no more visits from this supposed angel," Cain says, his voice turning serious again. His back straightens, and I'm seeing more and more of the hardened demon from before. "If Maverick returns, you are to tell one of us immediately."

I'm about to argue when I realize something. He said Maverick's name. I don't think I told him what the angel's name was.

"Do not interact with him. Do not even say a word. And especially, do not let him touch you."

All these commands. They are really pissing me off. It's like we've gone from being on the same level to him looking down his nose at me. Again. And I hate that more than anything.

I'm not a child. I'm not his little plaything, either.

What did these demons not get?

Maybe deciding to stay here was a mistake.

Unable to stand being in the same room as him, I spin around and stomp out of the office.

"Aria," Cain calls after me. "Aria, wait."

I don't. I walk through the library and down the long hall to the foyer. I can hear him behind me, following me but still keeping enough distance to give me space.

It isn't until I reach for the door's handle that he blurts out, "Where are you going?"

I pause. "I'm going to Joseline's," I say, making up my mind in that split second. "Oh, but I need *permission* for that, too, right? Since technically I'm still a prisoner here?"

"Aria," he begins with a heavy sigh, "you're not—"

I tug the door open. "Really? Because you sure make it seem like it."

He heaves a sigh. "Fine. Go to the witch's. But you are expected at work after."

Work.

Excitement bubbles up inside me. I haven't been to Purgatory in... Shit, it feels like forever. That means I get to see Charlotte, Antonio, and Sting again. Other people besides broody demons who like to try and control my life. *Normal* people.

I glance down at my everyday attire—jeans, sweater, and sneakers—and realize that means I have to change.

Without saying another word, Cain rubs his forehead, looking distressed, and strides back toward the library, leaving me alone. I wait until he's out of sight before closing the door and rushing back up the steps to get ready for the day.

Stepping out of the Town Car, I wrap my winter coat tighter around my body. One thing I don't miss about work is the "uniform" requirement. I've been spoiled with wearing only jeans, comfy leggings, oversized sweaters, and sneakers for so long, now that I'm in skin-tight pants, a halter top, and three-inch heels, I'm struggling just walking down the sidewalk to Joseline's apartment building. Not to mention it's colder than a witch's tit out here and I can't stop shaking, even with my winter layers on.

When I get to the front door and the buttons to call the apartments upstairs, I pause. Any other time, I'd call up and tell her I was coming, but I have a nagging bad feeling after running into her on the sidewalk with that warlock and those witches. Lucky for me, it only takes a few minutes for another person to walk out of the building, so I use the opportunity to slip inside without being buzzed.

I'm not sure what I'm expecting. But if this feeling is wrong, then there'll be nothing to worry about. It'll just be a normal surprise drop-in.

After riding up the elevator, I get to her door in record time. Again, I raise my hand to knock, to do the sensible and normal thing, but hushed voices drift from inside. The words are too hard to make out, but it sounds like another language. Like a spell of some kind.

Fuck formalities. I grip the handle and test it. The door's unlocked.

Slowly, I make my way inside. I recognize Joseline's voice immediately, and from the quick jumble of words, it definitely sounds like she's performing some kind of spell. But it doesn't seem like a spell I've ever heard her cast before. She's speaking fast, angrily, and loud bangs mimic her cadence.

My dark magic detector suddenly goes off the rails. Tingles shoot up and down my leg, straight to my toe. My pulse speeds up, and my internal 'oh shit' meter flashes. This can't be good.

On light feet—well, as light as I can manage in these blasted heels—I creep down the hall to the first room. The door is cracked open, and I shift my body into an awkward angle to get a good look into it.

What I see freezes me to the core.

Joseline kneels in the middle of the painted pentagram on the floor—painted in what looks like blood. She's topless, her breasts smeared with more blood, and she dips her hands into one of the bowls in front of her. Another bowl has feathers sticking out of it, and when I press my face against the doorjamb for a better look, I realize it's not just feathers but an actual chicken with its head twisted, neck broken.

Oh my…

This is dark magic. *Dark, dark* magic.

I knew it! I knew something was up! But I never thought Joseline would do this kind of shit. And then lie to me about it?

Fury sparks inside me. The swanky apartment on the expensive side of town. The lush furniture and fancy decor. It's all making sense now. Is there even a rich roommate? I'm starting to think not. She's been using this new power to better herself.

What an idiot. She's going to get herself killed.

Unable to watch this go on a second longer, I push the door open hard enough for it to hit the wall with a loud bang. She whips around and jumps to her feet, eyes wide the second she sees me.

Surprise.

"Aria!" Glancing down at her nakedness, she quickly hugs herself and searches for something to cover her breasts. She snatches a towel from her bed and holds it against herself. "What—What are you doing here?"

"What the fuck are you doing?" I throw at her instead. I point at the strange blood-painted symbol on the floor. "What is all this? You're doing dark magic now? Are you out of your freaking mind? And is that a chicken? You killed a chicken?!"

"Aria, stop. It's not what you think. It's—"

"Don't lie to me anymore, Joseline. Don't you fucking dare." I turn to the other room down the hall, the one she'd claimed was for her mysterious roommate. Before waiting for her to answer, I storm to it.

"Aria, don't!"

Throwing the door open, I find it completely bare. Empty. Not even one piece of furniture inside.

No roommate.

I can't believe this. I never thought Joseline would ever lie to me about anything. The truth of her deceit cuts me like a knife straight through the heart. I never in my wildest dreams thought she'd stoop this low or do something this extreme.

Now I'm starting to wonder if I really knew her at all.

I whirl on her, anger buzzing inside my chest like a swarm of hornets.

"What?" she snaps back, her body rigid. "You don't want me to lie to you, fine. Here it is. I don't have a roommate. Never have. It's just me. Are you happy now?"

"Are you going to conveniently leave out the fact that you're covered in blood, half naked, and kneeling in the middle of some demonic symbol? Whoring yourself out for a fluffy carpet and an apartment on the upper east side?"

She bristles at my words. "I'm not *whoring* myself out to anyone! I'm just giving myself a better life, the one I've always wanted."

"And at what cost, Joseline? Your life? Your soul?"

"You should talk," she huffs. "You talk about me whoring myself, but look at you!" She points to my wool coat and heels. "You've been fucking three demons. Living high on their blood money."

"You know I didn't have a choice in that! Murray—"

"Yeah, yeah. I know. Murray sold your soul to replace his. I heard the bullshit excuse," she says. "Well, it seems like he did you a favor because you've sure been enjoying the perks of it, haven't you? While I've been working my ass off in two jobs trying to keep a roof over my head. Where's the fairness in that?"

"Oh, so this is *my* fault?" I shout. "You're trying to blame this on me?"

"Not once did you think to ask if I needed any help." Her voice continues to rise, combating my anger with a heaping dose of her own. "We were supposed to be in this together, and you just dumped me."

She isn't serious, right? She can't be. Does she know how ridiculous that sounds?

Half the time I've been with the demons, I've been fighting for my life. I haven't been sitting pretty on some golden throne, sipping tea and eating crumpets. What gives?

I cross the hall and glare at her. "The only thing dark magic is going to do is get you killed," I say. If anyone knows about how badly it can affect a person's life, it's me. Look at Sayah. "It's not worth it."

She gestures to the apartment in a grand sweeping motion. "Really? Because look what it's got me. Everything I could've ever wanted and more."

I shove past her toward the door. Tears sting my

eyes, the rage quickly turning into heartache. "Then you can get dragged to Hell all on your own, because I want no part in this."

"Yeah, well, I'll see you there!" she yells at my turned back.

Resisting the urge to say something more, I march out of her apartment. The poisonous mixture of fury and grief spins through me like a whirlwind, but as I step into the elevator and press the down button, the tears come without permission.

Joseline was the last tether I had to my old life, the demon-free life that was full of hopes and dreams, even as shitty as it was. And now, without her, I can't help but feel like I've lost that part of myself completely.

All that lies ahead of me is a dark and sinister road, and it's leading me straight to Hell.

CHAPTER TWENTY
ARIA

"I missed you, girl," Charlotte says, beaming like she normally does. Tonight she's wearing the sexiest shade of fire-engine red lipstick, a short snakeskin print leather skirt, and a see-through fishnet shirt to draw all eyes to her red lace bra and ample cleavage. The kind porn stars pay a small fortune for, and she has it naturally.

Lucky bitch.

To finish off the ensemble, she has a collar around her neck with metal spikes. Like a dog might wear. Not my thing, but to each their own.

"Where in the world have you been?" she asks, leaning over onto the bar counter and wiggling her backside.

I spin on the stool. Losing Joseline in my life pulls at my heart. I still can't believe she would do something so stupid as to use dark magic to better herself. She knows the consequences of getting involved in that stuff. I can't believe she's been lying to me all this time.

Thinking about it again makes my eyes prick with pending tears. Thank God for Charlotte. Her larger-than-life personality is what I need right now to deal with it. The distraction helps, and Purgatory is a place that thrives on fantasy and distraction.

"I've been all over the world, ironically enough," I say. "We actually just got back from Scotland."

She gasps. "Scotland? Holy shit. What were you doing over there?"

How to even explain this? Where do I even start?

"There's... There's a lot I need to tell you later."

"Later?" Her voice rises. "Honey, you're telling me right now. I need to know." She takes two glasses from underneath the bar and then a bottle of some kind of liquor. At that moment, Antonio passes behind her with an armful of crates.

"You better not be touching my alcohol, girl," he snaps.

She wiggles a middle finger at him before pouring us each a shot. To my surprise, Antonio only rolls his eyes and brings the crate to the back room. If it were Sting, he would've given him an earful. I guess Charlotte has more sway with the elf.

Leaning her elbows back on the counter, she slides my glass over and smiles. "Go on, chicka. Spill."

And I do, starting with our second run-in with Sir Surchion at the harbor, Cain getting hurt and nearly dying on us, then going to Cold's Keep, the necromancer, the Scotland pack and the Black Castle, to now. It's a loooong story, even when I take out all the parts about my shadow and the relics, but Charlotte stays locked in through the entire thing.

When I finish, I wait for her reaction. As expected, it's priceless. Her brows shoot up and her mouth drops open, but instead of saying anything, she picks up her glass and throws back the shot.

She squeezes her eyes shut after swallowing to counter the burn before saying, "That was way more than I was expecting."

I pick up my own drink and bring it to my lips.

"I was thinking you'd say you were on a sex-cation or something."

I spit out all the liquid in my mouth at that one. Embarrassed, I wipe my mouth with the back of my hand while Charlotte takes a nearby rag and starts wiping up my mess.

"I'm sorry but sex…cation?"

"You know. A trip just so you and your man can get it on? A sex-cation."

Is that actually a thing?

Charlotte bursts out laughing. "I'm guessing you've never heard of it."

I can't help it. I laugh right along with her. "Can't say that I have."

"Hmm… well, since you went with two out of the three demons, it's easy for my mind to go that way. Right into the gutter."

Heat crawls up my neck because in all actuality,

she's absolutely right. Dorian, Elias, and I had shared the night together… *All* together. And it was one of the best nights of my life.

"Now that Cain's back, what does that mean for Dorian and Elias?" She points to the wing necklace around my neck. "You're wearing his emblem. Is Cain the one you've decided on?"

"Yes—No! I mean, it's not like that," I stammer pitifully through my defense.

She bats her long lashes. "Oh, so you're not choosing, then?"

"I… I…"

She waits a few seconds for me to find my words, but I'm so flabbergasted, I couldn't form anything coherent if my life depended on it.

Finally, she grabs the same bottle from under the bar and refills my glass. Scooting it closer to me, she says, "Hey, it's better if you don't have to. Right?" She winks. "The more the merrier, I always say."

Now it's my turn to snatch the drink and down it in one swig. It scorches my throat going down, making my eyes water, but it's just the distraction I need at the moment.

"Excuse me, but I believe there are tables out there waiting on orders." Cain's silky voice glides over my skin from behind me, making goosebumps rise. I whip around to find him standing there, just inches away, his handsome face a mask of hardened indifference like usual.

When his icy blue eyes flicker from Charlotte to

me, my heart kickstarts into overdrive. I hop off the chair a little too quickly and wobble on my heels. His hand shoots out and grasps my arm to steady me.

"One day I'll get the hang of it," I say nervously as I regain my balance.

He doesn't even crack a smile. You'd think, after all he's been through, nearly dying and all, he would've loosened up a little. But nope. He's just as stiff and guarded as ever.

I wonder if it's because of the angel's ring and how I've refused to take it off. He's probably still pissed at me, but whatever. He doesn't understand. None of the demons do. To finally have Sayah out of my life? I'll wear an anchor around my neck if I have to.

"We'll get to them right away," Charlotte says, referring to the waiting customers. "No worries."

Releasing me, Cain turns back to her, lips pressed in a tight line. "Will you be expecting a visit from Viktor tonight?"

Charlotte turns pale, and her head whips toward the front doors. Fear sparks in her eyes, like I've never seen before, and I don't understand why. Isn't Viktor her lover? Last time we'd spoken about him, she'd seemed genuinely enamored with him. Has something gone wrong?

That's when I see it. A faint purple and yellow bruise peeking out from under the collar around her neck, and my stomach drops.

Oh my God…

He hurt her?

She's obviously trying to hide it with the choker, and she's afraid of something—or someone—walking into the club tonight. Viktor is the only one who makes sense.

"I…" She swallows roughly. "I don't think so."

Cain nods, and I can't help but get the feeling that he knows the truth behind her fear, even if she hasn't told him a thing. "I think it might be best to avoid any more distractions tonight," he says. "Don't you agree?"

It's not really a question. More like a warning.

Charlotte's gaze drops.

He glances at me one last time. "Aria," he says as a goodbye and walks away.

When he disappears down the back hallway, I look back at Charlotte. She gives me a shaky smile, one that isn't as genuine and doesn't quite reach her eyes.

I want to ask her about the marks on her neck, or what Cain meant about Viktor visiting, but she looks so shaken, I decide they're questions better off left for another time.

"Man, what crawled up his bum?" Charlotte walks around the bar, grabbing her apron, order pad, and pen as she does. She's doing everything to put on an indifferent face and pretend like everything's okay. But honestly, it only makes me more concerned. I've never seen her like this before. "That demon needs to learn how to relax, am I right?"

I nod, but I'm too distracted to even have heard what she said. I can't stop thinking about those bruises and the terrified look in her eyes. Even now, as she strolls over to a table full of rowdy customers, she keeps stealing glances at the door, as if she's waiting for someone to burst through at any second.

When she catches me staring, she quickly averts her eyes back to the couples and scribbles down their orders.

We work for a few hours like that, purposefully avoiding each other, the tension building. As the night progresses, more customers fill the seats and dance floor, and things get busier for both of us. I'm running back and forth between the bar and the tables like a freaking ping pong ball. And on three-inch heels, it's exhausting.

At some point in the night, I spot Cain again. This time he's sitting in one of the couch booths at the rear of the club, in the most shadowy, secluded part away from the stage. He sits with two other men, talking business no doubt. The man was on the verge of death only days ago, and not even that is slowing him down. But Cain really isn't the type to take a break. Even if it is greatly, *greatly* needed.

Stubborn as a mule. That's what he is. Stubborn as a demonic, Hell-raised mule.

Mid-sentence, he glances my way and meets my eye, surprising me. Before the whole fiasco with the dragon, it would have annoyed me how we'd just spent what I thought was quality time together, getting closer, and now he's as distant as ever before. Hot and cold, hot and cold—it's Cain's specialty. But after almost losing him, I've decided I'm done complaining. It's just the way he is. Maybe I should expect it and move on.

"That demon needs to learn how to relax." Charlotte's voice buzzes by my ear. I whip around to see her striding by, tray of empty glasses in hand. She nods for me to follow her back to the bar. "What he needs is a good lay."

My eyes widen. "What do you mean?"

"I used to get guys like him in the BDSM club I used to work at all the time. Control freaks who had sticks so far up their asses, they would come in at least once a week to release that tension. To let someone else take over for a change." She starts unloading the tray and putting the dirty dishware in the sink. "An hour with one of the dominatrixes and they would come out new men."

I pause, considering her words. Yeah, it's true Cain has control issues, but would doing something as silly as taking over during sex mellow him out? It sounds bogus to me.

"Do you really think something like that would work?" I ask her, voice low.

She nods. "Oh yeah. Definitely."

I glance over my shoulder at the back table. Again, Cain is looking my way, cold eyes piercing into me but face as unreadable as ever.

When I turn back to Charlotte, she has a hand on

her cocked hip and a brow raised. "Have you ever tried being more aggressive in the bedroom? Switch it up? Take charge?"

I can't believe we are even talking about this right now. My stomach fills with jittery nerves. She might be okay with talking about her sex life so openly, but I'm still new to it.

"I'll take that as a no." She chuckles. "Well, maybe you should. Might be something you want to consider next time you two are bumpin' uglies."

"Oh my god, Charlotte. You did *not* just call it that."

She laughs again. "I just like to see you blush," she admits. "Besides, there's no reason to be shy about it. Living with three sinfully hot demons? We both know you're not a saint, and that's fine. There's nothing to be ashamed of."

She's right, I know. I am still getting used to all this change with the demons. Hell, with myself, too. Confidence has never been a strong suit of mine, but maybe it is time I try something different. I need to give myself more credit than I do.

"So..." I begin, eyeing Charlotte as she comes back around the counter. "What you were saying about Cain... How would I even go about something like that?"

She grins. "Oh, honey. I thought you'd never ask." She wraps an arm around my shoulder and squeezes me tight from the side. "When is your next break?"

"Uh—" I glance at the clock at the back of the bar. "Thirty minutes, about?"

She taps the dimple in the middle of her chin. "Tell you what. I'll let you have my break tonight, too."

"You don't have to—"

"Ah, but I do," she insists, guiding me across the room again. "'Cause I have a lot to teach you, and not a lot of time to do it."

She flicks a finger Cain's way, and when I look up, he's in the middle of a heated conversation with the two other businessmen, but his gaze continues to slide my way throughout the exchange. I'm suddenly not too sure about this idea…

CAIN

"We'll be in touch," Dalmer says as he rises to stand and rebuttons his suit jacket. The man next to him, Bechem, stands too. As the ones who oversee all of the drug dealings on Glenside's streets, they are useful acquaintances to have. Especially when it comes to making money.

Personally, I don't care too much for cartels and the drug trade. It's a messy business, but we wanted our hands in everything we could to… spread our influence and power that way. And the money it manages to rake in is always nice.

Once Dalmer and Bechem leave, my gaze sweeps

the crowd for Aria. I had been so distracted during my meeting, just by her closeness, that there were several times I considered excusing myself and going over to her.

But to do what? Pull her into my arms? Hold her? Kiss her? I wasn't sure.

One thing was for certain, I wanted her to take Maverick's damn ring off. But there are only two ways to get a demon ring off a person's finger. Death or the demon removing it themselves, and neither of those will be happening any time soon.

I probably should have told her who Maverick really is… but that would require also confessing that my father has her in his sights. Initially, I didn't want to worry her about Hell-matters, but it's clear I won't be able to keep it from her for much longer.

We've been trying to get back to Hell, but it seems Hell is coming to us.

As much as I don't want to frighten her further, I'll have to tell her. To protect her.

After waking up from that dream… No, that *experience*, only to find out that I'd been teetering between life and death for days—it had affected me. Maybe more than it should have, but it did. Now I was reexamining things. Wondering what it was I really wanted in this eternally damned life of mine. And the only answer I could come up with was…

Her.

Aria.

It's one of the few things I have no explanation

for. But now that she's decided to stay with us and hunt down the rest of the relics, I can't help but ask myself why. Does she feel this strange pull, too? Or is this entirely self-serving, a way to get out of the contract and live the rest of her life free of us?

I'm so lost in my thoughts that I don't even notice Charlotte approaching the table, but when I look up, she's standing there with a mischievous smirk on her face.

"Yes?" I ask, confused as to what this could be about. She's one of the longest-standing Purgatory employees, but even through all that time, she's rarely approached me to talk. Not unless something has gone very, very wrong.

"We have a disgruntled customer in Red Room number six," she says. "Refusing to pay for his session, giving the bouncers a hard time, destroying things. The whole bit."

I stare at her for a long moment. Surely she wouldn't have come to me unless it was something that couldn't be handled by other means. The rowdy guest must be a powerful supernatural if they need me to get involved.

Sighing, I stand. "Number six?"

"Yep. And you might want to hurry." She runs her tongue over her top lip. The sexualized gesture strikes me as odd, given the circumstances. But Charlotte has always been flirtatious, so I brush it off and she hurries back toward the crowded dance floor.

Readying myself to face a possible fight, I square

my shoulders and sigh before crossing the club and heading toward the back hall where the Red Rooms are. When I make it to the door labeled 'six,' I listen for any noise to clue me in to what I'm in for. Expecting shouts, curses, bangs, I'm surprised to hear nothing but silence on the other side.

Absolute silence.

Odd…

I open the door and step inside to find the place is not only dark, but it's empty.

Confused, I wonder if I've walked into the wrong room.

The door clicks shut behind me, and when I spin around, there's Aria, dressed in a sheer black lingerie dress and stockings with garter straps and matching bra and thong. My gaze roams over her, unable to believe what I'm seeing but loving every second of it. In the darkness, the dim red glow of the emergency light illuminates every delectable curve of her body. My heartbeat races, and my cock stiffens in my pants just at the sight of her.

It takes an extra second to find the ability to talk again. She's stunned me in the best possible way.

"There's no rowdy guest in here, is there?" I say, my voice coming out in a husky whisper. It barely sounds like my own.

She glances away briefly, a bit shyly, before looking at me again. "No," she whispers. "Just me."

"Good. I prefer that." I almost growl the words as my pants strain from my erection.

She smiles, and it's then that I realize she's wearing makeup. Red painted lips, pink cheeks, darkened lashes and eyes… The touches only enhance her natural beauty but replace her innocence with a darker, more mysterious look, bringing out the boldness I know she likes to keep hidden. But not from me.

I step toward her, the need to bring out that side of her clouding my senses, but before I can grab her, she presses a hand against my chest and pushes me backward several steps. The back of my knees hit the red pleather couch, and I fall onto the cushions.

"What's this all about?" I ask her, confused as hell but secretly enjoying the surprise of it all. Aria circles the couch until she's behind me, grasps one of my wrists and puts it into one of the designated straps on the high wooden back. As she yanks it tight and secures the latch, my eyes widen.

"Aria…" I warn.

She's quicker this time, snatching my other hand and strapping that one down, too, so that my arms are splayed out like I'm some kind of offering.

Of course, I could rip myself out of these leather bindings easily, even without my demon form, but part of me is curious where she's taking this. Part of me is enjoying the game of it too much.

When she comes back around to join me on the same side of the couch, she stands before me and looks me over. Her gaze drops to my lap where my erection is tenting my pants, and she grins.

"Who put you up to this? Was it Dorian?" I ask her, but she shakes her head.

"Everything doesn't need to have a motive to it, Cain," she says, inching closer. "Sometimes it's best to just live in the moment. Let things happen."

I hear her words, but this is so unlike the woman I know that I can't help but wonder who's behind it. There has to be something else.

She must be reading my thoughts because she says, "I figured it's time we both tried something new. You relinquishing some of your control to me, and me…" She climbs over my lap one leg at a time so that my cock is perfectly nestled in between her thighs. I can feel the heat of her through my pants. It calls to me. "Me finally showing you just how much I want you."

Her words make every muscle in my body clench.

Oh fuck…

Out of instinct, I go to reach for her, wanting nothing more than to press that gorgeous body against me and claim her mouth with mine, but I'm quickly reminded of the tethers holding my arms in place. A growl slips past my lips.

"I think you need to let me out of these," I say as nicely as I can manage, although my pulse is thundering with need. "You'll like what comes next. I promise you."

She narrows her eyes on me. "Nice try." She bends forward, and all I can look at are her gorgeous

ALL SHOT TO HELL

breasts pushing forward in her bra, straining to come out. I groan at the sight.

Soft fingers find skin under my shirt as she draws the tucked fabric out of my pants, her touch on fire. She takes her time, her gaze never leaving mine, undoing one button of my shirt at a time.

"You sure this is the game you want to play?" I warn her, my voice raspy as I struggle with holding back my own explosive desire.

She swallows loudly, but when she pries open my shirt, a wicked grin steals her expression. "Oh, definitely yes, this is what I want."

She runs her hands down my chest, then leans against me, kissing me all over. I inhale her sweet scent of honey and her slick. Fuck, she's so turned on, all I can think of is ripping off her thong and ramming into her, making her scream my name as I pin her to the wall.

She bites my nipple, and I groan. "Harder," I demand.

Her nails dig into my side, and I hiss as she obeys me, her sweet tongue licking after each bite, soothing the ache.

"You are going to be in so much trouble when I get free," I tease.

"Is that so?" She leaves a trail of kisses down my stomach, her fingers already pulling at my belt. Tugging down my pants and boxers at the same time, she frees me.

My cock jerks to attention, and Aria makes quick

work of wrenching my pants off and throwing them somewhere behind her before falling to her knees between my legs.

I can't stop staring at her beauty, at the way she licks her lips, looking at me while grasping my cock. Her sweet mouth slips over my tip, and my heart hammers in my ears. My body thunders with the build of arousal. Her mouth is everything.

She takes me deeper, while her fingers grip my thighs, holding on as she inhales all of me, her tongue flicking over my shaft.

I hiss, throwing my head back, the sensation pure, carnal pleasure. My hands curl into fists, my wrists straining against the restraints. But I don't try to break them… not when Aria wants me this way. So I give her what she wants. All of me.

Fire and desire twist inside me.

My balls ache with the need to fuck her, to unload in her. I'm not used to being the one who has to submit like this and not take charge. I'm the dominator, the one in charge at all times, but I am loving the way she's taking what she wants and not holding back. It's so fucking sexy.

She bobs up and down, her mouth sucking, building an unstoppable friction. My chest rises and falls with her, my hips rocking to match her rhythm. She's killing me, and it takes everything to not release into that sweet little mouth of hers.

"Enough," I growl. "I need to taste you. I want your pussy on my face, now."

She deepthroats me one more time to remind me she's the one holding the reins during this wild ride, and I half-laugh, half-groan, then she slips her mouth off me with a popping sound.

"You didn't like that?" She bats her eyes, knowing exactly what effect she has on me. Kneeling before me she's so innocent, so tempting that I'm close to breaking free from my shackles. She has no clue that I'm a predator watching over her, willing to do anything to ensure she never leaves my side.

"I'm going to own every part of your body, devour it, mark it as mine," I say. When I stare into Aria's dark eyes, I lose myself.

She stands up and slips her hands to her thong, which she pulls down, then steps out of. My heart starts to pound as my gaze goes straight to the apex between her legs. To the thin, straight line of hair while everything else is shaven.

"Get your pussy over here and spread your legs over my face."

"You're the one supposed to be taking orders from me," she says. "You're not supposed to be in control here."

I smirk. "You can't tell me you don't want it, too. Come here. Let me worship you."

She almost rushes toward me, her breath quickening. She makes me insane with arousal.

I slide lower on the couch… well, as low as the restraints permit me. Aria steps up on the couch and straddles my lap again, and the whole time I can't take my eyes away from her pussy, how it glistens.

"Come closer, gorgeous. Take hold of the bar over your head and kneel up on the back of the couch," I command, and she eases closer.

She reaches up and takes hold of the frame used to hold my restraints, and she lifts one knee, placing it on one side of my head, then just as quick, places the other on the other side.

And me, well, my head is caged in by her gorgeous thighs and her wet pussy. My cock twitches as I inhale her sexy scent.

"That's it, now widen and come down just a bit more."

"Not sure I can—"

I push my mouth up to her fire and take her lips with mine. She moans so loudly, so beautifully. She's so wet and primed, so ready for me to take her. The sounds she makes only push me to lick her faster, to tongue-fuck her until her whole body trembles.

Buried in her pussy is everything I crave, and my own resolve to hold back dissolves. I tug my arms, the straps breaking with ease, my hands starved of her spectacular body, her curves.

Her cries and her rocking herself against my face have me so close to the edge, except I'm not even close to being finished with her.

I reach up and grab one of her tits, then wrench the lace fabric out of my way.

"You cheated," she moans, but as I suck on her and

pinch her nipple, her protest morphs into a delicious scream. I push my tongue into her while pulling and squeezing her breasts. She's drenched, and I feel her getting closer.

And there's only so much a man can take... I grip her hips and push her, just enough that I can slip out from between her thighs. Her juices cover my face, her scent is all over me.

Swiftly, I'm on my feet and turn to my gorgeous little thing, still clinging onto the bar overhead, her head twisting to look at me with desire gleaming in her eyes.

Her inner thighs are glistening with her arousal, and I reach over and grab her ass. "Now I'm going to fuck you, and you're going to scream so everyone in this place hears you. I will show you what truly being claimed means."

A small, amused whimper falls past her lips. I reach over, wrap my arms around her delicious body, and bring her back with me, her curvy ass pressed against my chest. I carry her to the side of the couch, and she slides down until her feet touch the floor. But before she can make a move, I snatch her hips and snap them back, her bare cheeks against my groin.

"Hey," she protests.

"Bend over." I run a hand up her back, forcing her forward to lean over the armrest.

She looks back at me over her shoulder, and there's no sign of fear, but one of absolute need. I gently nudge her legs open, and the tip of my cock finds her entrance like we're made for one another.

"You will always be mine, you understand that, Aria?" I state, and already I feel her hips lifting, readying to accept me. From the beginning, I've been drawn to her, intoxicated by her, but she pushed me away, even if her body craved mine. But now, gone is the shy girl, replaced with a powerful, sex-confident vixen I adore.

"Fuck me, Cain. Please, make it hurt."

I don't give her a chance to change her mind and slide into her. Any chance of being slow is wasted on me and how horny I feel. That lucid dream in my half-dead state left me needing her more than I ever thought possible, and I'm ready to take my fill.

I ram into her, driving myself fully into her. She screams, her body arching, and I love seeing her this way. Barely holding onto my control, I hold on tight as she wriggles her hips. Reaching forward, I take her hair and wrap it in my arm and gently tug her head back. Then I plunge into her, completely taking her, rough and hard.

"Oh, Cain, I'm so—"

"Hush. You don't come yet," I mutter, one hand in her hair, the other sliding around her waist and to her swollen clit. I strum it, needing to push her closer and closer until she can't take another second. I thrust into her tight core, over and over.

Her body buzzes, the sounds she makes growing louder. My Aria is so close now. I feel her tightening around my cock, and there is something so innocent and alluring about her. I never relent, slamming into her, our bodies falling into rhythm.

"Cain, please," she begs.

I grab her elbows and wrench her back so that she's flush against my chest. Wrapping my arms around her chest and middle, I keep myself buried deep inside her and fuck her harder in this new position. I love the way she bounces against me.

Unable to do anything but take it, her head rolls to the side, exposing her neck, and I run my tongue up the artery to the curve of her ear. She shudders.

"Come for me. Let me hear you," I rasp against her skin.

Almost instantly, her gorgeous scream rings through the room, her body bursting with spasms. Her pussy squeezes my cock, sucking at it, and I lose all control. As much as I wanted to hold back, the sensation of coming into her, flooding her with my seed takes me to another realm.

A growl rolls past my throat, and I orgasm so hard my whole body rocks. I don't know how long we've been on our high, but when I look down, I've released her and she's collapsed over the couch, breathing heavily.

"Shit, Cain, that was incredible."

"I am not even close to being finished." I pull out of her and stare at her pussy dripping with my seed, with her dripping climax.

"Oh, but I have to get back to work," she tells me, at which I laugh.

"I'm your boss, and I say we aren't finished fucking." I can barely resist not taking her this very moment as she lays with her ass in the air and her offering spread for me.

"I love you like this, all wide and wet."

As if to regain some semblance of control, she wriggles off the couch and stands before me, so stunning and all mine.

"I like this look," I say. "You should dress like this more often."

She arches a brow. "Ahh right, so no underwear and my breasts on display."

"Exactly."

"Fine. Then you need to be naked."

"Deal."

Her mouth drops open as she realizes the web she walked into so easily. She shakes her head and goes to retrieve her underwear while tucking away her gorgeous, round breasts.

"I never said we were done. We have a lot of catching up to do, you and I." Before she can respond, a shuffling sound comes from the door. I cross the room and open it to find Charlotte startled, clearly caught. Her gaze dips down my naked body but quickly jerks up to look me in the face. Aria is by my side, covered up.

"Were you... spying on us?" Aria asks, looking horrified.

"Not spying, exactly. But it did sound like you were having a good time." She smirks. "Besides, it's only fair, seeing that you got an eyeful of me and Viktor on your first day."

Aria gasps and looks at me, then Charlotte. "Wait, wait? I thought these walls were soundproof."

Charlotte laughs then says, "Oh honey, they aren't *that* soundproof."

I shut the door in her face and turn around to Aria, who's a lot more shocked than I expected. "Take your clothes off," I insist.

"Are you mad? Everyone out there heard us. I can't…" Her cheeks blush, and I take her into my arms.

"They haven't heard *anything* yet." I am way past the point of not taking this further, my cock already stiffening. "Now, where were we?"

CHAPTER TWENTY-ONE
ARIA

Some time after work, I walk down the stairs toward the dining room for dinner, but I'm met by Cain, who half-steps out of the parlor. My stomach flips at seeing him, knowing that most of my time at work had been spent being fucked relentlessly by him, but when I catch sight of his grim expression, my gut twists into a tight knot instead.

"Aria, we need to talk," he says before walking back inside.

Not good.

Having no idea what this can possibly be about, I wrack my brain for a reason he might want to have a serious conversation with me. I thought we were past this. The only thing I can come up with is what happened between us in the Red Room, and I had thought that had gone rather well, myself. I sure enjoyed it, and I thought he had too.

So what could this be about?

As I step in, I find Dorian and Elias there, too. Dorian's perched on the arm of the oversized chair while Elias is pacing in front of the window. He stops when he hears me enter, his face a mask of mixed emotions.

"Oh, I didn't expect this to be a community meeting," I joke and let out a nervous laugh. Like usual, it's just me laughing, though. Everyone else is deadly serious. Even Dorian. It's unsettling to see him without so much as a smirk on his face.

Cain gestures to the couch for me to sit, but I'm suddenly so nervous I refuse. I bounce on my toes instead.

"What's going on?" I eye them all carefully. "What's this about?"

"That ring," Cain begins, nodding toward my hand where Maverick's emerald sits. "It's about time we explain to you what's been going on. The truth."

"The truth?" My throat tightens. What does he mean? They've been lying to me about something? "I- I don't understand."

"That ring belongs to Maverick," Elias blurts out as if he's been waiting to say it for ages.

"Yes, and? I know that," I reply. "The angel. He told me his name."

"No, not an angel," Cain says sharply.

"The complete opposite actually," Dorian huffs. "He's—"

There's a rapid pounding at the door. Everyone's attention snaps toward the foyer, but no one moves.

The *boom, boom, boom, boom* comes again, more forceful this time, making the walls shake.

Slowly, Dorian stands. "What the hell?"

The quick sound of Sadie's footsteps rush into the hall, but Cain hurries out to stop her. "I got it, Sadie. Thank you."

The three of us follow, filing into the room behind him. Elias and Dorian look worried, but I'm not sure why. It might be because the last time someone was beating on our door, it was a pack of werewolf bikers looking for a fight.

Dread seeps into my bones as I watch Cain move toward the door. But before he can even grab the handle, it flies open on its own, and in stumbles Joseline. She falls into the center of the foyer, panting hard, and deathly pale.

Heart hammering, I rush over to her and drop to my knees. "Shit, Joseline! What happened? Are you okay?"

She grips my arms, eyes wild with terror. Sweat clings to her forehead, and although her mouth opens to speak, she can only utter a bunch of incoherent sounds and point to the doorway. It's like she's seen a ghost or is being chased.

Or both... Chased by a ghost?

I look up to see Maverick strolling inside, a lopsided grin on his face. Joseline scoots closer to me, panicked, holding onto me for dear life.

Elias is on top of Maverick suddenly, snarling furiously as he twists his arm and brings him down to his knees in front of Cain. Maverick hisses in pain but doesn't fight.

Instead, when he looks up at Cain, his form begins to shift before my eyes. His limbs grow longer, spindly. The silvery wings jut out of his back, and two horns curl from the top of his head.

I gasp in disbelief. No, not an angel at all. He's a demon.

"Is this how you say hi to your little brother?" he asks Cain, who's grown rigid with fury.

Brother?

The ring. I glance down at my hand and remember what Cain had said about his father giving him his. If Lucifer had given all his children one, then Maverick isn't just any demon. He's another original sin demon.

Fury lashes through me. I've been lied to! Tricked! Maverick played me like a fiddle, and I fell for every word.

No wonder Dorian and Elias wanted me to take off the ring that night. Why hadn't I just listened to them? I'm such a fucking idiot.

Cain stares down at Maverick with black eyes, his lip curling in disgust. "You're no brother of mine," he spits. "Not anymore."

Elias takes the opportunity to punch Maverick across the face. One hard hit, that's all it takes, and Maverick is spitting out blood onto the floor, his cheek swelling within seconds. For everything he's done, I wish he'd hit him harder.

But to my surprise, Maverick laughs through it all. "I see you still have your pet." His gaze finds Dorian. "Or should I say, *pets.*"

Dorian crosses the room in two long strides, but before he can grab him, Elias lands another swift blow to the side of his head. Blood cascades down his neck from his ear.

That's when Maverick's head lifts, and the dark eyes I once thought to be warm and welcoming land on me. Now I see the evil lurking in his gaze, and I hate myself for not seeing it sooner.

"Aria," he greets as if we're old friends. My stomach turns with hatred. "You enjoying that ring I gave you?"

"Don't talk to her, you piece of shit," Elias barks at him, raising his fist again.

"I suggest you stop pummeling me for a second or else our little Joseline here is going to have a one-way trip to Hell sooner than expected."

Everyone freezes in place.

"What did you just say?" I ask, my voice rising.

Knowing he has our attention now, he grins broadly. Red stains his teeth. "The pretty witch here has sold me her soul in exchange for great riches and a taste of dark power. Isn't that right, dear?"

"You didn't…" I whisper, praying that he's lying again. There's no way she'd be *that* stupid. Not to get wrapped up in a demon contract.

Joseline doesn't reply. She only stares at me with

pure desperation in her eyes, and I know what he's saying is true.

My heart plummets. "Release her from the contract," I demand. "Release her."

"That's not quite how it works, Aria," he replies sweetly. "But you know that."

Fucking asshole.

I grip the ring on my finger and try to tug it off, but as if glued on, it doesn't budge. Not even a wiggle. My heart drops.

Oh no. It's stuck!

"How about you amend her contract, take your ring back from Aria, or I'll rip you apart limb by limb?" Elias growls.

Dorian steps forward. "I think you mean 'and,' Elias. Not 'or.'"

"You know what? You're right. Amend the witch's contact, take the fucking ring back, AND I'll rip you apart, limb by limb. That sounds much better."

"What say you, brother?" Maverick calls to Cain, who hasn't moved a muscle since this entire thing started. "Do you want a piece, too?"

Cain's body is so rigid and stiff, it looks like he's about to explode at any moment. The black veins line his marbled skin, and I can feel the immense dark power radiating off him in waves.

Unsure what else I can do, I hold my breath, waiting for the boom.

But it doesn't come from Cain.

A man steps across the threshold and looks upon the scene with bored eyes. He's dressed in a polished black suit, red dress shirt, and matching tie, appearing as if he's about to hold an important business meeting here, of all places, or maybe go to a ritzy wedding. His hair is dark, and his mustache and beard are neatly trimmed and sculpted to his handsome face.

As he takes another step into the house, Elias drops Maverick, and he and Dorian scramble backward, farther away. Stunned. Afraid. Two things I've rarely seen on them at the same time. Even Cain is affected by this stranger. The blackness has drained from his eyes and skin, and he stands there, mouth open, frozen like a statue.

The man's dark gaze meets his, and a pleased smile quirks the side of his mouth. He holds out his hands as if expecting a hug.

"Oh, Cain," he says, his voice deep but silky smooth. "My dear boy. Is that any way to greet your father?"

His... *father*?

But then that would mean this man...

He's...

Lucifer.

THANK YOU

Thank you for reading All Shot to Hell

Start reading book 4 in the Sin Demons series.
To Hell And Back

ABOUT MILA YOUNG

Best-selling author, Mila Young tackles everything with the zeal and bravado of the fairytale heroes she grew up reading about. She slays monsters, real and imaginary, like there's no tomorrow. By day she rocks a keyboard as a marketing extraordinaire. At night she battles with her mighty pen-sword, creating fairytale retellings, and sexy ever after tales. In her spare time, she loves pretending she's a mighty warrior, walks on the beach with her dogs, cuddling up with her cats, and devouring every fantasy tale she can get her pinkies on.

Ready to read more and more from Mila Young?
www.subscribepage.com/milayoung

For more information...
milayoungarc@gmail.com

facebook.com/milayoungauthor
twitter.com/MilaYoungAuthor
instagram.com/mila_young_wicked

ABOUT HARPER A. BROOKS

Harper A. Brooks lives in a small town on the New Jersey shore. Even though classic authors have always filled her bookshelves, she finds her writing muse drawn to the dark, magical, and romantic. But when she isn't creating entire worlds with sexy shifters or legendary love stories, you can find her either with a good cup of coffee in hand or at home snuggling with her furry, four-legged son, Sammy.

She writes urban fantasy and paranormal romance.

RONE AWARD WINNER
USA TODAY BESTSELLING AUTHOR

Want to read more from Harper A. Brooks? Subscribe to Harper's newsletter and get *Halfling for Hire* for free! http://BookHip.com/MCBDCN

Join Harper's reader group for exclusive content, sneak-peeks, giveaways, and more! www.facebook.com/groups/harpershalflings

Printed in Great Britain
by Amazon